"BEYOND MINDSLIP"
Tony Harmsworth

HEAT

HEAT

Reader Club

Sign up for Tony's no-spam Reader Club newsletter for a free e-book, exclusive content, and special offers.

Details can be found at the end of Heat.

HEAT

HEAT

Copyright Page

Thanks to these VIP Beta Reader Club Members: Alan Brewerton, Robert Brinkman, Annette Burgess, Gillian Elliott, Anne Graham, Terry Grindstaff, Jim Hewlett, Dean Howard, Scott Kreisler, James McCarthy, Averil O'Hare, Colin Pain, Joe Pedreiro, Ted Penfound, Linda Reed, Nigel Revill, Roy Straker, Susan Swinford, and Peter Watts who have contributed so much help in raising the quality of my story. I appreciate FormulaDriven of Reddit for checking my maths. Thanks for particular help from Wally Andrews – the real one, not the fictitious foreign secretary!

All rights reserved; no part of this publication may be reproduced or transmitted by any means, electronic, mechanical, photocopying or otherwise without the prior written permission of the author.

Edited by Melanie Underwood
Pre-edit by Wendy Harmsworth
Copyright © Harmsworth Publishing Ltd 2024
Cover: Author assisted by AI
ISBN: 9798338382233

Website: Harmsworth.net

Tony Harmsworth has asserted his moral rights.

Published by:
Harmsworth Publishing Ltd.
Drumnadrochit
Inverness-shire
IV63 6XJD

HEAT

Index

HEAT — 1
- Copyright Page — 5
- Index — 7
- Introduction — 11
- Author — 13
- Characters — 17
- Temperatures — 21

2032 — 23

- 1 Swelter — 23
- 2 Rising Tides — 29
- 3 The Kings Arms — 33
- 4 Royal Institution — 39
- 5 Number Ten — 47
- 6 Kigali — 51
- 7 The Shocking Truth — 55
- 8 Anxiety — 67
- 9 Trafalgar Square — 73
- 10 Moon — 77
- 11 Toase — 87
- 12 Tripoli — 93
- 13 Iceland — 99
- 14 North From Toase — 119
- 15 Sir Edward Gascoyne — 125
- 16 Crossing Borders — 133

17 Great Barrier Reef	137
18 Unrest	141
19 Unease at the Top	143
20 Violence	147
21 Briksfosarnet Glacier	157
22 Algeria and the Med	165
2034	*171*
23 Port Khalifa	171
24 Fireside Surprise	175
25 Le Bec de l'Aigle	181
26 Industrialisation	185
27 Cabinet	195
28 Building Cash	203
29 Hideaway	213
30 Excavation	227
31 Tourism	249
32 Southern Ocean	253
33 Summit	261
2037	*267*
34 Heatwave	267
35 Appeal	271
36 Maize	275
37 Starship	279

38 St Antonin-du-Var	289
39 Coast	293
40 Progress	305
41 New Forest	313
2040	*327*
42 Family Holiday	327
43 Alaskan Space Center	347
44 Riot and Murder	355
2041	*361*
45 No Respite	361
2042	*365*
46 Training	365
47 The Truth Will Out	371
2046	*375*
48 Departure	375
49 Was Anywhere Safe?	381
50 Communication	383
2048	*387*
51 Belts and Braces	387
52 Speed and Distance	391
53 The Storm	397
3668	*411*
54 Kepler-452 B	411

Tony's Books 415
Reader Club 418

HEAT

Introduction

Note for non-British readers – I write using UK English spelling, punctuation, and grammar, plus some US English words where appropriate as there are various nationalities within these stories.

Metric and British imperial measurements will be found in the story. There is a temperature table in the index which can be accessed while reading if you do not normally use Celsius.

*Reading **MINDSLIP – Evolution's Nemesis** before HEAT "Beyond Mindslip" would be beneficial and add to your enjoyment, but not essential. Some of the characters overlap both stories and there are numerous references to Mindslip events.*

Tony Harmsworth, 30th September 2024

I chose the title of this work carefully and included the words "BEYOND MINDSLIP" to explain that this is not a sequel to that stand-alone novel but does examine the future world a decade and more ahead of the first book's effects.

This preamble outlines what Mindslip was and introduces HEAT's follow up storyline.

Mindslip is never likely to be repeated. The odds against it are as astronomical as the size of the universe, but, at the time, it wasn't realised that the double supernova explosion of Betelgeuse would have more serious effects on the solar system.

In 2019, Betelgeuse, a giant star in Orion, many light years from Earth, collapsed and turned supernova, throwing out a vast cloud of debris in addition to many unwelcome forms of radiation. For some reason, still unknown, there was a second explosion the following day which, combined with solar mass ejections from the sun, showered the world with an unknown additional radiation. It caused every living creature on Earth to swap its mind with the mind of another creature. Most minds slipped into similar bodies, human to human, sheep to sheep, but not all. A large number slipped into other species, and even those who stayed in the same species usually changed age or sex. Absolute chaos ensued with men becoming women, the young morphing into the old and, amazingly some even entering unborn foetuses. The protagonist in HEAT is Geoff/Beth Arnold, a mid-thirties English astrophysicist who became a twenty-four-year-old Japanese female. Geoff's wife had changed into an aged greyhound; his twelve-year-old son into a Black African teenage boy; and his eight-year-old daughter into a French woman of twenty-two. You can imagine the problems Beth had trying to locate the family and then coping, and helping them cope with their new identities.

Read MINDSLIP to find out how it all resolved if you are curious.

The effect of the radiation on dear old Sol, caused increased surface activity including growing numbers of solar flares and coronal mass ejections. At first, they had little effect, but the problem was cumulative. The sun itself seemed to be heating up.

HEAT is the ongoing story, told in part by Dame Beth Arnold in first person, but also by a diverse collection of other minor protagonists.

Author

Tony Harmsworth was born Anthony Geoffrey Harmsworth on 19th March 1948 in Brocket Hall, Hertfordshire, which was being used as a maternity hospital after the Second World War.

His father, George, came from Boxmoor, Hertfordshire, and his mother, Williamina Robertson, from Preston Pans in Scotland.

Tony was educated at Welwyn Garden City High School and Bude County Grammar School, where he decisively failed all his A and S-level subjects in Pure Maths, Applied Maths and Physics, owing, in part, to severe hay fever, although he admits not working hard enough could have contributed to the failure. His IQ was Mensa tested to 158 in his last year at school. His lifelong interest in science and astronomy has inspired his writing.

As a teenager, Tony developed a deep scepticism of religion, read both the Bible and, later, the Quran, realising that they were nothing but ancient stories without any basis in reality, and became a confirmed atheist. Don't be surprised to find this influencing some of his stories.

Leaving school without qualifications, and thrown onto his own resources, he followed his soon to become wife, Wendy, to Manchester where she read modern languages. He tried a first career in sales, and, despite his youth, he was quickly promoted from salesman to supervisor and then became part of an advance team opening new sales areas throughout the UK.

Still only nineteen, he joined Top Rank prior to Granada's takeover. Seeking improved prospects, he moved to Ridings Stores, Loyds Retailers and then the Co-op holding down department management with the latter and quickly being promoted to store management with Loyds at just twenty years of age.

Now married, they moved to Basingstoke where several firms were relocating from London. A new post was created at Wella, which involved managing an innovative computer-controlled stock system from scratch. This appealed to his mathematical leaning. With Wella, he was soon promoted to Organisation and Methods, eventually becoming general assistant to the managing director aged only twenty-five.

In 1975, he was head-hunted by the cosmetics arm of British American Tobacco – Lenthéric Morny where he introduced new systems in the industrial engineering department.

He left here when he and his wife decided to break out of the rat race and relocate to Drumnadrochit in the Highlands of Scotland in 1978.

Discovering the lack of any tourist information about Loch Ness, he conceived, researched, and staged, the Loch Ness Exhibition. It was an instant success and made Drumnadrochit the capital of the monster world.

Discovering that his share of the exhibition[1] had mysteriously evaporated, he moved on to create a

---

[1] Detailed in his non-fiction book – Loch Ness, Nessie and Me.

manufacturing company in Fife, designed more exhibitions on Macbeth, Scottish History and Highland Heritage. In 1993 he staged Scotland's largest private heritage centre at Fort Augustus Abbey where, despite his atheism, they appointed him the first lay-bursar of any Scottish monastery.

Developing the tourism theme, he established high quality guided tours in the Highlands. In fact, his Discover Loch Ness tour company was the first to achieve the maximum five stars in Scotland.

As well as having written, according to one review, 'the most comprehensive and accurate book on Loch Ness', he got the writing bug and, at the age of seventy, began a new career writing science fiction. Not the space battles, star wars variety, but near-future realistic stories in the vein of the late John Wyndham, and with an eye on the environment. Perhaps because of his age, traditional publishers shunned him. Following the theme of his life, he struck out on his own regardless. Two of his novels have become UK Kindle bestsellers in SF categories, but he writes for enjoyment rather than income.

Now, at the age of seventy-six, he offers you HEAT "Beyond Mindslip".

HEAT

HEAT

Characters
Some readers like to be able to refer back to characters, so I have provided some information here. Please skip if you're not interested.

Scientists
Dame Beth Arnold – official astronomer – married to Gren Pointer. Beth is one of the main protagonists in this story.
    Martin Bishop – NASA computer nerd
    Ethan Cockridge – Canadian Space Agency
    Dr Linsey Delve – head of UKSA[2]
    Professor Janice Elsterd – Oxford University – sun specialist
    Ted Garve – NASA engineer
    Sir Edward Gascoyne – world famous naturalist and TV presenter
    Peter Gordon – solar expert from JPL[3]
    Sir Michael Harding – sun monitoring specialist
    Argos Homburg – top US astrophysicist
    Harry Kinsman – Head of NASA
    Daniil Kotov – Roscosmos
    Philippe Parodi – European Space Agency
    Sylvie Paulsdóttir – Icelandic home secretary.
    Sir Peter Watts – head of Jodrell Bank Observatory

Eco-Warriors
    James Buchanan – the founder and leader of EW

---
[2] United Kingdom Space Agency
[3] Jet Propulsion Laboratory

The Moon

Beatrice Ardent – farmer
Doc Lex Barrington – doctor
Astronaut Christine Daly
Astronaut Elena Esteban
Julian Hide – construction overseer
Dr Jason Ingersoll – a farming consultant
Commander Bert Lewis – Moonbase commander
Lucy Silver – construction engineer
Astronaut Dave Wilkes – communications officer

UK Government

Walter Andrews – foreign secretary
Sir David Brenner – science minister
Sir Charles Browning – defence minister – he was the prime minister during the Mindslip crisis
Beryl Charters – chancellor of the exchequer
Jack Easton – home secretary
Sir Joseph McKinley – cabinet secretary
Jenny McRoberts – prime minister
Gren Pointer – Mindslip rehabilitation minister – married to Beth Arnold.
George Smith – transport minister
Dame Diana Staunton – environment minister

Libya

General Ahmed – head of Port Khalifa forces
Colonel Asenath – helicopter pilot for Khalifa
Major Bashir – head of naval operations

Major Darius – head of construction
General Khalifa – president of Libya
Captain Gregory Mead RN – undercover UK captain
Ted Marston – British commando
Captain Mohammed – ship's captain
Colonel Omar – Khalifa's assistant

Africa
Esturu family – Destri and Bright. Children Mariam and Edu

Maldives
Umar, Mauna, Hamid, and Abbas

Great Barrier Reef
Dr Emily Hayes – lead marine biologist
Dr Adrian Head – coral specialist
Professor Terry Hughes – renowned marine biologist
Dr John White – Australian ecologist

Norway – Briksfosarnet Glacial Lake
Aakre family – Axel and Emma. Children Ingrid and Theo.

United Nations Security Council
Jefferson Barker – US president
Allain Fichefeux – French president
Leonid Gorlov – Russian president
Jenny McRoberts – British prime minister

Yong Zhang – Chinese president

Family
Angela Arnold – Wilson's wife
Caroline Arnold-Pointer – Beth and Gren's daughter
Emma Arnold – Angela and Wilson's daughter
Geoffrey Arnold-Pointer – Beth and Gren's son
Wilson Arnold – Beth's pre-Mindslip son
Malcolm Fletcher – Sandra's husband
Sandra Fletcher – Beth's pre-Mindslip daughter
Linda & Patricia – the Fletchers' children

HEAT

Temperatures

Temperatures are primarily in Celsius. This is a conversion table, and you can always find it via the index.

30 C	86 F	45 C	113 F	60 C	140 F
31 C	87.8 F	46 C	114.8 F	61 C	141.8 F
32 C	89.6 F	47 C	116.6 F	62 C	143.6 F
33 C	91.4 F	48 C	118.4 F	63 C	145.4 F
34 C	93.2 F	49 C	120.2 F	64 C	147.2 F
35 C	95 F	50 C	122 F	65 C	149 F
36 C	96.8 F	51 C	123.8 F	66 C	150.8 F
37 C	98.6 F	52 C	125.6 F	67 C	152.6 F
38 C	100.4 F	53 C	127.4 F	68 C	154.4 F
39 C	102.2 F	54 C	129.2 F	69 C	156.2 F
40 C	104 F	55 C	131 F	70 C	158 F
41 C	105.8 F	56 C	132.8 F	71 C	159.8 F
42 C	107.6 F	57 C	134.6 F	72 C	161.6 F
43 C	109.4 F	58 C	136.4 F	73 C	163.4 F
44 C	111.2 F	59 C	138.2 F	74 C	165.2 F

Let the story begin…

HEAT

2032

1 Swelter

James Buchanan turned over again. He could feel the sweat soaking into the sheets. This was no good. He'd never be able to fall asleep. What on Earth was the temperature? Why hadn't he bought the air-conditioner when he had the chance? Now they were as rare as hen's teeth. Jeez, surely it shouldn't be this hot in May, despite global warming. What was the government playing at? All those punitive changes to reduce emissions and the temperature was *still* climbing. Were they lying?

The top sheet already covered no more than the bottom foot or two of the bed and he'd long ago extracted his legs from it. He lifted his naked torso onto an elbow, decided he needed a drink and swung himself around to sit on the side of the divan.

The London traffic outside had begun its nightly hush. The sound of individual vehicles shushed by momentarily from beyond the open window, whispering along their journeys. Not a breath of air disturbed the curtains. The heat was oppressive.

He stood, walked to the drapes, and yanked them back so that even the hint of any breeze would find its way into the stifling apartment.

The moonlight gave the cityscape before him a silvery, ethereal feel. Lights burned in some of the flats and houses opposite and way in the distance, the taller structures were peppered with the glow of the odd fluorescent illumination ignored by the last departing office workers – or were some still occupied by diligent individuals trying to get ahead of the daily grind by burning the midnight oil in search of credit or promotion?

James looked at the alarm clock and was surprised that it was beyond midnight. It was quarter to three! Had he slept at all? He must have. He couldn't have lain awake for nearly four hours. There'd been a dream. Some strange scenario found him searching for his Lexus in a multistorey car park. It had become sinister, and he'd awoken suddenly, realising that he wasn't lost, his car was charging in the street outside and the malevolent stalkers had never been real.

He turned away from the view and walked into the hallway. The combination barometer cum thermometer read thirty-eight degrees Celsius. It shouldn't be possible in London, in May, at night. The antique thermometer only went up to forty-five Celsius. Would it explode higher than that and shower the hallway with mercury? Crazy! He relished the feel of the cold tiles on his soles. Now, there was an idea. He could sleep on the tiles. Savouring the coolest surface in the building, he continued onwards into the kitchen. It was even warmer in here. Of course, the hot water tank, lurking in its concealed cupboard location, would be warming the room. He welcomed it in the winter, but not in these sultry conditions.

Sliding up the sash window, an actual waft of cooler air momentarily met his naked torso. He stood motionless. The air stilled again. Had the draught just been wishful thinking?

HEAT

He grasped the cold tap and turned it on full blast. The violent jet of water splattered around the sink, some thankfully spraying his stomach and genitals and blissful cool drops meandered their way down his thighs. The force was lessened by the hurried application of his fingers. He grabbed and offered up a glass, filling and emptying it several times to allow the water to run cold, also cooling his hand as the liquid overflowed.

He drank. Oh, such rapture to swallow such cold nectar. How wonderful. He refilled and emptied it a second time.

Outside, a cat wailed. There was no view in this direction, just the building opposite about thirty feet away, many of its windows open, but all in darkness. He leaned forward and could make out the courtyard below, lined with bins of various colours pronouncing their diets of general waste, glass, recyclable materials, and food waste. The movement of the cat caught his eye. It leapt from bin to bin then onto a wall along which it began a stealthy patrol, studying the scene in search of vermin or copulation.

James turned away, took a third glass of water with him, and entered the lounge. There was a settee and one easy chair, a reclining leather chair no less. It would be cool. He threw himself into it, spread his legs and luxuriated in experiencing the cold leather on his back, bum, and the rear of his thighs. It wouldn't last, of course, his body would quickly equalise the material to his own temperature, but he'd enjoy it while the variance continued.

Strangely, he was thankful that the slinky Sylvia hadn't stayed the night. The heat was so overbearing. She'd worn just a slip of a dress and looked fabulous. How he loved her body, if not her difficult personality. His plan was dinner followed by slow, luxurious sex. He'd ordered in sushi which seemed ideal with some salad. They'd drunk a chilled Zinfandel and sat on the sofa; not cuddling, it was too hot for that but holding hands and listening to Fleetwood Mac.

God, her legs were magnificent. He knew it was a bad idea but gave in to temptation and caressed her bronzed thigh. He couldn't help himself. When Mindslip occurred, he had been ninety-one-years-old and hadn't had sex for nearly twenty years. Diabetes had wrecked his manhood as surely as if he'd been castrated. Suddenly nineteen-years-old and more handsome than he had ever been before, he could get laid more or less to order. An amazing transformation. Okay, he was thirty-two now, but that was still the prime of life.

'Too hot, Jimmy,' she whispered, shuffling away.

'Yes, sorry.' A disappointed acknowledgement.

'Think I'll head home. My place is cooler than yours.'

He hoped she'd ask him to go with her, but the invitation didn't materialise. The thought of sex, even the slowest and most gentle variety, no longer appealed in this heatwave. She didn't ask and neither did he. There'd be other nights for enmeshing their limbs. Big Love ended and Tango in the Night eased its head-pulsing rhythm from the stereo. Was it the thought of the hidden meaning in the lyrics that was enough to make her stand to go?

He jumped up and pulled her to him, grasping her buttocks through the flimsy material; God was she sans-underwear?

He promised himself: another time.

They kissed, extricated themselves from the clinch, then she called Uber and searched for her shoes. Within minutes the autonomous cab had arrived, and he showed her out. There'd be other times.

The leather chair had reached body temperature. He eased himself, stickily, from its grasp, visited the bathroom, took a two-minute cool shower, dried himself, and returned to tackle his bed once more, relocating to the opposite side to avoid the sweaty under sheet.

HEAT

2 Rising Tides

Hamid and Abbas were stirring after yet another night away from their home. Mauna yawned, sat more upright and squeezed the shoulders of her children. She looked out from under the peeling, painted timber of the awning of her father's veranda. The sea was calming and stretched into the distance, rippled with turquoise, cerulean and arctic shades of blue, highlighted by remnants of white spume and floating debris from the storm. Larger waves crashed onto the coral reef, but no longer breached its defences. In the distance, lights were still shining in beachside huts as dawn faded their brilliance.

'I'm hungry,' moaned twelve-year-old Hamid, the older of the siblings. Abbas was nine.

'Okay, let's go home and see if we can find something for breakfast,' Mauna told the youngsters as they rose, and brown feet and legs kicked up the loose sand beneath the decking steps. It took only a few seconds for one to find a broken palm frond and begin to chase the other in an invented game of tag.

The wicker shack door opened, and a number of adults emerged, stretching and yawning, some carrying coffee or tea and munching on something Mauna's mother must have had in the larder. They mumbled various grumbles such as, 'That was a baaaad baaaad storm'; 'What a surge'; 'They get worser and worser'.

A younger man ran off, shouting, 'Better check the boats.'

Mauna was now on her feet. She called to the lads, 'Come on boys, let's go check the house.'

The two youngsters ran up to her. Husband Umar joined them, and the kids scampered along the sand-covered road to the east. Signs of storm damage were everywhere. A palm tree blocked the road, a barrier to motor vehicles, but no obstacle to the family who jumped or climbed over the unexpected blockade to continue their journey. The boys walked along the trunk, Hamid turning cartwheels, his feet tangling in fronds causing him to tumble to the ground. He was up in an instant and running on with Abbas laughing in hot pursuit.

'Where is it?' Umar asked. 'It's gone.'

'Gone? Can't be. Not really gone?' said Mauna.

The boys came to a stop, looking towards a scattered array of posts, boards, and roofing materials. Their home had been demolished by the storm.

'How could that happen?' she asked her husband.

'It's wave damage, not the wind. Look, that's the base of the bed, it's been dragged down towards the water. The wind was coming the other way.'

Hamid came running back to his parents, and said, 'Mister Bee said that the island was sinking. Has it started?' Mister Bee was one of the teachers at the local school.

'Been going on a long time, son, and it's not the island that's sinking, it's the ocean rising,' said Umar.

'Mister Bee said sixty or seventy years, not now. Can't be happening yet!' the boy protested.

'It's the ice in the Southern Ocean that's melting, and the sea water is rising more rapidly.'

'Yes, I know dat,' the boy exclaimed, 'but he said it was also the water expanding as the temperature rose.'

'I s'pose so. Double-edged sword, I guess,' said his father. 'The two effects add to each other.'

'But what do we do?' asked Mauna. 'The house has gone. It's all gone.'

'Let's see what we can salvage,' said the man, trudging forward with a heavy heart. 'You boys run around and collect anything which is ours.'

'Boat's not there,' said Abbas, 'and the jetty's all busted up.'

'Okay, let's see what we can save,' said his mother.

Other Maldivians were arriving at the beach, plus some tourists who were staying in nearby holiday chalets which seemed to have survived the deluge. They could fly home in their airliners and carry on as normal in air-conditioned offices in their foreign countries, polluting the world and making the climate crisis worse. Here, in the middle of the Indian Ocean, there was nowhere left for the local people to run. Their islands were drowning.

HEAT

3 The Kings Arms

A rambling brick-built pub in Brixton, London, proudly portrayed a swinging sign outside depicting the king of clubs playing card and the words 'The King's Arms'. Inside, it was huge. Five large rooms were linked together, any doors having been long consigned to history, but sections of walls and supporting girders showed where the room divisions had once been. Room three was home to the bar.

Polished mahogany lined the back wall with dozens of shelves, which were concealed by every brand of whisky known to man and over sixty other bottles of spirits. More than ten of the whiskies had their own optics plus the usual gins, vodkas, rums – dark and clear – brandy and others.

The bar counter was a superb piece of timber, bevelled and rounded at the front and supported by another mass of mahogany panels inlaid with green leather. Behind it were eight pump handles for draught beers, several portraying artisan names like Bishops Tipple and Egham's Amber. Ten green leather-upholstered bar stools were lined up irregularly along the bar's length, several occupied, mainly by men in casual clothing.

The five rooms also contained mahogany tables surrounded by comfortable carver chairs as well as the usual wheel back versions. Around the walls, fitted green upholstered bench seats butted up against more tables with chairs on the other three sides. There was room for each table to become an intimate space, seemingly isolated from the next, in atmosphere if not physically.

HEAT

Music played over the speakers – too quiet to be intrusive, but too loud to allow any one table to overhear the conversations of another. The playlist was individual to the particular head barman or woman of the day, so it was never possible to predict what would be on the menu. Blondie, Oasis, the Beatles, Frank Sinatra, or myriad other artists who were favourites of the person running the bar that day or night. This was a big, busy establishment with a large number of employees.

This afternoon, there were maybe eighty or ninety people enjoying their drinks and, when James Buchanan walked in through the glass engraved doors at one end, the luxurious air-conditioning hit him full on. Delightful. It was nearly forty-degrees outside. He was also greeted by a constant babble of lively conversation, sufficiently confused to prevent any particular conversation or thread being comprehended.

An arm waved in James' direction from the window seat in room two. He acknowledged it and headed past it to the bar, nodding at several of those seated there. He quickly obtained a pint of Bishops Tipple, a strong dark foamy beer, and joined the group of around fifteen people sitting with the man who'd waved at him.

'Hi James, how's it hanging?' asked the waver.

'Not bad. Sorry I'm late. Traffic's a nightmare today and it's sweltering out there. Are we all here?' asked James.

'Hellish hot. Mary couldn't make it,' said a plump ginger-haired woman sitting at one end of the window seat, nursing a half pint of lager.

'Okay,' said James, 'I can report that we now have nearly a thousand in the WhatsApp group. They're primed and ready to go.'

'How many are London based?' asked the waver.

'More than seven hundred. I reckon at least a hundred or more will answer the call,' said James.

'Only a hundred,' said an overweight man in a stretched leather jacket. 'Doesn't seem that many.'

'It's a start,' said James. 'Once we start making a noise, the numbers will grow. The heat is intolerable, yet the government keep telling us how emissions are being reduced. People are angry. All we have to do is make them angrier.'

'When are you planning?' asked the waver.

James turned to two Asian men sitting on his right and asked, 'How're the banners coming along?'

Ashed replied, 'We've three canvas banners. One four metres and two three metres. We've also got thirty stiff-card boards. I've a couple here.'

He reached down and picked up a board, about eighty centimetres by fifty bearing the message:

STOP THE HEAT
FEWER LIES
MORE ACTION
NOW!

'Very good,' said James. 'Could maybe do with a few more. What about the other message?'

Ashed lifted a second board:

STOP THE HEAT DEMAND MORE WIND, WAVE, & HYDRO POWER NOW!

'Excellent,' said James. 'I'll let you know the date. I'll try to ensure it is a *really* hot day.'

'What do you reckon is happening, James?' asked the waver.

'I really don't know, Bert. We're definitely being lied to. They're saying emissions are down by forty percent over the last ten years. I checked that on several official sources and it seems correct, but how can it be? It's forty Celsius outside today and they recorded forty-four in Norwich yesterday and it is only May!'

'They must be lying about it,' said Adrian Watson, a long-haired, rebellious looking individual in jeans and eco T-shirt. 'The science says that if emissions drop then climate should normalise.'

'There is a lag, of course. It isn't an instant reaction,' said Barbara Beadon at the end of the table.

'Not that much of a lag,' said Adrian. 'I studied it at uni. It should be really noticeable by now. Something weird's happening.'

'They're all lying to us,' said another of the younger men on the window seat. 'It's a conspiracy for sure.'

'But why?' asked Barbara. 'What point is there in lying to us – not just us, but the whole world?'

'Something's going on. That's for sure,' said the waver.

'Okay. We have to make it clear that we're not putting up with it,' said James. 'We must force them to come clean. If it's not emissions, then what the hell is it? I've got to go. I'll message you all with the date and location. Bert, can you pop around to my place tonight?'

The waver nodded. James stood up and said, 'Hey, thanks, everyone for coming. Now get ready for action. Great job on the cards and banners, Ashed. Cheers.' He swigged the last of his pint and headed for the door.

Outside, he was hit by a wall of stifling heat.

HEAT

4 Royal Institution

I was sitting at the head of an impressive teak conference table in meeting room number four of the Royal Institution building in Albemarle Street. I'm the official astronomer, a post which used to be called Astronomer Royal before Britain became a republic. My name is Beth Arnold, and during one of the last honours events, I was made a dame, which is the female version of a knight of the realm. Dames and sirs would probably continue to be created even if they no longer had to pledge allegiance to the almost forgotten royal family. Mindslip had made them irrelevant. It was inevitable, however, that the word royal would continue to haunt many buildings and the institutions they held long into the future. There was no plan to change the building's name from Royal Institution.

I had been one of the key advisers to the government during the decade long Mindslip Crisis, mainly because my area of expertise had been the study of supernovae, and Mindslip had been triggered when Betelgeuse had exploded, twice no less, just over twelve years ago.

That fateful morning in 2019, Mindslip had magicked me from my original persona, thirty-five-year-old Geoff Arnold, into a rather beautiful, female, Japanese graduate in her early twenties. I was no longer a white English male astrophysicist with an eye on middle age. It was the mind which had been transferred, of course, so I had no new knowledge of Japanese and still retained all my expertise in astronomical physics. Thirteen years later, in 2032, my Japanese self is Geoff's original age.

Since Mindslip, as a woman, I had given birth to two younger children aged six and eight, fathered by my post-Mindslip husband, Gren Pointer, who today is the Mindslip rehabilitation minister in the British government. The changing of surnames on marriage seemed to be pointless with so many having changed sex, so I remained Arnold. Beth, rather than Geoff, was just a more sensible forename to suit my female form. Changing from male to female had been a real shock to me. Initially, memories of who I was had caused me serious distress. How could I, as a heterosexual male, suddenly become a woman? During that first year or so, hormones kicked in and my dread of a relationship with a male gradually diminished. I still remember all my male thoughts and attributes, but they have been augmented by that growing feminine awareness which spread through my being. Today, I am as much a woman as any who were born to that gender.

The clever design of the conference table I sat at, meant that it seemingly floated without support. Today it hosted five human beings. It could have catered for ten or twelve, but I'd only called my very closest colleagues and advisers for this meeting.

'I take it there is some purpose to our being here,' said Sir Peter Watts, head of Jodrell Bank observatory. He was a bearded man in his fifties who sat erect and allowed his left hand to fiddle with the pen which lay before him atop the obligatory notepad, and beside a glass and flask of iced water.

HEAT

'There is indeed,' I replied. 'All of us are aware of the ongoing flaring of dear Sol, but there are new concerns. We've just started to get on top of the CO_2 created climate crisis and now find that our hard work has been negated by the actions of our own sun.'

'The flares are mainly a problem to our technology, but they seem to be linked to the growing output from the sun,' said Professor Janice Elsterd, a highly respected astronomer who specialised in studying the sun at Oxford University. No one in Britain knew more about Sol. She continued, 'The solar maximum in 2025 has continued in intensity. When the flares are most common there is a distinct rise in the sun's radiation of heat.'

'Can we assume that the increase in coronal mass ejections, flares, heat, and sunspots is an effect caused by Betelgeuse? Will it subside? It's the fifteenth of May and the temperature outside is reaching a daily thirty-eight Celsius,' I said, looking at my tablet's screen then turning it so that the others could see the large figures 38.2°C. 'It hit forty-five in Great Yarmouth the other day.'

'The flares should cease tomorrow,' said Sir Peter, 'so the heat should fall away by Friday. The problem is that the temperature drop back is less on each occasion.'

A rotund individual with bald head, tufted eyebrows and horn-rimmed spectacles broke in. 'We still can't discover any mechanism whereby the Betelgeuse radiation could have caused these changes to the sun.'

The others all turned to look at Sir Michael Harding, another specialist in monitoring Sol.

'There must be something,' I said forcefully. 'It *has* to be connected.'

'I know,' said Sir Michael, 'but we can't demonstrate how.'

'Moonbase is still suffering but the new shelters are helping,' announced the fifth delegate, Dr Linsey Delve, head of the United Kingdom Space Agency. 'Radiation continues to take its toll. Greg Underhill died yesterday. That's all four of those who were building the radiation shelters. That extremely severe pulse of flares in January was devastating.' The UKSA chief was, despite being in her sixties, still a very slim and striking woman of East African origin, although, owing to Mindslip, her ethnicity was purely incidental.

'Did they finish the shelters?' asked Sir Peter.

'They did, but getting to and from the moon is now equivalent to playing Russian roulette. If there's an unexpected flare, life expectancy is drastically shortened for the astronauts who are en route. Although we get plenty of notice of coronal mass ejections, the radiation from the flares travels at the speed of light, and it's deadly,' Linsey said.

'Sorry to hear about Greg. I met him last year,' I said.

'Me, too. He had a wife and three young children,' said Sir Peter. 'He'd also been setting up an extra laser-reflector at Copernicus for us.'

'Is the ISS now secure?' I asked.

'Yes,' said Linsey. 'It cost an absolute fortune to lift it to a special retrograde geosynchronous orbit, but it's now stable and permanently in the shadow of Earth's magnetosphere. Getting to and from it is far more expensive though, and the risk of flares exacerbates the problem. Deep space radiation shields have also been put in place on the sunward side, so living on board is actually less hazardous than it was originally in low-Earth orbit. An alternative power supply has been installed because solar panels were no longer as effective in Earth's shadow.'

'What's the new power source?' asked Sir Peter.

'Atomic. Solves the problem.'

'I've been called to Number Ten for a meeting on Friday,' I said, 'and I really don't know what to tell them. Peter, if the sun continues to heat when these flares take place and they continue at the same frequency as they have been since Mindslip, what's the end result?'

Sir Michael added, 'The frequency of the flares has been fairly steady for the last eighteen months, but the sun's output continues to grow.'

'The flares have at least steadied. That's a hopeful sign,' said Linsey.

Sir Peter turned his tablet over in his hand, made a series of stroking motions and studied the screen. 'Do you want the short or the long-term prognosis?'

'Both,' I said.

'Expect life between the tropics to be impossible in eight to fifteen years. Say, 2050. That's the short-term.'

'And long?' asked Linsey.

'There is no long term. We'll need a new planet,' said Sir Peter, grimly.

'Seriously?' asked Janice.

'By when?' I asked.

'The sun's heat during the flare cycles increases the temperature of the oceans each time they occur. Antarctica is melting. The ice will be gone by 2050 even from the centre of the continent. There was no Arctic sea ice at all last winter. The algorithm tells us that, except for polar regions, we can expect temperatures over fifty C everywhere else before the end of the century, possibly much sooner. Not every day, but increasingly regularly. Humankind will be forced to live underground on those days.'

'What about on days without flares?' I asked.

'The problem is the general growth in the sun's output, not the flares themselves, that is just coincidental,' said Sir Peter. 'I haven't made a study of that aspect so I'm guessing, but I'd imagine, even when the sun's radiation eases when there are no flares in progress, air temperature would be over forty and could be pushing fifty. I was not joking when I said that we need a new planet.'

The assembly fell silent for a while then Linsey said, 'And that, folks, is out of the question! We don't have the technology to go planet hunting and the only logical place, Mars, is unlikely to provide a suitable environment for a population of humans to be viable. It's barely any more habitable than the moon and can't be reached without going through many flare cycles. The trip would likely be deadly.'

'So, the only hope is for the flares to stop, or at least reduce frequency, and there's no sign of that happening,' I said pessimistically.

'No,' said Sir Michael. 'They continue for about seven and a half days then pause for the same period, and there's been no change for over a year. We can hope that it's peaked, but there isn't any supporting evidence. As I said, the frequency has been steady for close to eighteen months. Prior to that, of course, they'd been increasing in regularity.'

'But why is the sun heating during the flares? Why is it connected?' I asked.

'We don't know. There are teams of scientists trying to find out, but so far, we don't have an answer,' said Sir Michael. 'We're not even certain it has anything to do with the flares. It is very difficult to measure the week on week increase in Sol's output.'

HEAT

5 Number Ten

The prime minister, greying fifty-four-year-old Jenny McRoberts, looked around the cabinet room, 'Your report, home secretary.'

Jack Easton, one of the youngest ministers, opened a folder and began. 'More small boats coming from the continent, though fewer than last year. Nothing we do seems to slow them down. However, there are others with bigger problems.'

'How do you mean?' asked the PM.

'As I told you over coffee yesterday, there is an armada of boats crossing the Mediterranean from Africa. They are attempting to escape the heat. Over eight thousand people are known to have arrived in Spain last month and a similar number in Italy. France is turning them away with military patrol boats. Those numbers are probably underestimates, as most boats make landfall and the occupants escape into the countryside, heading northwards. It's serious and only going to get worse, much worse.'

'Where are they heading? Are they aiming for Britain?' asked Walter Andrews, the foreign minister.

'From what we can make out,' continued the home secretary, 'most are *not* heading for the British Isles, but are making their way farther north with their sights set on Scandinavia and Russia. Britain is not far enough north in most migrants' minds. It could actually benefit us as marginally fewer numbers are crossing the Channel.'

'This is a worldwide trend,' said Dame Diana Staunton, the minister for the environment. 'Massive numbers are crossing into the United States. They're avoiding the normal borders and using boats to run across to Florida or up the Californian coastline. Australia and New Zealand are experiencing the same influx from the north, although the Kiwis seem to be better protected as the crossing is extremely treacherous in small boats. Even Tasmania is not cool enough for most migrants' wishes. Indians have been moving into the mountainous north of their country and there have been skirmishes with organised Sri Lankan gangs shipping ferry loads across the Palk Strait. They come from multiple directions and there is so much coastline that the Indian government is unable to control it. There is even the danger of military action over it. The Indian government is saying the Sri Lankans are doing it as a deliberate policy. South Korea and Japan are experiencing similar problems and, although they haven't admitted it, intelligence tells us that China's problem is worse than most.'

The PM turned to Sir David Brenner, the science minister, and asked, 'You've got something set up for us, I believe?'

'Yes, Prime Minister. Dame Beth Arnold, the official astronomer; Sir Michael Harding, a sun specialist from Cambridge; and Dr Linsey Delve, head of the United Kingdom Space Agency are arriving for a meeting here at ten thirty tomorrow. We're trying to keep the numbers small, but I'll be there. I recommend you attend, plus the home secretary and minister for the environment.'

'Anyone else here need to be included?' asked the PM. 'I don't mean, would you like to eavesdrop, but if you think you could make a valuable contribution let me know.'

'I should be there,' said Sir Charles Browning, the minister for defence. 'I know Dame Beth. She and I met several times during the Mindslip Crisis when I was PM. She's married to one of our junior ministers.'

'Who?' asked the PM.

'Gren Pointer. He's the minister for Mindslip rehabilitation,' said the cabinet secretary.

'That's a job which is likely to end soon. Very few people who became animals are still alive, just a few of the larger species. I'm not sure that it needs a dedicated minister any longer,' said the home secretary.

'Okay. The details and a video recording of the meeting will be circulated. Does anyone else need to be there in person?' asked the prime minister.

There was no other response.

The cabinet secretary said, 'Next item.'

HEAT

6 Kigali

The sun blazed relentlessly over Kigali, Rwanda, as a record heatwave gripped the city. The new and unexpected climate crisis had intensified the dry season, pushing temperatures to unprecedented highs. Hospitals in Kigali, particularly the main general hospital, were soon inundated with patients suffering from heatstroke and dehydration.

By mid-morning, the emergency department was overwhelmed. Hundreds of people, young and old, were arriving, but only the elderly were admitted. The hospital corridors buzzed with the frantic activity of doctors, nurses, and volunteers trying to manage the chaos.

The medical staff quickly set up triage stations to assess the severity of each case. Patients with the most severe heatstroke were given top priority. The treatment involved several critical steps, but resources were being stretched beyond their limits.

The most serious cases were immediately immersed in cold water baths, the most effective method to rapidly lower core body temperature. At least the hospital had a large number of baths and was not short of cold water. For those where immersion was not possible, evaporation cooling techniques were employed. Water was misted onto their bodies while fans blew warm air over them, facilitating rapid cooling.

Some patients were packed with ice and wrapped in cooling blankets, particularly around the groin, neck, back, and armpits, where major blood vessels are close to the skin.

HEAT

In the worst cases, intravenous fluids were administered to combat severe dehydration. Electrolyte imbalances were corrected using specially formulated solutions to restore sodium and potassium but the medical services in Kigali were not geared up to deal with a tenth of the influx they were experiencing.

Continuous monitoring of vital signs was essential, but with patients lying on the floors, on trolleys in corridors or slumped on seats, it was impossible to keep up. Some began to shiver, which is a counterproductive response that raises body temperature. When that was spotted, muscle relaxants like benzodiazepines were administered, but the supply of drugs would soon be depleted at this rate.

The sheer number of elderly patients quickly exhausted the hospital's supply of cooling equipment and IV fluids. Calls for additional supplies were made to neighbouring hospitals and international aid organisations, but none were able to provide support. The numbers dying were increasing. The crisis was turning into a disaster.

Medical staff worked in shifts around the clock. Volunteers, including medical students and retired healthcare professionals, were called in to assist. With the emergency rooms overflowing, makeshift treatment areas were set up outside under tents, but the relentless fifty-degree temperatures grew even higher under canvas. Even air-conditioned buses and refrigerated trailer units were brought in to be used as temporary cooling stations for milder cases.

Kigali's healthcare infrastructure was not designed to handle such extreme weather and the need for climate-resilient healthcare facilities became glaringly apparent. The government was put under severe pressure to do something – anything, but there was nothing which could be done to ease the crisis in the short term.

Lack of public awareness of what to do if affected by prolonged exposure to extreme heat was a further problem and hurriedly prepared public health campaigns were being cobbled together to educate the population on preventive measures. This was no easy task as many of the population didn't have televisions, radio or access to the Internet.

In the minds of most observers in other countries, and the aid agencies, the situation underscored the urgent need for global climate action. The Kigali Declaration signed many years earlier had called for accelerated efforts to combat climate change and invest in climate adaptation measures, but this was not global warming. Global warming was gradually coming under control. What was happening here was something new and not immediately obvious to less well-developed countries. It was the sun which was the problem. The life-giving sun was showing its indifference to lifeforms on the third planet.

As it set over Kigali that evening, the hospital staff continued their tireless efforts. The crisis was a stark reminder that the climate crisis was still not resolved, but science was beginning to show that everything was far worse than anyone had imagined.

HEAT

What would happen when the truth about the sun's growing output was revealed to an ignorant world?

7 The Shocking Truth

Sir David Brenner, science minister, showed me into the historic cabinet room at 10 Downing Street.

Harold Macmillan's enormous, tapered, green-baize-covered, lozenge-shaped table seemed strangely deserted with only six people standing at the far end of it holding bone-china teacups and saucers in a floral design.

David served me coffee and I placed a Bourbon biscuit in the saucer. I'd been in here two or three times during the Mindslip Crisis, although most Downing Street meetings had been conducted in the famous COBRA – Cabinet Office, Briefing Room A. This, however, was the actual cabinet room, where the senior ministers of the British Government met regularly to discuss policy and the affairs of state.

'She'll be here shortly.'

'Why are we in here?' I asked.

'There are meetings going on in both the other meeting rooms, Dame Beth,' he said as we slowly walked towards the other figures who were standing beside the double windows at the Downing Street end of the office.

I smiled at Charles Browning, the Mindslip era prime minister whom I'd worked with before, and David introduced me to home secretary, Jack Easton; environment minister, Dame Diana Staunton; and cabinet secretary, Sir Joseph McKinley. My advisers, Sir Michael Harding, and Dr Linsey Delve were already in conversation with them.

'How are you, Jack?' I asked. We'd had many meetings together in the past.

'Fine, fine. I'm intrigued about what you have to tell us,' he replied.

The door at the far end of the room swung open and Britain's sixth woman prime minister, Jenny McRoberts strode into her domain. 'Good morning, all,' she said, pouring a coffee and coming along the room to meet us, shaking Dr Linsey Delve's hand as they'd not met before.

The PM ignored her usual chair, the only one with arms around the cabinet table, and seated herself near the end by the windows. 'Please, take a seat,' she said, waving us towards the nearest chairs. The lozenge-shaped end of the cabinet table made it easier to see other participants, but with such a small group, it was hardly important.

Sir Joseph opened his laptop and set a recorder on the green baize. He said, 'This meeting has been called by Dame Beth Arnold, the official astronomer, to brief senior ministers over the current climate problems. Those present are the prime minister, home secretary, science minister, environment minister, defence minister, Sir Michael Harding, solar specialist from Cambridge, and Dr Linsey Delve, head of UKSA' – he paused, typed something into his laptop and continue – 'Dame Beth, please begin.'

I decided to stand. It would add more gravitas to what I had to say. 'Good morning, everyone. I don't bring glad tidings, I'm afraid. With other scientists including Sir Michael and Dr Delve, we have been carrying out a comprehensive study of the growing heat phenomenon we've all been experiencing over the last few years.'

The PM said, 'Yes, we all want to know when we're likely to get some respite. In Britain it hasn't been too bad, but our southern neighbours are really suffering, particularly the elderly and infirm. In Africa it's approaching calamity status. We've been very diligent in reducing emissions and most of the largest emission generating countries have been working with us. It seems to be having little or no impact.'

'I'm sorry, Prime Minister, but I cannot ease your concerns. The news I bring is probably more catastrophic than any of you will have imagined,' I said.

'Come on, Beth, let's have it. We can't tackle the problem unless we know the full extent and how much worse it might get,' said Jack Easton.

'I wish I could help you "tackle the problem", home secretary, but I cannot. Might I suggest that you allow me to present the findings before you quiz, Sir Michael, Dr Delve, and myself with any more specific questions.'

'Certainly,' said the PM. 'We need to understand what's happening without interrupting so, please, some patience. Start with the worst scenario, Beth, then we can hope to improve the outcome from that point onwards.'

'Yes, Prime Minister, but the worst-case scenario is that Earth is likely to be uninhabitable by the end of the century, if not well before. We are possibly facing the end of humankind, and, if not that, then the end of civilisation as we know it.'

'Oh, come now, Beth. Surely that is taking it too far,' said Charles Browning.

'No, Charles, this is what might be called an end-of-the-world scenario. It really is an existential threat. Michael, give them the specifics,' I said, and Sir Michael scrolled across his tablet screen then stood, his smart suit rather wasted as his oversized shirt made him appear untidy.

'Worldwide temperatures will exceed fifty degrees Celsius within twenty years. Sixty a decade later. Only the poles will maintain lower rates. This will mean that all life between the Arctic and Antarctic circles will be wiped out or will have to live underground. It is difficult to imagine any livestock farming at all in those temperatures and most crops will not survive either. The polar landmasses, mainly Antarctica, will see similar temperatures for around four months of the year and not much less the rest of the year because the whole atmosphere will be that hot' – he paused, tapped his screen a few times and continued – 'Even worse, the world's oceans will gradually heat to the same degree, although provisional estimates show that reaching fifty Celsius will lag some twenty years behind the atmospheric temperature. This will kill all coral reefs and almost all fish and invertebrates. Some might adapt, but not in any great numbers. Whatever we choose to call it, scientists are already referring to it as a mass extinction.'

I could see the shock passing over the faces of our audience. No one had expected the news to be so bad.

'The upshot,' I added as Sir Michael sat down, 'is that we will be unable to feed any surviving population. Starvation, famine, and the sheer heat, will kill billions and the remainder will only survive in underground shelters.'

Sir Michael rose again, 'The only way this can be prevented is if the output from the sun is reduced.'

'Why is it warming?' asked Sir Charles.

'We don't know. That is one of the problems,' said the Cambridge professor. 'The level of solar activity is growing. The frequency of flares is now constant, but they don't actually create the heat. The overall output of the sun is the cause of the rising temperatures.

'We are sure coincidence isn't involved here, so the supernova must have been the cause of the change, but we don't know why. There are numerous telescopes and satellites studying the sun but, to date, nothing has given us any clues as to the reason or if it is likely to change and return to normal. There is speculation, of course. The latest theory which has some merit is that gravity waves from Betelgeuse compressed the sun's outer layers. In effect, that caused more fuel to enter its nuclear furnace. There is currently no way for us to confirm it, but if that is true, there will likely be no reduction ever. The growth in output will continue for some decades and then stay at that level. It could also shorten the sun's life, but that is hardly likely to affect those of us experiencing the problem today.' Sir Michael sat again.

'You're serious about this?' asked Diana Staunton, the environment minister.

'Deadly serious,' I said. 'And some scientists give us even less time before the heat becomes unbearable.'

'So, what can we do?' asked the PM. 'You've heard about the heatstroke crisis in Rwanda a couple of days ago?'

'Yes,' said Sir Michael, 'and that's going to become the norm almost immediately for countries between the tropics and will gradually spread north and south from there. There will be no respite.'

'There are several aspects to this,' I said. 'Firstly, we are going to experience an enormous migration of people northwards, especially when they realise the heat will only get worse. That is hundreds of millions trying to reach more temperate regions – anyone with the wherewithal to travel. It's already happening on a small scale and will escalate rapidly, becoming a stampede. The increasing migration will not have escaped Charles' notice, and it will not be long before the Ministry of Defence will have to repel migrants. We thought the small-boat immigration of the twenties was a problem; what this will grow into is disastrous. The northern economies cannot feed and shelter the whole of the world's population.'

'You think we'll have to protect our borders?' asked Sir Charles.

'I guess that is a matter for government to decide,' I said.

'Indeed,' he said.

'And we'll do that, how?' asked Jack Easton.

'The French are already using force to protect their Mediterranean coastline. There are rumours that they have sunk migrant boats. They say they've just turned them away, but that might not be so,' said Charles, 'and it will not be long before the media manage to film a sinking.'

'They're sinking migrant boats! And you're considering the same? Drowning illegal migrants?' asked Jack.

'If what we're being told is true, it will be worse than that, we might need to use lethal force to stop our own people rioting... and we'll need to prepare for organised invasions from other nations if it's a matter of life or death,' said Charles.

'The heat will affect Britain, too. You're talking as if Britain is in some protective bubble. It isn't. We won't be able to survive here,' said Sir Michael. 'Maybe you should be formulating a plan to invade the Scandinavian countries to protect United Kingdom citizens and move them northwards?'

'Good God,' said Charles. 'Hadn't thought of that aspect.'

'What? Damn it!' exclaimed the PM. 'The more I hear, the more of a nightmare it's becoming. Beth, do you have any solutions at all?'

I replied, 'We have some ideas. Linsey, could you outline the current thinking?'

Dr Linsey Delve stood, an imposing figure, her smartly dressed slim Black figure and neat silver hair adding dignity to her appearance. 'There have been discussions about an ultimate solution,' she began.

'That sounds awfully like the Nazi final solution to me,' said Jack Easton.

'Jack!' scolded the PM.

'Sorry,' he said and slouched a little in his seat.

'Continue, Dr Delve,' said the PM.

'I've had several meetings with both NASA and Roscosmos. The last one, held in Iceland, also included ESA, CSA and JAXA.'

'That's the European Agency, Canadian and Japanese groups,' I interjected.

Linsey continued, 'We also tried to include the Chinese, but, so far, they've not been very forthcoming.'

The science minister, Sir David Brenner shuffled in his seat, 'And what have you come up with? Some sort of heatshield for the world?'

'No, Sir David, we're not capable of that sort of technology. I'll start with some background.' She scrolled through a page or two on her tablet.

'Firstly,' she continued, 'we all recognise that there are certain things which we are *not* capable of doing. We can't even contemplate Sir David's heatshield. That's totally out of the question. We are also *not* able to plan to go to another planet around another star. It is true that we now know of three habitable planets around nearby stars. They are eight, fifteen and eighteen light years away. With current technology, journeys to even the closest of them would take hundreds of years. I can, however, assure you all that scientists are putting every effort into finding near-light-speed propulsion systems. Ion drives are a possibility, theoretically, but we don't have a working model large enough to be useful yet.'

'What would an ion drive achieve?' asked Sir Charles.

'An ion drive doesn't produce an enormous force like a rocket engine but does provide a small thrust over a very long period of time. In that way, a ship would accelerate continually and might even approach the speed of light, but it is a slow process. Once a speed close to that of light is reached, time slows down for those on board,' replied Linsey.

'Relativity?' asked Jack.

'Yes. However, to complicate matters still further, deep space radiation will be a massive, possibly insurmountable problem for lengthy space journeys. Adding to our problems, the flares from the sun will be lethal during journeys within the range of the asteroid belt. We can't even get to Mars safely.'

'So, what *is* possible?' asked the PM.

'Sorry, Prime Minister,' continued Linsey, 'but I have to spell out the impossible before we can consider the more likely possibilities. Otherwise, nonsensical suggestions will muddy the waters.'

'Okay, I understand,' said the PM.

'Even going to Mars is out of the question during the sun's flaring. NASA have been looking at how to get from Earth to Mars while using the shadow of the Earth as a shield and while this could work during the early part of the journey, it is not the shadow of the Earth but the size of its magnetosphere which is important. Although it extends beyond the orbit of the moon it soon becomes too small to encompass the spaceship, so that concept fails too.' Dr Delve scrolled to a new page on her device. 'Of course, work is being done on shields for spacecraft and while there is a lot of promise in shielding small ships to the moon, and even to Mars, any ship capable of carrying a substantial crew and passengers would be too large to protect.'

'You're thinking of an evacuation but are currently unable to do it?' asked the science minister.

'Yes, that is the major thrust, but the challenges we'll face doing that are almost insurmountable. So far, we believe a population of several hundred or more could be housed on the moon, underground, but, of course, we could house even more underground on Earth, although it is easier said than done. We don't just have to house the selected individuals or families, but we also must feed them for generations, perhaps. The moon is not much more of a problem than Earth regarding that, but on the moon, there would be little chance of the abandoned population breaking in and destroying the fortunate protected few. If any of you have not considered the trouble violent, rioting hordes represent, I suggest you do so. It's a real threat.'

'Are you telling us that there is no solution to the problem?' asked the PM.

'So far, the answer is that we haven't found one. I'm flying to Reykjavik with Dame Beth on Friday for another meeting with the other space agencies. We are looking for a solution. We'll report back, of course. Can I now throw it open for questions?' she asked and returned to her seat.

The questions were numerous and tended to involve even crazier ideas than building a heatshield for Earth. Eventually a halt was called, and the PM called an urgent meeting of the senior cabinet ministers for the next morning.

'Charles, come to my office,' said the PM as the Cabinet Office emptied.

∞∞∞∞∞∞∞∞∞∞

'Have you any contingencies for this, Charles?' asked the PM, once they'd closed the door of her office.

'No, frankly, we were banking on the heat eventually reducing back to normal levels,' said the minister of defence. 'Can I suggest you change the senior cabinet meeting to Tuesday. I'd like to call in my military advisers and the home secretary to help us put some sort of strategy into place.'

'Yes, sounds sensible. I'll tell Joe to push it back. I don't think we should release this news to the full cabinet yet. We'll discuss that on Tuesday. I assume you'll eventually be thinking about declaring a state of emergency.'

'Not initially, Prime Minister. I believe we should deal with the crisis in phases. Martial law will be needed, but it is not our first line of attack.'

'Good. Okay. Brief me after your meeting and give me time to provide some input. I fear, whatever the outcome, we're not going to be very popular. Saving as many people as possible might be our only saving grace as a government,' said the PM soberly.

'You might be right,' said Charles Browning and he got up to leave.

'Wait,' the PM said, standing up. 'Do you think we should tell the public the truth about this?'

'Good God, no.'

'What? We keep it secret? How can we hide something which is so obviously taking place?'

'We must,' said Charles. 'If we tell people, it's the end of the world, there'll be anarchy.'

'You really think so? Surely the people will work together to try to mitigate the problem. I don't know but building shelters or the like.'

'I'll take advice. Not hopeful though, Prime Minister,' he said. 'In fact, I think you are very wise not to be telling the full cabinet yet. Keep those who know the truth close to you. Just the most senior ministers.'

'I'll give that some more thought. Good luck with your meetings.'

'Thanks, Prime Minister. I think we'll all need it.'

8 Anxiety

Mindslip had changed so much in the world. I had been a fit family man in my mid-thirties when it had struck. I had a beautiful loving wife and two beautiful children of eight and ten. Suddenly all of that had gone. My wife had become an elderly greyhound and lived less than a year; my eight-year-old daughter had morphed into a French woman of twenty-two; my son had become a Black lad, but he was only two years older than he had been. He'd gained the most amazing footballing skills, and ten years later he'd become a midfield genius for Tottenham Hotspur. He was also playing for England who continued to fall at the last hurdle in every international competition. Sandra, suddenly only three years younger than me, found she had a talent for cooking. Her adulthood was really difficult to manage – for her and for me. She learned quickly, however, and became a chef, winning a Michelin star and running the kitchen of the prestigious Montagu Arms in the New Forest. Both were happy in their new lives twelve years later, which was a great relief to me.

Personally, getting over the loss of Caroline took a while and was complicated by my becoming a young woman. I suffered a lot of harassment as I was physically extremely attractive. I began to see my old sex in a wholly new light with all its misogyny and selfishness. I learned the lesson of how badly men had treated women very quickly indeed by experiencing it first-hand. I recognised that even my pre-Mindslip self had been guilty from time to time.

It was difficult getting used to being in my new body. I was seeing my own body through the eyes of a sexually active very heterosexual man. For some considerable time, many weeks, I desired myself; what a ridiculous experience indeed. Can you imagine it, looking at yourself and having carnal sensations while doing so? Men wanted to date me, of course, but the thought of participating in a relationship with a man horrified me. In fact it would not be too wrong to say that I was sickened by it. In my new guise, and despite being illegal, I suffered catcalls, wolf-whistling, uninvited touching, ogling and sexual advances. It so angered me that I could see no future for myself in any sort of relationship. I tried to shut myself off from any contact with men.

However, Gren Pointer came along. He was an undeniably handsome, thirty-something man with strong features and a surprisingly gentle nature. I later discovered he'd been a woman approaching middle age before Mindslip and that probably gave him his caring nature.

Gradually, his friendship morphed into a closeness which started to make me feel uncomfortable, but hormones were at work within my new body. The dread of any physical contact with him eased. Such an extraordinary change which took place over almost two years.

Eventually, one evening it happened. We both lost our post-Mindslip virginities in an awe-inspiring manner. I suppose, after that, I could relax into my female body and truly become a woman.

Inevitably, we married and now have two other children of our own, childbirth being both an incredibly frightening yet wonderful event for me.

On the evening after the Downing Street meeting, we enjoyed dinner in the fabulous Royal Garden Hotel by Kensington Gardens and retired to our room. We talked about the climate crisis, but Gren eventually switched into romantic mood, and we went to bed.

Later, as we peeled ourselves apart, I couldn't help but think back to my old male sexual self. Was it better to experience the amazing, uncontrollable sensation of ejaculation, or the equally unexpected similarly surprising female orgasm and its gentler and more enduring post-coital glow? I had to admit that the latter was gradually winning me over, but I had the double joy of knowing exactly what he was experiencing too. A true Mindslip gift to those of us who changed sex.

We lay still, breathing heavily, my head and shoulders crooked in his strong arms, thrilling to his warmth.

'Love you,' he said.

'Yes. Me too,' I agreed, rubbing my fingers across his stomach.

'What are we going to do?'

I laughed and said, 'Well, you know, my new body has an unexpected talent; I'm more than happy to start again right now!'

'Shut up, vixen. I meant, what do we do about the crisis? Is it really going to be as bad as we think?'

'Worse. I think we'll be suffering as much in the UK as the more southerly countries.'

'People will be dying all around us,' he said.

'They will. Africa and other tropical and equatorial regions will become parched. Crops will fail. Hordes will head northwards, trying to find somewhere cooler, but by then we'll be fighting them off. I think the Med will become a killing field.'

'The French are already deliberately sinking migrant boats.'

I was shocked. 'Thought that was just a rumour.'

'Afraid not. We've seen video of it and, sooner or later, it will hit social media,' said Gren, tightening his grip on my shoulder. 'Same question; what should *we* do? For us?'

'Ask me again after the Reykjavik meeting.'

'What? You think there's a possible solution?'

'For our children, maybe, but not for the world.'

'The Arctic, Antarctic, the moon?'

'Not now, dearest. After the summit.'

'What about your older children?' he asked.

'Our two could be included. They're still young enough, but I can't see it stretching to Sandra and Wilson. Scares me what'll happen to them. Sandra being a Michelin-starred chef and Wilson a top footballer is hardly likely to pass the criteria for salvation. They're adults now so I don't see how they could qualify for special consideration.'

'Can't you pull strings?' he asked anxiously.

'I doubt it, not in all conscience and I don't want to raise any false hopes.'

HEAT

Minutes later, my glow was fading, and I heard his breathing change as he fell asleep.

I extricated myself and walked over to the window, sat in one of the easy chairs and looked at the moonlit gardens beneath. I was determined to do my best for Geoffrey and Caroline, even if I could do nothing for Wilson and Sandra.

HEAT

9 Trafalgar Square

Had James been rather optimistic when he decided that the protest should take place in Trafalgar Square, the rallying point being Nelson's Column? It was a huge space.

Several of his eco-warrior group thought he had. Many felt that they would be lost in the giant London square. The Metropolitan Police considered it a breeze. How many would attend a new eco group's first protest?

The message went out on WhatsApp to almost a thousand followers:

Now is the time to make a stand. Our government is lying to us about climate change. For a decade, we've been suffering under the regulations aimed to reduce emissions. They've told us it's working, that emissions are falling, yet what do we see? The growing heat has been escalating over the last few years. Unprecedented 45°C in parts of the south of England. ACT NOW! Join us in Trafalgar Square on Saturday the 15th at eleven in the morning and show solidarity. Help us get the answers. NOW! Forward this to as many people as you can.

The authorities were shocked. Trafalgar Square was filled to the brim with tens of thousands of people. Some carrying official banners and protest signs, others with their own homemade versions.

As James Buchanan climbed onto a plinth to make his speech, he was applauded by the entire assembly.

'My name is James Buchanan,' he shouted into the megaphone, 'and I run the EW group.' Cheers rang out, the banners were lifted and stretched out, official and unofficial placards were raised up and down.

'Friends. We have been lied to. We've spent the last twenty years, at great cost in both money and convenience, getting shot of fossil fuels. Now most cars are electric, gas boilers have been scrapped. Everyone has heat pumps in their homes. We've all suffered from the cost. But for what reason? Is it cooler now?' Screams of 'No' from the crowd.

'Exactly. It is forty-one degrees right now! Right here! It's crazy! The temperature just continues to rise. They've been lying to us. It's pretty obvious that fossil fuels had *nothing* to do with global warming. Nothing!' A chant of 'Liars, liars!' began and made it impossible for James to be heard. He let it die down before continuing.

The speech went down well. The crowd was orderly, until, that is, a couple of police officers approached the plinth and ordered James to climb down.

He wouldn't. He continued to shout through the megaphone. One officer managed to get onto the plinth and James did something he regretted. He pushed the man. He fell over, almost tumbling to the ground, but managing to hang on by his fingertips. That was it. James was arrested and the crowd became belligerent.

However, the demonstration had achieved its objectives. Questions were asked in the Houses of Parliament. What was happening to the climate? Were emissions really falling? Why was the heat continuing to grow?

HEAT

10 Moon

'Clear, at last,' Commander Lewis's voice came over the Moonbase intercom at 07.13 GMT.

The deaths at Moonbase over the last few years had instilled a new caution into the already careful management of the structure, which occupied a crater adjacent to Copernicus and the tunnels of new underground radiation shelters. Despite it having nothing to do with the slipping of minds, the term Mindslip Radiation had become the common expression for the bombardment of the moon and orbital spacecraft, by the increasing number of solar flares which had begun when Betelgeuse had turned supernova. The excited sub-atomic particles were, however, linked to the cause of Mindslip; Betelgeuse turning supernova.

Moonbase was now well protected from general deep space radiation, but the flares produced surges which breached the domes' defences. Flare radiation can reach the moon at the speed of light, so there was no way of receiving any warning. When they occurred, alarms sounded and everyone rushed to safety to minimise the effect. There's a little extra warning of coronal mass ejections and they could be equally dangerous. Damage to astronauts was inevitable. Resupply ships were scheduled for the sun's quiet weeks, but the base itself was vulnerable. All astronauts were called back to Earth while NASA, ESA and Roscosmos, in addition to other space agencies, considered the best way to proceed.

In 2030 the plan to strengthen Moonbase's protection was put in hand. Construction was almost abandoned as nearly every returning astronaut quickly showed symptoms of radiation poisoning and, although some survived, most succumbed to a painful and inevitable death. The survivors would never live a normal life again.

The heroic work undertaken by the volunteer crews saw tunnels dug into the surface. This offered emergency shelter, but it was only recently that the excavations had finally linked to a natural rille to provide permanent living accommodation during the period of flares.

When the first flare of each cycle was spotted, astronauts moved underground, not returning to the normal domes and their surface tasks until after the last flare and when a flare alarm sounded, there was a rush to get underground as quickly as possible. Airlock safety procedures were abandoned, and astronauts were often seen running into the tunnels still in their EVA suits, though that helped because the suits also provided a modicum of extra protection.

Moonbase was considered vital for the future of space exploration. It now provided water and hydrogen for fuel for ships which could soon be departing to Mars and even farther afield. Amazingly, nitrogen and other essential components of breathable air could be extracted from the regolith. It was a slow and difficult process, but once the method was mechanised it quickly provided the elements required. No one, however, had yet formulated a satisfactory plan to protect interplanetary spaceships from radiation during their journeys. There was much to do, much to learn, but, at least now, the work could be carried out safely.

Christine Daly's red ponytail swept leisurely from side to side in the moon's gravity as she made her way along a well-lit but very narrow corridor cut out of grey moonrock. Corridors were considered a luxury as they cost resources to create. They were only as wide as was necessary to move equipment or furniture along them. She wore a purple tracksuit with white go-faster stripes down the legs. To each side, numerous doors led to personal cabins – almost all currently empty. She stopped at number thirty-two and pressed the button which would alert the resident that a visitor had arrived.

'You awake?' she called into the microphone.

The door was an elongated oval, with a lip above floor level. It opened inwards, as did all personal Moonbase doors. It was protection against the loss of pressure in any public areas. The astronaut cubicles had similarly been excavated from the rock. There was no way that they could ever accidentally depressurise.

A crack appeared along the right of the opening as it swung inwards revealing Elena Esteban, a bronzed, mixed race woman with tightly braided hair, wearing matching pink sports bra and square cut briefs. She welcomed her Scottish colleague with a beaming smile.

'You're keen,' she said, stepping backwards into her crew living quarters to allow Christine to enter and close the door behind her. 'Won't be a minute.' She began to pull on the knee-length heavy duty socks which were needed in spacesuits.

'Can't wait to get outside again,' said the redhead, sitting on a chair beside a small desk. 'I've been going stir crazy. Doesn't seem long to begin with when you're suddenly confined for a week, but, my God, it seems interminable when you're nearing the end.'

'Had to abandon my drill, six metres into the surface when the last alarm went,' Elena replied, pulling on a tracksuit similar to Christine's, but in red, with yellow stripes. 'Hope it's not ruined the drill bit.'

'Should be okay,' said the other, casually looking around Elena's quarters. The door to the bathroom stood open and steam was escaping into the main room. Fans were struggling to extract it. Bathroom wasn't a fair description. There was no tub, only a plexiglass shower cubicle, washbasin, and toilet. It served its purpose, however.

The living area comprised some built-in drawers, desk, office type chair, a closet, comfortable easy chair, and an unmade three-quarter sized bed with drawers underneath. Elena hurriedly gave the duvet a shake. Under one-sixth Earth gravity, it settled unexpectedly slowly back to the bed. Another pull on one corner, the plumping of a couple of pillows and it was ready for the next slumber.

Both women in their casual outfits left the crew cabin and walked along the corridor. The word walk did not do justice to the light, extended strides they both exhibited, pushing off with one foot and almost floating a metre or so forward before landing on the other. Very graceful, and fast too.

Elena punched the green button on the canteen entranceway. Double doors swung outwards into the corridor. Inside, Bert Lewis at a nearby table, looked up from his toast and marmalade, raised his hand and smiled at the girls. Opposite him, Doc Lex Barrington swung around to see who'd come in and gave a wave before continuing to attack what looked like a coloured speckled omelette. The two men were also casually dressed, the paunchy, bearded, doctor in a black tracksuit and the commander in an outfit which resembled a flight suit in brilliant orange. The canteen was a thirty-metre crescent-shaped space in the command dome, utilitarian in design. A kitchen area was to one side with all the expected appliances; fridge, freezer, large and small ovens, a couple of microwaves, coffee machine, blender, two air fryers and all the expected utensils. The dining area was home to ten plastic-topped dining tables. Some easy chairs and a sofa were clustered around the huge window with its panoramic view of the lunar surface.

'Moooorning,' said the doc, stretching out the first syllable.

The women entered the kitchen area, prepared their breakfasts, and joined the men. Christine, eating from her cereal bowl, firstly wandered over to the panoramic window and surveyed the moon's surface which stretched away like a landscape painting from which all the colours had been mysteriously drained.

'So good to look outside,' she said. 'I was going stir crazy.'

'Yes,' said Bert. 'Wish this dome was protected. Hate living underground during these flare periods.'

One area in the protected tunnels also had a viewport, in fact, with a steel overhanging awning. The crew had taken some comfortable seats and put them facing it. As the regular imprisonment progressed, the crew could, increasingly often, be found sitting there, looking out from the wall of the crater, sometimes just chatting, at others playing chess or cards, or simply talking. The opening faced south so never saw the sun.

The four of them ate breakfast while discussing the tasks for the day.

'A new crew-ship is on the way, departing tomorrow with another two inmates for us. Should be here on Thursday,' said Bert.

'What's today?' asked Elena.

'Sunday,' said Lex.

'Lose track when we're stuck underground,' she explained.

Christine stood, gripped Elena's shoulder, and said, 'Come on sleepyhead, better get on with it.'

Elena swigged the last of her coffee and rose.

'Be careful,' said the doc.

'We will,' said one and, 'Always,' the other.

Back in the corridor, they turned left and glided about twenty metres to a more substantial doorway, a veritable airlock, with an array of lights, buttons, dials, and a video image which showed that it was currently empty. Elena hit the green button causing the circular portal to slowly swing inwards revealing a tunnel-like room, about ten metres long. On each side were hangers and lockers. Those on the left were bare, but on the right, there were five pressure suits and helmets.

The two women stripped to their underwear. The tracksuits and contents of their pockets were secured in their lockers, and each approached their own space suit. Christine's had the name DALY in a blue nameplate and, above it, a white saltire on a royal blue background – the Scottish flag, also known as the St Andrew's cross as the saint was crucified on a diagonal cross. Elena's was labelled ESTEBAN and sported the Spanish flag with its colourful coat of arms.

The suits were open above the steel waistband and up the back. The women climbed in through the waist, one leg at a time and worked their feet into the integral boots. Next, their hands reached into the arms and pulled the sides around themselves, pushing their heads through the steel collar. Now it needed teamwork. Elena sealed the waist of Christine's suit to the back and pulled each side together, sliding the double-fold airtight fastener from the collar down to the waist. Reversing roles, the Scot sealed the Spanish woman's suit. Each action was accompanied by verbal confirmations such as 'Top connection done,' and 'Neck link secure.'

Following a critical time-tested safety procedure, each in turn reversed up to a backpack which was fixed to the wall of the room. The backpack connected to the suit, and cables were plugged into the waistband and other orifices and secured. When that was done, they both checked instrument panels on their forearms and received green confirmation lights advising that the backpacks were correctly attached, fully charged and ready for use. Each took their own helmet and assisted their colleague to settle it into the collar, turn it through about forty degrees and apply the locking mechanism. Finally, they fitted their gloves, each examining the clasps to ensure they were airtight.

The final checks were that they could speak to each other on the radio system, that the suits had pressurised correctly and that all operating functions on their control panels were green.

'Hello, Dave, copy,' said Elena.

The fifth member of the current crew, Dave Wilkes replied, 'Copy you, Elena.'

'All checklists completed. Just about to leave Moonbase,' she responded.

'Copy that. Logging you out zero nine eleven hours. Stay safe,' said Dave.

'Will do,' both women replied.

Above the airlock, a red panel with white letters began to flash, 'VACUUM'.

They both checked the suit monitors on their right forearms as the pressure fell, for the collection of green lights which confirmed all was in order, then Christine leaned forward and punched the green button. The main door to the surface of the moon began to open inwards, swinging to the left. Some regolith in the entrance area which had been missed during the last hurried clean-up, was sucked outwards as if in a hurry to return to the landscape from where it had been so cruelly exiled by the last moonwalker at the end of the flare-free period. The regolith was an extremely fine powdery grit which clung to everything it came into contact with. Even the slightest electric charge on a suit or piece of equipment was like a magnet. Cleaning the legs of the suits after each EVA was essential to prevent the dust getting spread throughout Moonbase. It was also dangerous. Because of the lack of atmosphere, there was no erosion, and every particle of regolith had sharp edges. You did *not* want to breathe it in!

Elena stepped over the threshold, followed by Christine, who turned and hit a red button on the panel to the left of the open door. Lights flashed and it began to swing shut.

'Airlock closed,' announced Christine as the round, steel portal settled into place and the panel information screen advised, 'Airlock closed – depressurised.'

'Copy that,' said Dave over the radio.

She followed Elena to a storage shed and they both tampered with pieces of equipment which resembled giant yellow storage trunks with four pneumatic-tyred wheels. The tyres weren't rubber, of course, as that would not survive the extremes of the lunar surface, but a kind of reinforced plastic. The colour of the trunks was yellow so that they stood out against the regolith. Inside, they held tools and other equipment which was often required by astronauts during their work period outside. They could also provide an emergency supply of air.

'Artoo, follow me,' said Christine and the storage trunk fell in behind the astronaut as she headed along a well-worn track from Moonbase towards the lip of a crater. The other buggy, Detoo was similarly instructed to follow her colleague.

Elena stopped and looked to her left towards the canteen window. Doc and Bert saw her turn and they waved. Elena lifted her arm in response.

It was a strange sight for the two men, watching these figures in their cumbersome suits walking in the strange gait which was best for locomotion in one-sixth Earth gravity, followed by the two autonomous trunks, like obedient sheepdogs.

11 Toase

Hardly a breath of air stirred within the dim interior of the brightly coloured wooden dwelling of the Esturu family who were subsistence farmers in Toase, a few miles west of Kumasi, Ghana.

Destri, dressed in cut-down jeans and an unbuttoned red shirt with flip-flops on his feet, entered through the open door and clipped a young boy of about twelve years of age around the ear. 'Keep fanning your grandfather,' he shouted.

Quickly, the boy, in short brown corduroy shorts and nothing else, sweating profusely, began to pull and release a piece of string attached to an assembly of palm fronds above the old man's bed.

The room was poorly lit and windows were open to encourage any breeze to pass through the stifling environment. The floor comprised bare boards, covered by islands of colourful rugs. Cooking was done outside, so this was a living space. Some ancient, but still serviceable easy chairs, old cupboards and shelves, plus a table with four wooden chairs occupied most of the space. The boy sat in one of the easy chairs and pulled vigorously on the string to create a draught for the old man, lying on a single cot beside the door to the bedrooms.

His skin looked ghostly for an Asian man. He'd been Black until Mindslip which had also cost him a dozen years. Sweat beaded on his face, neck, and chest. The covering had been pulled down; Kwame Esturu didn't need to be kept warm, he needed air. A flannel covered his forehead, and the evaporating sweat on his body also lowered his temperature, but it was so hot that none of that helped him. Breaths rasped from the grandfather's mouth. He did not look long for this world.

'You're damn lazy!' shouted Destri.

The boy looked up and protested, 'I only stopped for a minute to wipe my face.'

'It second time I come and found you almost asleep. If happens again, will not be good for you! Understand?'

'Yes, Da.'

Destri bent down over the old man, removed the flannel from the creased forehead and replaced it with a fresh one. There was no cold water in this heat, the best he could do was to soak it in a bucket kept in the shade outside. This family did not have the luxury of a refrigerator, but did have a camping fridge which used evaporation to cool its interior. Inside it were essentials like butter, a jug of milk, cheese, fish, and meat.

A woman with braided hair and wearing a colourful dress entered carrying groceries, her ebony skin glistening where it was visible. 'How's he now?' she asked, laying a few staple foods on the table; eggs, bread, rice, a couple of tins.

'No better, Bright. It's the damn heat. See if you can get him to take some more water.'

She left the hut and shortly returned with a plastic beaker. She lifted the old man's head and offered it to his lips. He took some. Not enough really, but some. 'Doctor said he come later,' she said.

'Right. Nuffin he can do though, really.'

'No. Not really. Did you call your bro?'

'Yes, but can't get here for three days. Think he be too late.'

The old man coughed. He barely had the energy to do even that and collapsed back, struggling to breathe.

'It's not just your father. All the old people are suffering. Marielle died last night. Doctor wrote "heat" on death certificate. What we done to deserve this?'

'You know Moses taken his family north?'

'What he doing that for?'

'Said if he can get them to Europe, won't be so hot. Reckons he get a boat across the Med.'

'Heard others doing same, but what they going to do in Europe? They won't want them up there. Where they get food and work?'

'Guess they think only way. I dunno. Maybe we should do the same.'

'Your dad can't travel.'

'Fear he not hold us up much longer.'

'Don't say that! Got to have hope. I've been praying for him.'

'Prayers not much good, Bright, unless heat drops. Forty-seven degrees in centre of Toase this morning. Did you see field?'

'Yes. Mariam's watering what she can now.'

'Won't save crop. Actual leaves burning brown. Think it's had it. River's running slow too. Short of water if drops anymore.'

'Don't say that, Des, we can't survive winter if all the crop dies. Radio says rainfall is up, not down.'

'Won't all die, but no surplus, I think. Faster on that fan, Edu!'

The boy yanked the cord more vigorously. The old man's wispy hair was ruffled as the palm fan waved swiftly to and fro, back and forth.

The sound of a staff hitting the door called for their attention.

'Destri, you in there? How's Kwame?'

'Doctor. Come on in. He's real bad.'

The doctor, a distinguished looking fifty-something in tan coloured shorts and a sweat-soaked T-shirt entered the room carrying a black leather Gladstone bag. Mindslip had turned him into a Korean man and dumped him in Seoul. It took him a year to get back to Ghana.

Firstly, he took the pulse, then pressed a stethoscope to the bare chest, opened the patient's mouth and examined it before putting a thermometer under the tongue.

'Breathing's ragged,' he said. 'Pulse okay, but heart's weak. He should be in hospital by rights.'

'Can't afford dat,' said Destri.

The doctor removed the thermometer and examined it with a puzzled expression. 'Can't be that hot. He'd be dead if it was. Trouble is we can't get a good reading when the air is hotter than the body.'

'You able to do anything?' asked Bright.

'No. Keep fanning him and wetting his brow, Bright. The evaporation helps cool him. All we can do now is pray. They say the flares should stop today.'

'But that have little effect now. Tem'rature seems to climb anyway,' said Destri.

'Does seem that way,' said the doctor. 'I'll call in again tomorrow.'

'Wanna beer?'

'Much kindness, Destri.'

'Sit on de veranda. I bring em out.'

Destri joined the doctor on the narrow decking shaded by a rickety awning. He carried two open bottles of beer. 'Sorry, not cold,' Destri said as he handed one over and the two men sat on wooden chairs. 'What's happening to the world, Doc?'

'It's burning up, man. They say it was that supernova that hit us in 2019,' the doc said, draining half the beer.

'Yeah, looks real pretty in the night sky these days. Who'd've thought it'd cause such problems.'

'Was talking to friend of me in Kumasi, who knows a government minister. He's saying that there's a big conference at the UN to discuss it all.'

'Discussion solves nothing,' said Destri, sipping the ale.

'There's talk of asking northern countries to take in the sick and elderly from worst affected areas, like ours.'

'Too late for ma dad, I fear.'

'Don't give up hope. Flares stop tonight and it'll cool a little tomorrow.'

'But it don't cool so much recent.'

'No. Air everywhere is staying warm,' agreed the doctor. 'Sea in some places hits forty sometimes now. Crazy!'

'World going to end?'

'Dunno, wouldn't be surprised though.'

'Don't see northern places letting rest of the world into their land.'

'No. Might get violent. Guess time will tell.'

Bright ran out of the shack, 'Quick, Doctor. He's worse.'

The two men ran indoors, the doctor taking Kwame's pulse, then yanking the stethoscope from his bag. He pressed it against several parts of the man's chest, then put fingers to his neck and shook his head.

'Sorry, Destri, he's gone.'

Destri cried and Bright held his hand. The boy stopped pulling on the cord and the hot air stilled around them. Two half-finished beers sat on the table outside, growing still warmer in the heat.

12 Tripoli

What passed for a government in Libya met in the old palace in the capital. General Khalifa had called the meeting. He was a big man in every sense of the word: a commanding personality, heavily built, tall and aggressive. He'd come to the attention of the military during the long-gone Muammar Gaddafi regime and became increasingly influential. Mindslip morphed him from a well-built forty-year-old Arab into the imposing Black thirty-year-old Ugandan he was today. Once he'd found his way back to Libya, proved his identity, and reclaimed his rank, he swiftly rose to become the country's leader. There were no challengers. As head of state, he was fair, except when it came to any opposition and, during the last fifteen years, he'd reinvigorated the economy, increased the police force to reduce crime, cut out much of the previously endemic and infamous Libyan corruption, and tourists were returning in droves to visit the nation's fascinating coastline and inland heritage. The standard of living had improved, and Libya was able to shed its pariah statehood.

His background was curious. Before Mindslip, he was startlingly well educated, obtaining science degrees at Oxford in England and was a post-graduate at the Massachusetts Institute of Technology. He then spent four years working in the pharmaceutical industry in Belgium. Fluent in eight languages, while education is never wasted, he had apparently thrown away his academic career when he joined the Gaddafi regime as a lowly lieutenant. His climb was rapid, and his promotions not necessarily obtained through military merit. He'd gathered others around him, and they behaved almost like a mafia within a faction of the late Gaddafi's military. He never upset his superiors and knew how to endear himself to those who held more power than he did, until, that is, he became more powerful than them and discarded them out of hand. Ruthless was the best descriptive word for his rise. Corrupt until he got to the point where he began to stamp it out in all things Libyan. Genius was the most apt description for his abilities.

Today, his cabinet met in a luxurious, air-conditioned conference room at his palace in Tripoli. From his office, he watched them arriving on a television monitor. They were all hot and sweating, having come in from the forty-eight degree heat of the courtyard where he ensured they were all kept waiting for a sufficient number of minutes to cause stress. The military members dare not loosen their collars and the others wore smart suits and ties, not ideal in the heat. He wanted them hot and bothered when he marched into the meeting room from his ultra-cool office. The last day of the week-long flaring of the sun was always the hottest, so perfect for his agenda. Make them sweat. Finally, he gave the order for them to be shown into the cabinet room.

Khalifa strode in through double doors, held open for him by two of the smartest soldiers he could find. One, close to two metres tall, was muscular and dressed in a spotless khaki uniform with crisp white shirt; the other, a female with knee-length khaki skirt, military jacket, and white blouse. On her head was a white cotton shemagh scarf worn as a keffiyeh. She was slim but well-endowed, exactly as Khalifa liked them.

As he entered the room, the two ornate doors were closed behind him, their golden panels reflecting the sunlight streaming into the room from a large window directly behind the general's seat, which, itself, could almost be called a throne. Three walls were honey coloured with the contrasting one a darker shade. Impressive gilt-framed pictures depicted Gaddafi and other famous individuals. There were two oil painted scenes of cavalry battles plus an incongruous Hubble image of galaxy M31, the erroneously called Andromeda Nebula. Other pictures were a false colour representation of the influenza virus in shocking pink and amethyst, and a vastly enlarged electron-microscopic image of a microchip. Khalifa liked science and wanted it to be prominent in his palace.

Eight men sat around the ebony table in ornate red upholstered seats. Three military and five civilians: the ministers of employment, defence, health, science, and the chancellor. He'd handpicked all of them for their intelligence, education and, most important of all, their loyalty to him and commitment to his anticorruption policy.

Khalifa looked hard at the science minister and barked, 'So, what have you learned?'

The nervous minister played with his pen, tapping it on his notepad as he spoke. 'I still have information and data arriving, sir, so my report is not yet complete, but it is as you thought. The flares themselves are not causing the heat. That is being generated by the sun growing in temperature. Even if the flares stop, the heat will continue to rise. Even in periods without flares, the air temperatures are rising worldwide. The best estimate I can give today is that our country will become uninhabitable within ten to fifteen years, perhaps even sooner. Some might live underground. As you requested, we're exploring how that could be achieved, but living as we do today will likely be impossible.'

'And what other data or information are you expecting? Will it change anything?'

'I have more data arriving from NASA daily, but the US is starting to be difficult about releasing information. As this climate problem worsens, I believe they might be considering the data to be, let me say, "sensitive" to their own defence needs. It is so bad, they are becoming worried about what will happen to their own population.'

'It is as I thought. Thank you, Saad.' Khalifa turned his attention to General Fathi. 'Your report, please.'

The three-star general was a more confident individual than the science minister. He shuffled his papers then scrolled down his tablet. 'Sir,' he began, 'the acquisition of the craft is more problematical than we first thought. Most of the shipbuilders around the Mediterranean are inundated with work. I don't understand why that should be so unless others are thinking as we do. I have commissioned eight ferries capable of holding between four and six hundred people, plus some landing craft. We're also buying any serviceable ships which come onto the open market. I really need to know the details of the plan to be able to look for alternatives.'

'Yes, Fathi, I think you, General Ahmed and Mr Saad had better stay behind when this meeting finishes. Saleh, how are people surviving this heat?'

The health minister opened a folder and pulled out a couple of pages. 'Sir, it is not good. The elderly are dying and there is nothing we can do about it. They could tolerate the situation with air-conditioning, but few houses have it. Last week we lost fourteen hundred people, mainly the elderly, because of the heat and, this week, we have already passed two thousand. And those are the ones we know about, sir. There'll be others who haven't registered the deaths.'

'Thank you, Mr Saleh. Mr Saad, you and the two generals stay behind. Meeting closed,' said Khalifa.

The others made their way out.

'Come closer,' said Khalifa, and he waved the three men to move to his end of the table.

He waited for the double door to be properly closed then said, in a conspiratorial tone, 'Ahmed, how did the survey flight go?'

The two-star general opened his laptop. 'Very well, sir. Here's some footage.' He turned in his chair and pressed a button on a remote control. Blinds closed over the windows and a projector screen lowered from the ceiling at the far end of the room.

Aerial video footage of the ocean began to run on the screen. A coast was being approached. There were cliffs plunging into the sea. Snow covered the land, but not totally, there was bare rock and, in places, what looked like scrub vegetation. As the flight continued, a fast-flowing river was crossed, and the aircraft approached a crescent-shaped bay, several kilometres wide, before heading back out to sea. The video ended.

'This is a map, sir,' he said, handing over an A2[4] sized document.

'Is the bay suitable?' asked Khalifa.

'Most certainly. It'll cost, but it can be done.'

'Okay. You've been asking what the overall plan comprises, and I think it's time to reveal the details but remember, I want no leaks. Only the four of us are privy to this and it's vital it stays that way.'

---

[4] A2 is four times the size of A4. 42cm x 59.4cm or 16.6 inches x 23.4.

13 Iceland

I flew into the Icelandic capital with Dr Linsey Delve, head of the United Kingdom Space Agency. I'd been here many times to make use of the clear winter skies for astronomical purposes and for conferences. It was a convenient halfway house for those of us from Europe meeting with our Canadian and American counterparts. When the Chinese were attending, they could fly directly over the roof of the world, cutting down the journey time considerably.

The flight into the island was always interesting. It was a beautiful island, even more so in the snow, but on this occasion, there was little white in the scene. Of course, the island sported active volcanoes. Gren and I had come more than once just to look at the lava flows and hot springs, and one occasion to bathe in one.

The airport was about twenty miles from the capital. As VIPs we were quickly ushered through customs and passport control and emerged into the main concourse.

The Icelandic equivalent of the British home secretary, Sylvie Paulsdóttir, was there to meet us. She was also an astrophysicist so would be participating in our meetings. She had already greeted and was accompanied by Harry Kinsman, head of NASA, and Peter Gordon, a sun specialist from the Jet Propulsion Laboratory in Pasadena. We'd met both before. I'd met Harry on several occasions and always found him fascinating and amenable. Peter, not so much so, and I'd had to react strongly to his roving hands more than once in the past. *Why can't these lechers just take no for an answer?* I was sure I'd be fending him off again at some point in the coming days. He never seemed to learn the error of his ways.

Sylvie guided us through the busy atrium to a luxury Mercedes people carrier which sped off to join Highway 41 towards the capital. I ensured I was sitting beside Harry to avoid Peter's attentions.

We were all being accommodated in the five-star Reykjavik Edition Hotel. Arriving late morning, once we'd checked in, Sylvie took us to lunch in a private dining room where we joined Ethan Cockridge from the Canadian Space Agency, Daniil Kotov from Roscosmos, the Russian Space Agency, and Philippe Parodi from the European Space Agency. Argos Homburg, a top US astrophysicist was also present. Sadly, the Chinese Space Agency had decided not to send a delegate on this occasion. That wasn't unusual as they often did their own thing as regards space exploration and we regularly sent them Minutes of meetings they didn't attend.

Over lunch, most of us kept the conversation off the climate, but I was sitting next to Argos. Both of us were astrophysicists and astronomers so it was natural that our chatter soon diverted into the subject of Betelgeuse and the sun. Twice I had to put my hand onto his sleeve to hush him while waiting staff were nearby. He was either unaware of the confidential nature of our proposed discussions or was just naturally too open. Having been involved with government for over a dozen years, I was probably savvier when it came to secrecy.

Sylvie arranged for coffee to be awaiting us in Studio Two, a compact meeting room set out with a central conference table.

I noticed Peter Gordon keying frantically on his laptop. A couple of images flashed up on the big screen, then he shut his machine, and the pictures vanished.

Harry Kinsman, the fifty-four-year-old distinguished looking white administrator of the space agency took the lead. He didn't stand. He just cleared his throat and began, 'Thank you all for coming. We are facing an existential threat. If it doesn't wipe us out, it will nevertheless destroy our civilisation. Peter, please provide us with the latest data.'

Dr Gordon, the solar specialist from JPL, swung around in his chair to face the screen on the wall, opened his laptop again and showed us a graph. 'This first graph shows the solar output since Mindslip. You'll notice that there was no dip in radiation after 2019, but it continued at more or less the expected level until the solar maximum of 2025. The blue line shows what we would then normally expect, a slow reduction in heat for five or six years until the solar minimum and then a return to maximum levels. If you look at the red line, it shows what has actually occurred. Instead of the sun's output reducing after 2025, it continued to rise. Hence our current problems. This is even more pronounced because the sun was entering a cooler phase around Mindslip, and the 2025 maximum was expected to be little warmer than average.'

He took a long draught from his coffee cup and continued, projecting a new graph showing the next twenty years. 'As you can see, we're projecting the output to continue to rise. This has an cumulative effect because the atmosphere doesn't get time to lose its heat between maximums and that exacerbates the problem. The work we've all been doing to remove carbon dioxide from the atmosphere and bury it in the oceans, plus the move from fossil fuels should have been mitigating the rising heat, but that is not the case.'

Philippe Parodi broke in, 'Those figures. Where are they based upon?'

'We used Houston as the base for the figures,' replied Peter.

'You're projecting fifty-five Celsius *in Houston by 2040*? That's only eight years!' said the head of ESA.

'Yes. It's a lot worse than we originally thought,' said the man from JPL.

'And what time of day, month or year is that?' asked the Russian.

'Late July.'

'And it would normally be what in late July?'

'Thirty-three or thirty-four C. Ninety Fahrenheit.'

'You're projecting a hundred and thirty-one Fahrenheit in just eight years' time?' asked the Canadian.

'We are,' said Peter sombrely.

'How does that equate to us?' asked Sylvie Paulsdóttir.

'I don't have figures for Iceland,' said Peter, 'but I'll get my guys to produce them for you when I get back.'

'That's normal daily temperatures?' I asked.

'Yes. Not particularly hot days. We can expect variations between fifty and sixty.'

'Sixty!' exclaimed Daniil. 'Sixty Celsius?'

'Yes.'

The Russian threw up his arms and collapsed back into his seat, exasperated.

'Your last set of figures for London said forty-one C,' I said. 'Has that changed too?'

'I'm afraid so. The problem is that the overall atmospheric heating spreads rapidly. You can expect a continual forty-seven in London by 2040. Let me put the extension graph onto the screen,' said Peter, turning to his laptop and tapping a few keys. 'Here you can see 2050. Houston fifty C in winter and possibly sixty-five in summer. That's one fifty Fahrenheit. As a consistent daytime temperature, the human body cannot survive such heat.'

'That is so much worse than we expected, and sooner too,' said Linsey Delve.

'Yes. The world will not be habitable below sixty degrees north or above sixty degrees south. Oh, yes, healthy, young individuals might survive for some time, but I fear that none of us in this room would be able to live through it,' said Harry.

'Okay,' I said, 'we're meeting here to decide what to do. We could obviously create habitable regions within the Arctic and Antarctic circles, but how many could they support and what about the production of food?'

'Even that could be temporary,' said Peter. 'In our opinion, we must assume that Earth's surface will be completely uninhabitable from about 2075 or earlier.'

'You're saying we in Iceland are in the same predicament?' asked Sylvie.

'You have a few more years than Britain or Canada, but yes, no one escapes.'

'We're going to have to live underground?' asked Dr Cockridge. 'Even us Canadians?'

'Sooner or later, yes,' said Peter.

'Let me add some slight hope to proceedings,' said Harry Kinsman. 'We've been throwing a huge amount of money and technical resources at it, and we might be able to mitigate the worst... but only for a favoured few.'

'How do you mean? Explain,' said Daniil.

'I have two astronautics experts flying into Iceland this afternoon,' said Harry. 'They could not be with us today but will offer some ideas tomorrow.'

All eyes turned to the head of NASA.

'I need to ask you all a favour, however,' he added.

'Fire away,' said Philippe.

'The president of the United States has asked me to get all of you to commit to secrecy,' Harry said.

'I must tell our president and science ministers,' said Daniil.

'Yes, indeed you must, but the commitment is to vow not to speak to anyone about the project before

HEAT

speaking to your own heads of state. They will understand the reason for the secrecy and will give you guidelines as to who else might be taken into your confidence. The president is, as we speak, contacting all the heads of state of ESA countries, plus the UK, Canada, Russia, and Iceland.' Harry looked sternly at each delegate in turn. 'Do you give me your word?'

'I don't like secrecy. It often comes back to bite you when you least expect it, but will do as you wish,' said Philippe,

There was a chorus of yeses from the others.

'In that case,' he said, 'we meet back here at ten tomorrow and the scientists will give their presentation.'

∞∞∞∞∞∞∞∞∞∞

You could not imagine two more different individuals. Martin Bishop was a typical computer nerd, pockmarked white skin, tousled hair, spectacles forever slipping down his nose, and thin as a rake. I discovered later that Mindslip had changed him from a fifty-something IT genius into an eight-year-old kid, so now he was still only twenty-two, but a genius with decades of experience.

The other appeared more brawn than brains. Ted Garve was built like an American linebacker with one of those thick muscular necks, six feet six inches tall and broad-shouldered. They attached a storage device to a desktop computer which had been provided on one of the tables and Garve was soon checking links to the Bluetooth projector to cast images onto the screen on the wall.

Harry said, 'Martin and Ted are two of our most respected astronautic scientists. Both have had extensive involvement with the International Space Station and Ted was responsible for lifting it into a special geosynchronous orbit to keep it clear of the worst of the solar flares and hide it within Earth's shadow.'

'I've not been clear on how that works,' said Peter Gordon, the solar expert from JPL.

'How do you mean?' asked Martin.

'Well, once the flares pass Earth, they close in again as the radiation moves onward. Why would the ISS be safer in a geosynchronous orbit?'

'The magnetosphere extends way beyond the orbit of the moon and it's the worst of the radiation we are concerned with,' said Martin using his hands and fingers to emphasise each word and to draw circles and lines in the air. 'The bulk of the danger from flares is diverted far enough to have significantly less effect.'

'That's why we also had to position additional shielding,' added Ted. 'The sunward side of each module now has a water-filled shield.'

'I didn't know,' said Peter.

'Many of the changes have not been publicised,' said Harry. 'What's important is that the ISS is crewed and operational again.'

'Right,' said Peter, taking a sip from his glass of sparkling water.

Harry stood and looked at all within the room. 'This is a top secret brief. I cannot emphasise strongly enough the serious repercussions which might arise if it were to become common knowledge prematurely.'

He fiddled with his pen, spinning it around between his fingers then continued. 'We cannot save the world. We cannot save any substantial number of the population. There will be death and destruction caused by the heat on a massive scale. We may not be able to save more than a few thousand but know that we must try.' He pressed a button on the Mac and an illustration of Noah's Ark appeared on the screen, animals walking up a ramp. Two elephants, two rhinos, two lions, two sheep, cattle, pigs, chickens, buffalo, and so on.

'We must save what we can, but what is being proposed is no Noah's Ark. We cannot be sentimental about species. This image immediately shows the problem. We cannot take elephants and rhinos. We must concentrate on animals which can be of value in the future and those must be taken, not in twos or fours, but in large enough numbers to ensure a viable population to return if it ever becomes possible.

'Noah's Ark was always impossible, anyway. We now know that you cannot build a viable population with just two animals. Just another Bible myth. Dozens are needed as a minimum. Sorry, elephants and rhinos are *not* among our selected species.'

'Thank God. No snakes then!' said Sylvie.

Everyone laughed and it broke the tension.

'No, Miss Paulsdóttir, no snakes!' Harry turned to look at the screen. 'That does not mean that we are abandoning everything else. There are already DNA banks in several locations around the world and the cleverest minds are trying to determine how we can best maintain these libraries through this disastrous interregnum. There will, however, be arks of sorts. Martin, explain.'

The geek stood, pushing his spectacles back up his nose from where they immediately began to slip. 'We are planning four refuges for humans and domestic animals. Refuge one will be in the centre of Antarctica. This is already under construction. Refuge two will be at Moonbase and, again, work is already underway. The third will be an enormous space station which will be parked beside the ISS. It is at the planning stage. The fourth refuge is a starship. Its protection from radiation is the biggest problem; it will be along the lines of the third refuge but powered and heading into interstellar space. It is unlikely that animals will be included in the starship or orbital refuge.'

'You've selected a target for refuge four?' I asked.

'Trappist-1 F is favourite at the moment,' he replied.

I laughed. 'That is a real longshot!' I said scornfully. 'We can't trust that any red dwarf star can support a habitable planet for humans. Have you assessed LHS 1140 B? That's also attached to a red dwarf and has all of the same problems.'

'What you say about the red dwarf planets is a concern. We actually prefer Kepler-452 B, but the distance is even more of an obstacle,' Ted added without enthusiasm. 'LHS 1140 B is, as you know, larger than Earth and gravity would be an extra obstacle.'

'What's the distance?' asked Sylvie.

'Trappist-1 about forty light years and Kepler-452 sixteen hundred light years, but it is a star similar to Sol, and planet B is extremely promising,' said Ted.

'LHS 1140 is about fifty light years,' I said.

'Sixteen hundred light years! How long would that take to reach?' asked Sylvie.

'Don't ask. We'll discuss that later,' said Martin.

'You've come up with some faster-than-light drive?' asked the Icelander.

'I regret not,' cut in Harry, 'but for now let's go through each of the refuges in order.'

'We need to be fairly sure of a habitable planet before we set off for it,' I said. 'Imagine arriving after a two-hundred-year journey and discovering that none of the Trappist-1 planets are suitable.'

'We're doing everything we can to study potential planets, and with greater urgency. All other projects for the James Webb Telescope have been postponed. Same with Hubble,' said Harry.

'Will people still be able to live on the surface in Antarctica?' asked Linsey.

'Only for short periods,' said Ted. 'Martin's the expert.'

The geek stood up again, flicked his finger over the mouse and a drawing appeared on the screen. It portrayed a network of tunnels running parallel to each other with substantial tracts of solid rock between them. Crossways joined the tunnels and there were many larger spaces.

'To give an idea of scale,' began Martin, 'the main grid of tunnels are planned to be up to fifty metres wide and twenty high. The whole refuge is some twenty miles in diameter. It is located east of the pole in an area of stable geology. The exact location is currently top secret, although we guess it will soon break. The larger spaces are the size of football stadia. This is where domestic animals will be housed; vegetables and fodder crops will be grown. You'll notice, surrounding them are smaller storage areas for feed etc.'

'What animals are being selected?' Linsey asked.

'A final selection has not been made,' said Martin, 'but a provisional list includes cattle, pigs, sheep, goats, chickens, turkeys, geese, tilapia, salmon…'

'Fish?' asked Ethan in surprise.

'Yes. A fish farm is no more problematical than the farming of domestic animals,' said the geek. 'In fact, it might be simpler to undertake as long as care is taken with water conditions.'

'How many people will it hold?' I asked.

'Again, no final figure has been set, but we believe it will be between five and eight thousand,' said Martin.

'What?!' Daniil exclaimed. 'Just one in a million will be saved. Are you serious?'

'Well, there are the four refuges,' Harry added quickly.

'But one in a million. It's horrendous,' said the Russian.

'We know,' said Harry, 'but one in a million is better than none.'

We all fell silent, contemplating how few would be saved or, more likely, how many billions would die a horrible death as the world roasted.

'How confident are you that such a number can live indefinitely underground?' asked Philippe Parodi. 'What work has been done?'

'We're pretty confident,' said Ted. 'At least in refuge one, we have plenty of available space being provided. We are less confident regarding the orbiting refuge and starship. That could be as few as two thousand, which is about the minimum viable population which could survive.'

'And the moon?' asked Daniil.

'We think eight thousand, similar to Antarctica,' said Harry.

'How will humans who've been living on the moon for a few decades adjust to life back on Earth?' I asked.

'With difficulty, for sure,' said Ted.

'What will happen when the general populace learns what is being planned?' Linsey asked.

'We've left that to another part of government in the US and we guess your own governments will have to plan individual strategies for the drip-feeding of information,' said Harry.

'There'll be riots!' said Philippe. 'They'll hate us for the secrecy. There was a large protest in London recently. Tens of thousands demanding to know why the drop in emissions hasn't had any effect on the overall climate.'

'We know. It'll be the tragedy of our plans that the numbers who will try to attack or invade the Antarctic refuge, will gradually be dying out. The heat will take the oldest and youngest first, but everyone will die eventually,' said Harry.

'It's a nightmare,' said Ethan. 'Will the refuge be protected?'

'It *is* a nightmare, and, yes, there will be a military contingent among the selected people,' repeated Harry. 'They will be well aware that if an invasion were to succeed, it could be the end of everything.'

'Okay,' I said. 'Practicalities – how are we going to get thousands of people to the moon and sufficient livestock to feed them?'

'We don't know yet,' said Martin, 'but they will be one-way journeys. We won't need reusable craft, well, at least, for people. If they do return, they will be empty.'

'But hundreds and thousands of cattle and chickens; that will be a logistical nightmare too,' I said.

'The cost will be huge,' said Ethan.

'Yes,' said Harry, 'but we've nothing else to spend the money on other than these refuges. Defence budgets could be trimmed to just cope with migrants and rioters.'

'Surely, getting larger livestock to the moon will be too challenging,' said Philippe.

'We're not so concerned about that,' said Harry. 'They'll have to be moved in small numbers, though. As far as the moon is concerned, it's producing the fodder for the livestock which is among the greatest challenges. Yes, we can ship it to the moon while we're still able, but growing it hydroponically underground, well...' His voice trailed off.

'It will be more than challenging,' agreed Peter, slumping back into his chair. 'There's a school of thought which suggests off-world refuges should only carry hydroponics.'

'For fodder, or you mean no livestock at all?' I asked.

'No livestock. Just crops which can fulfil nutritional requirements,' he replied. 'Time to turn the world vegetarian, perhaps?'

Linsey cleared her throat and asked, 'Martin. What propulsion system are you planning for the starship?'

'That's Ted's domain,' the geek said, and Ted stood to take over.

'We're working on an ion drive,' said the big American. 'It will provide continuous acceleration and deceleration at the other end. In mid-journey, speed will approach that of light.'

'And the power source?' asked Linsey.

'Experiments are currently being carried out using nuclear reactors,' said Ted.

'What sort of acceleration?' the head of UKSA asked, following up on her power source question.

'Our target is one tenth of a gravity, but work is ongoing,' said Ted. 'It might only be possible to use one hundredth of a gravity owing to the Coriolis effect. Tests are being conducted.'

'What's that?' asked Sylvie.

Martin broke in, 'The problem is that the ship will be disc shaped and rotating to provide gravity for the passengers. The direction of travel, and more crucially acceleration, however, is through the hub which means that any acceleration is being applied through the rotation. Weird things can happen when you do that. The Coriolis effect is one of them. It could make onboard sports impossible, because if you throw a ball, depending on where you are along the axis of the rotating disc, the ball is unlikely to get to where you were aiming. How inconvenient that will be to ordinary life is unknown. Hence the tests.'

Linsey bent over her tablet and frantically began calculations. 'Forty light years would take nearly a century with tenth g acceleration.'

'Not for those on board. Probably more like fifty to sixty years. Time dilation,' said Ted.

'Still a lifetime on board a metal prison.' Linsey punched some more figures into her tablet and said, 'So, Kepler-452 doesn't take that much longer.'

'No, not for the people on board, but a couple of thousand years will have passed on Earth,' said Ted.

'What about the impact problem?' I asked.

'What's the impact problem?' asked Ethan.

'As the ship's speed increases, the chance of space debris causing damage increases exponentially. We all see meteor showers when Earth passes through a comet's tail, even decades after the comet has visited. Similar debris is sure to be encountered en route. A grain of sand being impacted at close to the speed of light could pass through the entire ship. A tiny shower of dust could possibly destroy the ship utterly,' I said, unenthusiastically.

Ted answered, 'We're not unaware of the problem. Work is underway on magnetic forcefields.'

'But there'd be no time for the forcefield to work,' I said. 'The dust shower would be approaching at close to 186,000 miles per second. How could any force field react quickly enough?'

'I see what you mean,' said Ted, 'but we're not thinking of bending the object's path around the ship. The magnetic field we're working on will make the front of the ship slick, as if covered in oil, a sort of quantum oil slick. It has a slight slope, so dust particles will slide off.'

'You already have this?' I asked.

'No, but there is a high level of confidence,' said Ted.

'This is all very well,' said the Canadian, 'but how are we going to construct these huge arks. I understand the possibilities on the moon, but not for the orbiting refuge or the starship. Digging tunnels and caverns is far easier and cheaper than manufacturing and launching sections of an enormous vessel.'

'If people are living in zero g in the orbital refuge, their bones and muscles will deteriorate pretty quickly,' said Peter.

'It will be rotating to provide one g at the outer edge,' said Ted.

'How will the people be selected to go to the moon, Antarctica or the two space arks?' asked

Philippe. 'I foresee corruption and violence in the process.'

'Me, too' I said.

'I guess there'll be a committee,' said Harry.

'We don't want to be throwing everything into saving people, if those saved are just the privileged and politicians,' said Ethan. 'Remember Douglas Adams' book where they put all the telephone sanitisers, hairdressers, insurance salesmen, PR executives, and management consultants on a ship, just to get rid of them. They were told that they were so essential they were on the first ark to get things ready for the rest of the population!'

'...when in fact the rest of the world was just getting shot of them,' said Martin, bursting into laughter.

There was a brief interlude when everyone relaxed, thinking about Adams' Golgafrincham Ark.

'Seriously, the choice of who goes will need to be done with great care. It has the potential to be a catastrophe on top of a disaster,' said Daniil. 'Do you think the project will be international or will those who construct the refuges be people from their countries. Would seem most unjust.'

'We'll need to put some trust in politicians to resolve it,' said Argos Homburg, speaking for the first time. 'It is scientists and agriculturalists who'll be needed. Not a bunch of selfish administrators.'

'Like us!' I said and laughed.

'We're thinking that it will be eight thousand on the moon and in Antarctica, but more like half or a third of that on the space vehicles,' said Harry. 'I imagine the healthiest, youngest, best educated and fittest will be selected.'

'I don't like that word, "selected", Harry,' said Daniil.

'No, it smacks of the very corruption we're concerned about,' said Ethan.

'A lottery?' asked Linsey.

'It won't be our problem,' said Harry. 'Someone will have the responsibility, but it's hardly going to be us.'

'Can I suggest we learn more about these two spacecraft? We need to report back to our governments, and we must have the best possible information on how the refuges will be constructed and launched,' I said.

'Good idea, Beth,' said Daniil. 'Come on, Ted, Martin, fill us in with some detail.'

'Well said, Daniil,' said Harry.

The screen filled with illustrations of the two vessels. They were enormous.

'We'll have to construct them in sections which can be fitted onto the SpaceX starship boosters,' said Martin. 'The shape of each component will have dimensional restrictions. The technical aspects to the project are considerable.'

'And it will all have to be done in the same special geosynchronous orbit as the ISS to protect from the ongoing flares,' added Ted.

'Surely, people will notice the vastly increased number of launches,' said Phillipe.

'They certainly will,' said Harry, 'so we will eventually have to come clean about what's going on.'

We all settled down to study the presentations, drawings, and technical data. For now, the lottery or selection process had to be relegated to the fringes of our minds. Could I save Gren and our children? What would make us essential to one of the refuges? I began to contemplate how to build a case for our survival, then realised I was using my status within science to my advantage. It was the very corruption we were trying to avoid.

14 North From Toase

Kwame was gone. Dead and buried. There was no longer anything to keep Destri Esturu and his family in Toase. Bright's mother had a big family so there would be many relatives to look after her. Their crop would produce barely enough to feed them and none to trade. There was no work to be had. Once the funeral was over, the sad group of four re-entered the colourful but dilapidated wooden hut which was home.

God, it was hot. Destri pulled the knot of his tie downwards and threw the jacket onto the back of the easy chair. He pulled Bright to him, her bare shoulders tacky from the beading sweat, but pleasant to his touch despite the heat. He tightened his grip, hugging her to him, his eyes desperate to hold back the droplets of tears shed for the loss of his father.

'Just us now, Bright,' he whispered, planting his lips on the smooth, ebony cheeks of the woman he loved. 'Think it's time to go.'

'Go? Go where?' Bright spoke softly, curiously, worriedly.

'Time to follow Moses. Time to head north. We can't stay here, the heat will kill us, the crop's failing and there's lawlessness coming. We in danger, Bright.'

'Lawlessness?'

'Was chatting with the minister. He says gangs in Kumasi are raiding stores and amassing supplies. Police let them. Too hot for anyone to care. Only safety in north. Cooler places.'

'No relief there, Des. Ma cousin in Dedougou say it just as hot there.'

'Don't mean Burkina Faso, Bright. I mean we head for very north. Sweden p'haps, or Norway. Finland. Russia maybe.'

'How us going to get there?'

'Bit by bit. Take it slow. Keep selves to selves, bother no one, just slow, steady travelling.'

Bright pulled away and looked up into her husband's anxious face. Tears still ran down his cheeks, attempting to navigate their way through his black, patchy beard. 'You mean it, man. Don't you?'

'I mean it. We must go. We must look after selves. No one else matters. Northern borders no problem, sparsely guarded. We'll have no trouble 'til the sea. Once we in Algeria and through desert, we're halfway there.'

'You serious!' Bright exclaimed in disbelief. 'You want 'bandon friends, relatives and run away?'

'That year I had in un'versty, a professor told me the wise man retreats in the face of insurmount'ble danger, the hero faces it, but risks self and family. He right, Bright. Running is the only way, but we'll do it properly.'

Bright stood, defiant, hands on hips, the sober dark dress adding to her fierceness. 'Well, I not leaving!'

'Then you'll die here, and I'll die with you, and Edu will die, and Mariam will die, and relations will bury and mourn each other until, one day, there no one left to mourn. We must go. We no choice if we going to save ourselves. Must, Bright. No other option… and best to be among the first.'

'Moses went 'cos he knew others were going. We not first, Des.'

'Then they get the worst trouble. By time we reach the coast, there'll be multitudes on the move. We be lost among numbers.'

They stood, glowering at each other, then Bright burst into tears and they were in each other's arms again.

'No rush, Bright,' Destri whispered, caressing his wife and holding her tight. 'Start getting essential clothes packed into that big uni backpack. No cases. Light things for heat. Spare shoes. Medical stuff. I'll get water containers from town. Need to think about food which won't spoil. Check our store. I got some cash. Must take care. I'll close savings account. Banks no good where we headed.'

'You really mean it?'

'We no choice… and don't speak of it. Keep it to ourselves or us'll have that crazy cousin of yours, Kwadwo, wanting join us. He mad. Will hinder, not help.'

'My mother!'

'No. This no journey for old folks. She plenty family round her. Must save selves. Keep quiet. You say goodbye to your mother day before we leave. Understand?'

'Oh, Destri.'

'Do you understand, Bright? I am right on this. Us four are important. Can't take no one else. Understand? I mean it. Tell no one.'

Bright pulled away, tears running down her cheeks. She looked at him. So strong, so handsome. She nodded reluctantly.

∞∞∞∞∞∞∞∞∞∞

The heat was oppressive again, although, for a pleasant change, a breeze was visiting the hut. Destri's old university backpack stood on the chair, Bright still adding more socks and underwear. She turned in some trepidation as the door opened. She'd invented lies to cover the packing process, but she was never a good liar.

Destri opened the door, then immediately shut it and locked it. 'Where's kids?'

'Out playing. Think it football. Amazed they don't feel heat. S'pose they back soon. Why?'

He lifted a bag from under the table and extracted its contents, laying them side by side on the tabletop. A ten-inch hunting knife in a scabbard, a domestic carving knife, three paring knives, a crowbar, a screwdriver, a hammer, and a plastic box of assorted nails, screws and other bits and pieces. Bright watched as the armoury took shape then drew in a sharp breath as she watched her husband extract something wrapped in cloth from under his belt.

He carefully removed the covering. It contained a heavy metal object. He laid the material flat on the table and positioned its contents centrally. A nine-millimetre semi-automatic handgun was revealed.

'A gun!' A deathly whisper from Bright.

'If it them or us,' said Destri, 'I choose us.'

Alongside the weapon he placed four dusty, khaki boxes of ammunition he'd extracted from his trouser pockets. Relieved of the weight, he was able to loosen his belt.

'Look, Bright, this lever is safety on gun. Can't fire while that is closed. Remember that. Important. This is the clip of bullets.' He removed the clip took out some bullets and reloaded them. 'That's how it's loaded. Got it?'

She nodded.

He wrapped the pistol again and slid the weapon into a side pocket of the backpack. 'It's loaded,' he said. 'Put the spare ammunition in the backpack. Ensure it not pressing against me when I'm wearing it.'

The selection of knives was slid into a long pocket on one side of the backpack. 'You got everything?'

'Yes,' said Bright. She lifted another, smaller backpack from the floor. 'Contains hard cheese, 'nough bread for a few days, cured meat, dried fish and other non-perish'bles. Four litres of water. Kids' bags also have water and some more clothes.'

Bright showed Destri two smaller packs. A golden, worn, one-eared, one-eyed teddy poked out of the top. 'Made them choose one toy each for a special holiday.'

'They know we travelling? They've not mentioned to anyone?'

'Yes, but not soon. No, told them it secret. When you thinking, Des?'

'Tomorrow. When dusk falls. Where's money?'

'Hidden. I'll wear a money belt when we leave,' said Bright. 'Transport?'

'Managed to borrow that old Jeep from Sabir. Collect tomorrow afternoon. Fresh oil and full tank.'

'Borrow?'

'Told him a week. We'll be long gone before he realises.'

'Oh, Des, he don't deserve that.'

'No, but this time for burning bridges, hon. Sorry. Will leave note here, tell him help himself to crop and anything we left behind.'

They hugged, anxious tears again running down Bright's cheeks.

15 Sir Edward Gascoyne

Sir David Brenner, science minister: Dame Diana Staunton, minister for the environment, and home secretary Jack Easton were already in discussion in COBRA when the prime minister joined them and sat in the usual central seat on one side of the table.

'Glad you could all attend,' she said.

'No problem,' said Jack, 'but why the sudden urgency?'

'David and I have been discussing the climate problems and he suggested we make time to listen to Sir Edward Gascoyne, who, of course, we all know as probably the most famous environmentalist in the world.'

'Wonderful man,' said Diana. 'I was watching his latest BBC series, *The Atmosphere*, just last night. Fascinating. Such a shame that Mindslip turned him into an old man.'

David said, 'He's just returned from South America and has some rather disastrous news for us. I convinced the PM that we should give him half an hour to put it over to us directly. He'll be here in a few minutes.'

Jack said, 'I must ask you to be careful how much you let him know about our knowledge of the eventual situation. He's hardly the type of person to spread rumours, but nevertheless…'

'Yes, okay. We're all aware of how delicate the situation is,' said the prime minister as there was a knock on the door and Sir Joseph, the cabinet secretary entered, closed the door behind him and waited.

'Yes, Joe?' said the PM.

'He's here, ma'am,' he replied.

'Please show him in.'

Jenny McRoberts stood as did the other three. The door opened again, and the cabinet secretary brought in the famous television presenter. He was in his late eighties and silver haired with a neat beard which took years off his appearance. However, his wrinkled suntanned face and stenotic back, which made him appear to be falling forward, added the years back on. He was well loved by the British public, a national treasure, and Jenny quickly moved forward and shook his hand.

'You know David and Diana, of course, and this is the home secretary, Jack Easton,' said the PM.

Pleasantries were continued and he was offered a seat directly opposite the prime minister. The cabinet secretary sat beside him with a digital recorder. The three ministers sat beside the prime minister, Jack on her right, and Diana and David on her left.

'Sir Edward, I asked you to present the details of your recent visit to Mato Grosso to members of the cabinet. Thank you so much for agreeing,' said David.

'I'm honoured. I didn't expect such prestigious members to be here. I'm guessing that you have more than a passing interest in the ecological affairs of Brazil,' said Sir Edward in his familiar educational lilt, but also with the authority of one who is an expert in his field.

'You are very astute, Sir Edward,' said the prime minister. 'We have concerns about the climate crisis for ourselves too.'

'Of course you do, Prime Minister,' he said, knowingly.

'Please explain why you felt it important to speak to us.'

'Well, on my return last week, I talked to David, who I know well, and it was he who suggested this meeting,' said Sir Edward. 'Next week, I'm going to a conference staged by UNFCCC[5] and that is likely to have international coverage.'

'Please educate us,' said the PM, 'as you have done with all of us through your wonderful documentaries.'

'I should say,' he replied, 'that our findings and filming on this occasion might not be suitable for general viewing. I have had many critical attacks over my documentaries showing animals attacking their prey and being harmed by natural situations, but what I have seen in the Brazilian Pantanal goes beyond that. It might not be released for general consumption.'

'We're listening, Sir Edward,' the PM said.

'The Pantanal is the largest wetland on Earth, or rather, it was. It extends into the Mato Grosso and into parts of Paraguay and Bolivia. It covers some sixty thousand square miles, so larger than the whole of England and Wales combined.' He paused to let the sheer size of the area sink into his audience's minds.

'Climate change has caused frequent fires to develop. Sometimes these have been caused by natural means such as lightning strikes, but during the twenties we saw more and more deliberate destruction

---

[5] United Nations Framework Convention on Climate Change

by farmers. In 2024, an enormous blaze destroyed three thousand square miles, but that is nothing compared with the scale of fires we are seeing today. Today's fires are almost entirely owing to the heat this region is experiencing. The wetlands have been drying out and, with temperatures sometimes reaching forty-eight degrees C, any spark will ignite tinder-dry brush.'

He poured water from a jug into the glass before him, his hands revealing the signs of newly diagnosed Parkinson's disease, which had begun to afflict him. Sir Joseph quickly assisted by taking the jug and completing the action.

'I am no longer as steady as I once was,' Sir Edward said, laughing off the affliction, 'but no matter, I do my best.'

He paused to drink then continued, 'What I have seen is nothing less than a catastrophe. The entire Pantanal is on fire. I don't mean parts; I mean the entire wetland. The heat is so intense, drying out anything not actually in water, that it burns spontaneously. It is devastating. Animals are dying. They cannot be rescued, anything unable to outrun the flames is doomed to a fiery death. This includes people. Over ten thousand natives of the region are believed to have lost their lives, staying behind to save what they can, then discovering they are encircled and there is no longer any escape. Roads are littered with the burned-out cars and trucks of people trying to leave the area but have been caught in the fires when fanned by strong winds.'

He drank again and dabbed his lips with a white linen handkerchief.

'I've seen giant otters lying dead in dried-up creeks, armadillos never stood a chance. Jaguars panic and become trapped, macaws cannot outfly the flames, the rheas are disorientated and run aimlessly. These are all endangered species, and they are being lost to the world. I cannot imagine the overall scale of the loss.'

The same white linen handkerchief now dabbed his eyes as tears developed. Jenny heard a sob from Diana who also had been unable to control herself on hearing the distressing account.

'It isn't just the animals. There are no hospitals now operating in the region. People and, in particular, children fill surrounding hospitals as they suffer from respiratory illnesses brought on by the acrid smoke.

'Reptiles and amphibians are at the greatest risk. They cannot escape, but howler monkeys are dying from smoke inhalation; I've witnessed them falling out of the trees. I've seen jaguars, anteaters, and tapirs with such severe burns that they've had to be put down by SOS Pantanal volunteers. It's soul destroying.

'I have personal friends working for Ecologia e Ação who are telling me that even when they believe they have stopped the fires, they continue to smoulder in layers of dense, built-up vegetation which then flare up unexpectedly. With the area being so vast, it's impossible to control. While I was there, the Brazilian air force dropped over two hundred and fifty thousand gallons of water on the fires. That may sound an enormous volume, but I need to remind you that the fires are covering an area as large as England and Wales combined. Their actions are no more effective than spitting into a bonfire.'

'Is there any hope for the region at all?' asked Jack.

'No, Home Secretary. It is destroyed, gone. An area larger than England is littered with blackened trees, dead animals, and scorched earth. I've seen skeletons of alligators at the edges of dried-up pools. They will one day become fossils, as they are covered with the falling debris of burned vegetation and thick dust from the smoke. It is gone. It's all gone,' he sobbed, 'There's no longer anything we can do to save it.'

His tears continued to flow, and the handkerchief caught them, and sometimes hid them.

'That's it,' he said, finally, and sat back in his chair.

'Sir Edward, I cannot thank you enough for coming to update us today,' said Jenny McRoberts, hurrying around the table and bending to hug the famous man. 'I'm sorry that it's caused you such grief and personal distress. Sir Joseph, will you take Sir Edward somewhere where he can recover his composure. Tea perhaps in cabinet room two.'

Sir Edward leaned on his stick and heaved himself out of his seat. Sir Joseph helped him towards the door, but he stopped and looked around at the PM and her ministers. He cleared his throat.

'Thank you for listening,' he said.

'Despite the sad nature of what you had to say, Sir Edward, it has been a pleasure,' said the PM.

'You know…' he said, and hesitated as if deciding whether to finish his sentence. Everyone looked towards him, and he did continue, 'You know, what I've seen will be happening here soon enough. I suspect that is why you were so interested.'

'Thank you, Sir Edward,' said the PM and returned to her seat. Sir Edward took that as a dismissal and turned to leave with the cabinet secretary.

When the door shut, the home secretary said, 'He knows.'

'Of course, he knows,' said the minister for the environment. 'He's just returned from the battlefront and the news is the worst.'

'So, what do we do?' asked Jack.

'We battle on,' said the PM.

'I think we should begin to prepare the populace for the truth. It'll be worse for us if we don't,' said Jack. 'That last protest in Trafalgar Square was all about suspicion that we're lying to the people over climate change and, of course, we are.'

'Bring it up at the next senior ministers' meeting. For now, we say nothing,' said the prime minister.

HEAT

16 Crossing Borders

The third day was all desert. The odometer of the ancient Jeep no longer worked, but Destri believed they must have travelled close to fifteen hundred miles from home. Crossing into Burkina Faso was not a problem. They were asked the reason for crossing the border and a visit to Bright's cousin in Dedougou seemed to satisfy. The land here was bush country and wildlife was abundant between the villages and small towns. They stopped once and filled the Jeep with fuel. Bright entered a store and obtained fresh bread and fruit. So far, so good.

Crossing into Mali the next day was not so simple. They were questioned for nearly an hour at the northwest crossing at Lonani and ultimately turned away. There was talk of visas but obtaining one would mean a trip back to Ouagadougou and that was the last thing the family wanted. They could be kept waiting months for permission and the granting of visas. No. They couldn't wait. They headed back a reasonable distance then struck out towards the northeast and found no one manning the border into Niger.

There was no proper road there. The terrain was rocky with a little scrub vegetation, but also characteristics of desert. A red and white painted, official barrier blocked their way. No one emerged from the two portacabin-style huts. Where were the guards? Perhaps it wasn't manned continually. Destri sounded the horn. There was still no sign of life. Cautiously, he slid the pistol under his belt at his back, pulling his shirt over it to ensure it was concealed from view. Bright looked at him, full of trepidation.

'Be careful, you,' she said.

He climbed out of the vehicle and walked to the fence. The barrier was padlocked shut. He shook the fixing, but it was too secure to be broken without a determined attempt.

'What you doing?' asked Bright anxiously.

'Don't know, hon. It's locked. Seems no one around. Could break the lock, though.'

'No!' she exclaimed. 'Can't do that. If they come back, they'll know someone bin through. They'll hunt us down.'

Destri looked at Bright, considering what she'd said. 'Will drive along the border fence. See if another way through.'

He climbed back into the Jeep, knocked it into four-wheel drive and slowly drove alongside the border fence southwards, the whole family bouncing around as the suspension did its best but failed to compensate for the rough terrain.

After about forty minutes and perhaps ten miles, the border continued. Usually, it was timber with barbed wire along its top, but sometimes just coils of wire. They came up to another section of five-bar fencing.

'Look,' exclaimed Bright, pointing ahead. 'Fence is broken.'

Right enough, the timbers had been flattened by something driving at them.

'There's tracks, like tank or mechanical digger,' said Destri. 'Someone bin through here definite.'

'It's not us who done it, Des, but only we know that. If we drive through, we get blame. Sure thing.'

'No. We have tyres. Obvious this was broken by something much more 'stantial,' he said as he left the vehicle and walked cautiously towards the flattened structure.

'What you doing now?' asked Bright.

'Checking for nails and things sticking up. Don't want a puncture.'

He lifted a plank to one side and propped another against one of the still-standing fence posts. He jumped back in and revved the engine. They bounced over the remains of the border barrier and followed the tracks of the previous culprit.

The Jeep crossed a rise, Destri crawling slowly so he could stop if there were people ahead, but there was no sign of any life and nothing to stop them. In the distance, a few hundred metres away, the road from the official border stretched away, deserted in both directions. It was roasting hot and a gentle breeze from the south wasn't helping matters. Sometimes a gust would toss some sand into the air; they all wore bandannas to protect their faces.

Destri pushed the Jeep's capabilities to open distance between them and the crossing. Now they could aim for Ayorou and the main RN1 route north to follow the River Niger into Mali. A busier crossing might mean more amenable customs officers. They could only hope. A few miles later they pulled off the road, drove up a side wadi to hide themselves and made camp for the night.

The children grumbled and moaned that it meant another night of cured meat and dried fish. Water was running short. They'd need to fill their containers at Ayorou before another attempt at entering Mali.

Shortly after they'd set up for the night, Bright saw a snake. Quick as a flash, Destri was after it and a second or two later the spade had decapitated it. He threw it to Bright with one of the sharp kitchen knives.

'I'll build a fire,' he said. 'Fresh meat tonight and bake some of those potatoes.'

He scouted around, collecting dried bush plants and soon had a vigorous fire burning. An hour's cooking saw the flesh fall from the substantial serpent's skeleton. It was good eating. Fresh meat as a change from their dried fish and cured meat. The baked potatoes were welcome too.

As night fell, Bright told a story to the children, and they turned in for a well-earned sleep. Destri lay with the pistol under his pillow. He needed to be ready for any eventuality.

17 Great Barrier Reef

In the early dawn of a humid summer day, a group of dedicated naturalists gathered at the marina in Cairns, Australia. Their mission: to conduct a comprehensive survey of the damage inflicted upon the Great Barrier Reef by the increasing output of the sun. Among them were marine biologists, ecologists, and climate scientists, all united by their passion for preserving one of Earth's most magnificent natural wonders, the huge coral reef which borders the north-eastern coast of Australia, unique in its diversity and size.

The team boarded the research vessel *Coral Guardian*, equipped with state-of-the-art underwater drones, temperature sensors, and diving gear. As they sailed towards the outer reefs, across turquoise and cobalt mottled seas, tall and distinguished looking, Dr Emily Hayes, the lead marine biologist briefed the team on the survey's objectives.

'We'll be focusing on coral bleaching, species diversity, and water quality,' she explained. 'Our data will help us understand the current state of the reef and predict future changes.'

Upon reaching their first survey site, the team donned their diving suits and plunged into the crystal clear waters. The initial sight was both breathtaking and heartbreaking in equal measure. While some areas still teemed with vibrant corals and colourful fish, others were ghostly white, a stark reminder of the bleaching events which had plagued the reef in recent years. Some of the coral had turned a pale tortilla brown.

Dr Hayes was able to point to a bleached section of coral and via a built-in microphone in her diving mask told the others, 'This is a direct result of prolonged heat stress,' she said, referring to the elevated sea temperatures that caused corals to expel the symbiotic algae living within them, leading to their bleached appearance.

'It seems much worse than it was last year. Also, at first glance, the number of species of fish seems to be reduced,' said Dr John White, a well-known Australian ecologist.

'You were here last year, John?'

'Yes, Emily. I've been to roughly this spot each year for the last seven years. The bleaching is spreading more rapidly. I think much of this coral is dead; look how brown algae is growing on sections of it. That only happens when the polyps have died.'

Over the next few days, the naturalists meticulously documented their findings. They used underwater drones to capture high-resolution images and videos, allowing them to analyse large sections of the reef without disturbing the delicate ecosystem. Temperature sensors recorded the water's heat levels both at the reef's edge where the deep ocean met it and at various locations towards the coast. It would provide crucial data on the extent of thermal stress. The bulk of the bleaching seemed to be in the top couple of metres of the water.

Later, during a press conference, Dr Hayes said, 'One of the most alarming discoveries is the widespread bleaching in shallow water areas, which span two-thirds of the reef.'

Dr White added, 'We've noted that parts of the reef have been exposed to nearly three months of hotter-than-normal temperatures, a critical threshold for severe coral bleaching. There is a danger the reef will not recover. The water temperature is averaging over thirty Celsius, and peaking at close to forty.'

Dr Adrian Head, a coral specialist said, 'We've also been conducting interviews with local fishermen and indigenous communities who have witnessed the reef's continual degradation over the years. Many spoke of the declining fish populations and the increasing frequency of severe weather events, which had further stressed the reef's fragile ecosystem.'

Dr Hayes continued, 'Professor Terry Hughes, the renowned marine biologist, joined us for a segment of the survey. He shared his insights on the historical context of coral bleaching. He had noted that the first mass bleaching event occurred in 1998 and that such events had become increasingly frequent and severe. Especially since 2025.'

Despite the grim findings, the naturalists were determined to find solutions. They discussed strategies to enhance the reef's resilience, such as coral gardening and breeding heat-resistant coral species, but that would take time. They also emphasised the urgent need for global action to reduce greenhouse gas emissions and mitigate the impacts of climate change. Of course, at this time, they too believed that it was all part of the global warming which had been occurring. The increasing output of the sun was still an unknown factor to all but a select few. The world had, indeed, reduced emissions, but the sun's increasing output negated it.

After the press conference, they gathered to discuss the conclusion of the survey. Dr Hayes addressed her colleagues, 'Our work here is just the beginning. The data we've collected will inform conservation efforts and drive policy changes. We must continue to fight for the survival of the Great Barrier Reef. However, its urgency is now much greater than before.'

Copies of their studies were sent to naturalists and climate scientists worldwide, but would they have any effect?

18 Unrest

James Buchanan was met outside Brixton police station the morning after the eco-warriors' fourth demonstration against climate change. It was almost as if he'd been personally targeted when the violence began. Whether he had or hadn't, the group had already made up its mind. The government was lying about climate change and the EWs were onto it.

He climbed into the back of one of the group member's cars and they sped off to the Kings Arms. There were plans to make, members to recruit and action to be considered.

It wasn't just Britain which was suffering from eco groups protesting the rising heat. In Tokyo there had been a full-scale riot. Cars rolled over and burned, shop windows smashed, and violence against the police, and it was only quelled when the army moved in and took control, firing rubber bullets and teargas into the mob.

In Washington, a well ordered but enormous protest took place in the grounds in front of the White House. Armed police held their ground and, to be fair, there were only a few scattered violent incidents.

In the Kings Arms, planning was underway to cause more disruption in the capital the following weekend. The WhatsApp group was growing by the minute as more ordinary people started to rebel against the heat.

The question was clear. How could the global temperatures still be rising when the authorities claimed that CO_2 emissions had drastically reduced in almost every developed country?

Either it was a concerted policy of lies over the effectiveness of reducing emissions or there was some other cause for the heat and that meant that government lies were even more sinister.

James was determined to force government to come clean.

19 Unease at the Top

Home secretary Jack Easton, science minister Sir David Brenner, secretary of defence Sir Charles Browning, and minister for the environment Dame Diana Staunton, sat in visitors' chairs in prime minister Jenny McRoberts' office in Downing Street.

This was unusual. The four ministers had requested an unscheduled meeting with the PM. They were unhappy with the government's position over the climate crisis.

The PM looked sourly at the group. 'What is it now?'

Jack Easton replied, 'Prime minister, the EW group has now become the largest protest movement in the UK. They've overtaken Just Stop Oil, and the membership is willing to jump at every invitation to vent their feelings.'

'We've already agreed to hold our stance on the release of information. I don't see the point in this additional meeting,' said the PM.

'Jenny's right,' said Charles, 'we cannot second guess established policies. Wally Andrews is in Washington at the moment and the Americans are taking the same position. We cannot tell the world that it could be the end of civilisation.'

'Yes,' added the PM, 'if we do that then it will be obvious that sanctuaries will be on the agenda. It will become impossible to build refuges if the construction teams are facing disruption from these eco groups. We must stand firm.'

'Well,' said David, 'three of us disagree with that policy for very sound reasons. The public no longer believe what we're telling them about the heat. The public consider that we are lying, but they don't know why. The public are starting to disbelieve the scientific data on emissions. The public no longer trust us, and we must do something to re-establish that trust urgently.'

'To hell with the Americans telling us what to do,' said Diana. 'The people deserve the truth.'

The PM looked angrily at the environment minister and said, 'So, you expect me to go onto national television and announce that within a decade everyone will die and that we are trying to save about one in a million people in refuges. One in a million! It sounds ridiculous, but everyone will be scrambling for ways to be those one in a million. It will be chaos.'

'Jenny's right,' said Charles. 'If the general public know they have less than ten years to live, what will happen to the economy, industry, jobs. People will leave their jobs and try to enjoy their last years. There could be thousands of suicides – do you want that on your hands? Food production could grind to a halt, and mass starvation could hit the population. Think about it.'

'Sorry,' said Jack, 'those arguments don't work. We govern for the people, not for ourselves. We *are* lying. We really are and it is not good enough. People have the right to make their peace with their families, and their God!'

'The policy stands,' said the PM.

'I want to bring it up in full cabinet,' said David.

'*No!*' said the PM. 'As senior ministers, we have *made* our decision, and we're not going to revisit the issue every time Buchanan stages one of his demonstrations. *That is an end to it. Understand?'*

'You'll be receiving my letter of resignation,' said Diana.

'I will regret having to accept it,' said the PM. 'Please rethink. How will it look if you, the minister responsible for the environment, decide to throw in the towel? You are valuable to this government. We need you. You're respected. Please don't do it.'

Diana responded, 'I, more than anyone else, am being seen as both incompetent and lying by the general public. I can't tolerate that.'

Charles said, 'Diana, this whole matter is covered by the Official Secrets Act. You cannot explain why you are resigning.'

'You can't tell me what I can or can't do. I might join EW and spill the beans. How will it look if I tell the truth, and you jail me?' Diana said with real passion.

'Don't do it,' said the PM. 'This meeting is over. Jack, David, are you resigning too? I want to know *now!'*

'Prime Minister,' said Jack, 'you really need to take our points seriously. Eventually the news will break, especially when rumours about the refuges circulate. We really must come clean. I won't resign. I can do more good as a member of the cabinet, but I will continue to bring this up at every opportunity. I am certain you are getting this wrong. Frankly, the whole cabinet should be made aware of the situation. It is not right that it's just the ten senior ministers who know.'

'David?' asked the PM.

'I can do better by keeping my post, but I'm telling you right now that I, too, am sure that you're wrong and I'm also sure that the balance of the cabinet will come around to our way of thinking when they are made aware,' said David.

'I will *not* tolerate lobbying of other ministers. This is still a state secret,' said the PM.

'Not listening to us will be a mistake,' said Jack.

'I *am* listening, but I'm *not* for changing. Now, this meeting is over. I have work to do!'

'You're no Margaret Thatcher, Jenny. You're making a bad decision,' said Diana who got up and walked straight out of the office before giving the PM time to respond. Jack and David followed her. Charles remained seated.

'You're with me on this, Charles?' she asked.

'One hundred percent,' he replied.

20 Violence

It was less than one hundred kilometres, but the journey across the Republic of the Niger, once part of the Songhai Empire, to reach the RN1 motor road took almost three days. There were no proper roads and the only homes the family saw blended into the desert so well that they seemed to be part of it. Occasionally, people would come out of buildings and watch the old Jeep trundle by, and once a shot was fired, but they didn't know if it was aimed at them or just a warning shot to keep away.

Part way through day two, they approached a small community – half a dozen houses plus a trading centre and shop. Fuel was available, but only in jerrycans. Destri filled the Jeep, finding it difficult not to slop the diesel in the process. He bought a full jerrycan to take with them. There was a dedicated spot for it on the back of the vehicle. Bright entered the trading room and bought fresh meat, dried meat, vegetables, and milk. They also managed to fill their water containers.

Destri was apprehensive throughout the visit. He didn't like the suspicious glances they received, and three men came over, wanting to buy the Jeep. Destri felt behind his back to ensure the gun was ready to pull if needed.

No, he didn't want to sell. His French was hardly adequate to make himself understood. He began to feel threatened and, as soon as Bright and the kids returned from the shop, he hurried them aboard and spun the Jeep's wheels as he put his foot to the floor to get away.

HEAT

They put as much distance as they could between them and the village before pulling away from the dirt track and making camp several kilometres north where some scrub trees were growing closely enough together to hide them from view. After they'd left the track and parked the Jeep a hundred metres away, all four of them went back with a broom and to drag some blankets to conceal their tracks from view. Destri worried that the villagers who wanted to buy the Jeep might come after them to obtain it by other means.

Destri slept fitfully that night and was thankful to wake and find that his fears had been unfounded.

Now the terrain was changing. They were on the approach to the Niger River and the vegetation was lusher. It continued to become greener, but there was a new hazard – areas of water from the last flood. They had to make many detours because Destri was too worried that the Jeep might become stuck in waterlogged ground. Fortunately, the wet areas were beginning to dry out, so the danger wasn't as bad as he'd first imagined, but he took great care through the next few kilometres.

Suddenly, they came across a properly paved road and turned north. An hour's driving later, they realised that the road was leading back to the west, so U-turned and sped the other way. Dusk was falling when they approached a substantial bridge.

'Think we cross morning,' he said quietly.

'Why, Des? More distance from border the better.'

HEAT

'Worried about more communities. Let's hide away for night and cross early, Bright.'

They turned off the road and hunted out a concealed area where they could camp without being seen.

∞∞∞∞∞∞∞∞∞∞

The eastern sky was already becoming a luminescent flaxen-tinted, powder blue colour as Destri rose. Taking the pistol, his first task was to walk around the campsite, ensuring there had been no visitors. He checked areas on the approach where he and Bright had swept footprints out of the sandy ground. If anyone had walked in to investigate, they would have left spoor. There was nothing. They'd survived another night.

Returning to the Jeep, he primed the barbecue grill and let the heat intensify. The bag of provisions they'd obtained the day before included some sausages, tomatoes, eggs, and some slices of morcilla.

Destri poked his head in through the canvas flap and shouted, 'Come and get it!' then returned to the heat and put the sausages and morcilla onto the grill.

Bright and the two children soon appeared. Bright made tea, while the aroma from the cooking meat filled the air around them. Destri placed a pan on one side of the grill, added a little oil and cracked the six eggs into it. The sliced tomatoes were added to the grill and breakfast was almost ready.

They tucked into their feast, then packed everything away to prepare to depart.

Back on the paved road, they crossed the bridge and continued to head eastwards at a leisurely pace, passing through a few settlements, and noticing how they were watched with great suspicion.

They came to a halt at an isolated trading post. There were no other vehicles visible, so it seemed relatively safe.

'Mariam. You stay in Jeep. Keep your head covered. This is a Muslim country. If you sees any car or truck approach, you hit horn once. Just once. Single short blast. We'll hear and come running. Understand you?'

'Yes, Da,' she said.

'Don't leave Jeep for nothin. Understand?'

'Yes, Da. I know.'

Destri gave her a peck on the cheek and ruffled her hair. 'Won't be long. Edu, you come wiv us. Don't say or do nothin.'

The two parents and the boy entered the trading station.

Inside, the walls were mostly unpainted timber with some windows through which light streamed, illuminating dust which filled the air. There was a smell of flour.

Just inside the door, to the right, a man in his thirties, was crouching beside an open sack and the reason for the aroma of flour filling the air became clear. Destri guessed, from seeing his tanned, white skin colour that he must have been a Mindslip race-change victim. Few Europeans lived in the African bush. He was filling kilo plastic bags with the creamy white powder ready for sale. He looked up at the family and said, 'Mornin.'

'Mornin to you too,' said Destri. 'We'd like some eggs and fresh fruit, please.'

He stood. 'This way.' He made his way through the avenue of shelves to a long wooden counter displaying a wide variety of products.

Bright selected pears, more tomatoes, eggs, cheese, and milk.

'You not from hereabouts?' said the man.

'No. Visiting relatives in north. Come through from Ghana. You don't look from hereabouts either,' said Des.

'Mindslip effect,' the man said in an irritated tone of voice. 'How you gonna pay?'

'I've got cedis. Can you trade those?'

'Want two hundred francs for what you got there,' he said.

'What'll you take in cedis?' asked Destri. 'Two hundred is about five cedis, I think.'

The man laughed. 'Guess you want bank rate. This ain't no bank, and I don't give no bank rate.'

'Just a fair exchange.'

'Twenty cedis,' the shopkeeper said.

Now, Destri laughed. 'Nah. Seven.'

'No chance. Fifteen.'

'Ten.'

'Twelve, final chance,' he said defiantly, hands on hips.

Destri produced two five-cedi notes and two ones. 'Harsh deal,' he commented.

'Good to do business wid you.'

Bright put the goods in a hessian bag, and they quickly left the shop. Mariam hadn't budged. They were soon in the Jeep and travelling east once more.

The road was quiet, the odd car heading the opposite way and a few trucks. At one point, a jet-black, four-wheel-drive pickup streaked past them at high speed, kicking up clouds of dust, and vanishing into the distance. Quite a few people were on foot or cycling, often loaded down with boxes and baskets, heading to markets in one direction or another.

The Jeep passed the black pickup, which was parked on the roadside, three men standing around it, talking. One hefty individual was leaning lazily against the bonnet, an automatic rifle hanging over his shoulder. Destri did not like the way his eyes followed them as they passed alongside. It unsettled him and he increased speed.

'Keep eye on rear,' he whispered to Bright, who turned in her seat to look backwards along the arrow-straight concrete road surface.

A few minutes later, she said, quietly, 'Somethin comin up behind us fast, Des.'

Her husband put his hand to the vibrating mirror and steadied it so that he could better see the approaching vehicle. It was the same pickup and, as before, it was travelling at high speed. Probably it would just shoot past and continue on its way, but he felt uneasy.

The pickup did not overtake. It followed them at a distance of forty or fifty metres, matching their speed. Destri eased off the accelerator a little, dropping their velocity enough for their tail to notice.

He felt even more uneasy when the black four-wheel-drive slowed to the same reduced speed.

A series of trucks and cars came the opposite way, and as if on a signal, when the road was clear, the black pickup accelerated, came alongside and one of the men in the passenger seat made a clear sign for Destri to pull over.

He slowed gradually and drove onto the rough ground on the right of the highway. He hoped this was some sort of routine check.

'No one speak. Leave talk to me. Jus' keep quiet. Mariam, Bright, cover faces,' he said earnestly.

The pickup pulled across in front of their Jeep. The men jumped out, the large man hefting the rifle from his shoulder and carrying it across his body. He swaggered up to the Jeep.

In good French, he said, 'Get out,' and waved the gun at them.

Quietly, Destri said in their own local dialect, 'Do what he say, stay opposite side of Jeep to them.'

He climbed out himself, reassuringly feeling the pistol tucked into the back of his trousers, hidden by the loose shirt.

In poor French he said, 'How can we help yous?'

'Where you from?' barked the gunman.

'Ghana. Making way to visit family in Algeria for wedding.'

A second man walked around the front of the Jeep and pulled the veil off Bright. 'These your kids?' he demanded.

Bright nodded.

'Yes,' said Destri. 'Edu is ten and Mariam is twelve.' Would the man realise the lie? Mariam was fifteen. Des was trying to protect her from being abducted.

'What you got for trade?' asked the armed man.

'Nothin. Nough food for day or two and few Ghanaian cedis.'

'How much? Show me.'

Destri reached into his side pocket and pulled out a synthetic leather wallet. 'Need it for food and fuel,' he said, handing it to the man.

The gunman passed it to the third man who opened the flap and removed the colourful Ghanaian notes.

'How much?' asked the gunman.

'Two hundred and twenty,' said the other, folding the banknotes and putting them back into the wallet and slipping it into his pocket. Destri tensed.

'Search Jeep,' said the gunman.

The two men pulled out bags and began to spread the family's belongings over the ground. They poked and prodded the clothing, looking for anything which might be concealed. One of the men grabbed Bright's arm and twisted it around behind her back. 'You're hurting,' she cried.

'We don't believe you. Where's the valuables?' asked the gunman, pushing the barrel of the automatic rifle into Destri's throat.

'We've nothin. We're jus visiting relatives,' whimpered Des.

'Where's wedding gifts?' the man snapped.

'Posted them ahead. Visit s'posed to be s'prise,' Des said nervously.

'Liar!' He lowered the barrel and circled the Jeep slowly, looking into every nook and cranny, tugging off Mariam's veil and looking at her lecherously. He returned to face Destri once more, again pushing the weapon into his chest.

'Okay, get walking. We'll take the Jeep.'

It was that 'now or never' moment. Destri's hand had made its way behind his back. He felt the hilt of the pistol, fumbled to disable the safety then gripped it ready for action.

'You can't jus leave us here wid nothin,' he cried.

The man pushed the weapon harder into Destri's chest. 'Don't tell what can or can't do, man. Get walking or we'll keep the women too. The girl will fetch a good price. Twelve my ass!'

That was it for Destri. He quickly brought the pistol around from under his shirt and fired into the man's chest. The gunman's eyes were full of surprise. A second shot and he fell, lifeless to the ground.

Destri picked up the rifle, pointed it at one of the others, and said, 'Take him, put him in your pickup.'

Cautiously, the two men came around to the driver's side of the Jeep and lifted the body, keeping their gazes fixed on Destri. 'He's dead. You killed he,' one said.

'Take him to pickup. Throw him in back and sit in the cab. Do it now!' Destri shouted.

Bright and the children started to repack their belongings and return them to the Jeep. The men hefted the body into the open back of their vehicle and Destri waved them into the cab. As soon as they were both seated, he checked the rifle's safety was off, took casual aim and shot both men through the head.

He reached into the cab, retrieved his wallet and cash, took money from each of the bodies, then positioned them as if they were in natural driving and passenger positions and shut the doors. He then leaned into the back of the four-wheel-drive to take the leader's cash before pulling a dirty piece of tarpaulin over the body of the gunman. For a moment he wondered if they should take the pickup and leave the bodies in the Jeep. He decided against it. The vehicle might be well known hereabouts, and it could cause trouble.

Returning to the Jeep, he hid the rifle in the luggage area, then, shaking all over, he jumped in, started the engine, and drove onwards.

'Oh, Des,' said Bright. 'Did you have to kill them?'

'I did what necessary,' he said, his voice trembling dreadfully. 'Keep fingers crossed that can put distance between us and they before someone stops to check why they parked in middle of nowhere. They seemed do lot of that, so hope others keep clear rather than curious.'

21 Briksfosarnet Glacier

Heavy rain and spring meltwater caused the river to be in spate. Axel was concerned that if the level rose much higher, the vegetable garden and chicken compound could well be flooded. Should he relocate the chickens now or give it another day?

The river ran from the glacial lake beneath the Briksfosarnet glacier just northeast of Bergen. There'd been a meeting of townspeople of Klakverk to discuss the situation. They were all concerned about the increased flow, but like Axel, no one wanted to take emergency measures unnecessarily. If the rain stopped, and the forecast said it should tonight, then the threat may pass.

The pickup truck turned in from the road. It was Emma, bringing the children, Theo and Ingrid back from school. The kids ran inside to change, and Emma came over to where Axel was studying the raging torrent.

'Even higher today,' she commented.

'Yes. Was thinking of moving the chicken compound, but it's such a lot of work and it might be for nothing,' he said.

The children, Theo fourteen and Ingrid twelve ran out of the house and down to the river and vegetable garden dressed in jeans and T-shirts. It was unseasonably hot at thirty-five degrees.

'Okay, you guys dig us half a sack of potatoes,' he said, tossing a spade to Theo and a fork to Ingrid.

'Thought they were saying that climate change was almost beaten,' said Emma. 'I can't ever remember it this hot at this time of year before.'

'You're right. I read that with the amount of carbon dioxide being recovered from the atmosphere and the switch from fossil fuels, warming should have stalled. Maybe they got it wrong.'

'Or they're lying,' said Emma, always more distrustful of government than her husband. 'I think the glacier's shedding more water this year. Bet that's adding to the river.'

'Yes. Arne was up above the lake the other day, hunting and said there's a lot of ice calving. Some quite large blocks are floating in the lake,' said Axel.

He pulled a few radishes and carrots, Emma tossed them into a bag, and they headed back to the house, leaving the children working on their potato harvest.

∞∞∞∞∞∞∞∞∞∞

Overnight, huge blocks of ice which had calved from the Briksfosarnet glacier, had gradually made their way towards the lower edge of the glacial lake. The wind had picked up, causing the blocks to crash into each other and tumble. The authorities had decided that there was a real danger of the moraine dam being damaged so two rangers were in a mountain hut overlooking the outflow of the river from the lake ready to sound the klaxon if necessary.

At seven in the morning, the largest block of ice was run into by a smaller, flatter iceberg. It caused the largest berg to roll over and grind against the moraine which held back the lake. The rangers watched in horror as the gravel started to flow with the river. A river in spate became a flood and the moraine dam was on the verge of collapsing. The rangers looked at each other, fear crossing their faces. One rang the police department of Klakverk, the other hit the dam siren button.

A rising and falling wail suddenly filled the dale. It could be heard miles away. It meant one thing – the dam might be failing. Get out now! Evacuate! Run for high ground!

The siren woke Emma. Axel was sleeping through it, but suddenly, the door burst open and Theo and Ingrid, in their night clothes, burst into the room. 'What's happening?' shouted their son.

By now, Axel was awake. He knew immediately that the siren meant the glacial dam was near to breaking. 'Quick, everyone. Dress. And despite the heat, dress warmly, we need to be prepared for anything.'

Theo grabbed Ingrid by the arm and pulled her out of the room and through to their own bedrooms. Emma threw on jeans and a heavy shirt as Axel did the same. He also yanked four anoraks from the hall cupboard which had not been worn since winter. The heat of spring had left them surplus to requirements. Now they might need them as they headed into the hills to avoid any flood.

The rise and fall of the siren told them that the emergency was still in progress. If it had changed to a long, continuous siren it would have meant that the crisis had passed. The family dashed outside.

Dawn was breaking and, looking east, they could see the glacier in the distance. The lake, of course, was hidden by the moraine dam, but the river outflow seemed to be stronger.

'Let the chickens out, Theo,' shouted Axel, and open the compound so that they can escape if they need to.'

'Don't want them to get lost,' cried Ingrid.

'They won't,' assured Emma. 'Chickens always come back to roost if it's safe to do so.'

'Once you've done that, Theo, come back here and stand with your sister. Keep watching the dam. If you see any change, shout for us. We're going to pack some essentials.'

Theo unlocked the pickup, and the two adults ran into the house. Emma packed food, drink, and important documents while Axel filled suitcases with clothes, shoes and other essentials.

'There's more water coming!' shouted Theo from outside.

Axel ran out to check the situation. 'It's giving way. Come on, Em, we've got to go. *Now!*'

They threw the cases and bags into the back of the pickup, the children jumped into the backseat of the cab and Axel started the motor, checking that there was sufficient charge. It read 140km, which should be enough.

'Should've put it on charge last night,' said Emma. 'Didn't think.'

'A hundred k should be sufficient.'

'We going to town?' asked Theo.

'No, we'll take the Aksdal road up into the hills. Klakverk's in direct line of the flood.'

'Oh, God! Mum!' exclaimed Emma and dialled a number on her smartphone. It answered on handsfree, and Emma said, 'Mum. You heard the alarm. What are you doing?'

'Don't panic, dear. I'm on an evac bus with Auntie Brina and Uncle Magnus. Are you safe?'

'We're heading to the Aksdal road. Should be okay when we get to it.'

'Can you see the dam?' asked her mother.

Emma swung around in her seat and, just at that moment, the dam gave way. 'Oh my God,' she said, 'It's given way! Speak later.' She cut the call.

'Talk to me! What's happening,' Axel said, gripping the steering wheel as he negotiated the multiple Z-bends on the road from their house. 'I daren't stop to look around. We're still below the surface level of the lake.'

Emma turned in her seat to look out of the back window. 'Dam's washed away, raging torrent heading down the dale. Still got a mile or so to cover before it hits home.'

'Here's the junction!' said Axel. 'Hold tight.'

He swung the pickup around a one-forty degree turn to the left, tyres squealing, and for a moment, it seemed it might turn over. Ingrid and Emma cried out, but Theo stoically held onto the grab handle above the door. The vehicle's low centre of gravity, helped by the weight of the battery, seemed to keep it glued to the road as Axel gunned the accelerator and it leapt forward, all 300kw of power driving both axles.

'Still need to climb a hundred metres or so,' he informed them.

'I can see the house,' cried Emma. 'It's almost upon it. Oh, God, it's just lifted the whole thing and carrying it away.'

'What about the chickens?' asked a panicky Ingrid.

'Don't worry. They'll swim,' said Axel as he wrestled the pickup around another hairpin bend.

'Chickens can swim?' asked Theo with some scepticism.

Emma looked at him severely with a 'not in front of your sister' scowl. 'Of course they can!' she said confidently.

Foaming water unexpectedly burst over the outcrop of rocks to their right.

'Hang on tight. It's going to hit us!' shouted Axel, gripping the steering wheel even more tightly.

The road bent to the right. Axel accelerated again, but now they seemed to be driving through water, littered with branches, leaves, and other debris, which was rushing across the road from behind and the right. The vehicle seemed to be lifted off the road, but still maintained some traction as he wrenched the wheel to the left at another hairpin. The water tipped them almost onto their side and there was a grinding crunch as the bodywork came up against a rockface. As it bounced back to level, still in a metre of rushing water, the wheels seemed to grip once more, and it lurched free of the water and was again accelerating up a slope of at least twenty-five percent[6]. A branch

---

[6] 25% slope = 1 in 4 gradient.

had secured itself behind a wing mirror and Emma rolled the window down to dislodge it.

'Are we clear?' Axel asked, still driving flat out, but also pumping the brakes to ensure they'd not been affected by the water.

Another surge of water rushed by beneath them. Where they'd first been hit by it was now under three metres of water. They'd escaped death by a matter of seconds. The whole valley had become a lake, but the lake was moving. As the deluge moved west, less and less emerged from where the dam had been. The worst had passed.

The pickup took another sharp bend and came to the crest of a hill. Axel pulled over and stopped. They had the most amazing view down on Klakverk and the distant fjord. They got out to watch.

The temperature outside was already increasing, but standing on their own feet after such a pell-mell journey was a relief in itself.

The torrent had reached the town, and some buildings were being washed away towards the fjord. Others stood there, jutting out of the water forlornly.

'We were lucky,' said Emma. Axel gripped her hand as her other arm surrounded Ingrid's shoulders. Theo, still trying to be brave, stood, hands on hips, staring back towards where their home had been.

'Do they really swim[7]? Chickens, I mean,' he asked. Axel gave him a meaningful shove.

---

[7] In case you are worried – yes, they can swim, but whether or not they could survive such a torrent is debatable.

HEAT

22 Algeria and the Med

The old Jeep, a relic from better times, rattled and groaned as it navigated the rough terrain of northern Mali. The vehicle, though aged, was a sturdy four-by-four, capable of handling the rough terrain they would face. The morning sun blazed overhead with heat that would normally put midday to shame, but there was no such thing as normal heat these days. The sun cast long shadows across the parched landscape.

Destri gripped the steering wheel tightly, his eyes scanning the horizon for any signs of danger. Beside him, Bright clutched the map and occasionally glanced back at the children. Mariam, protected by a scarf, stared at the landscape, her thoughts a whirlwind of fear and hope. Her younger brother, Edu, wore a floppy hat and clung to his favourite toy, a one-eyed teddy bear, his eyes wide with curiosity and anxiety.

'Are we going to be okay, Ma?' Edu asked, his voice trembling.

Bright turned to him with a reassuring smile. 'Yes, my love. Just need be brave and stick together.'

Their journey took them through the vast expanse of the Algerian desert. The heat was oppressive, and the Jeep's old engine struggled against the shifting sands. They encountered other travellers, some heading south in search of water, others like them, moving north in a bid to escape the extreme temperatures.

The Sahara, with its vast, unforgiving expanse, tested both their endurance and the Jeep's reliability. The family had to navigate through areas known for their harsh climate and potential dangers, including remote regions where terrorist activities were a concern. Despite the risks, Destri was determined. He had studied the route meticulously, avoiding the most dangerous zones and sticking to trails frequented by others. The days were scorching, with temperatures often exceeding fifty degrees, and there was no option but to stop and shelter under a makeshift awning. The nights brought little relief and they rationed their limited water supply carefully to ensure they could make it through.

One evening, as they set up camp, Bright noticed a group of Tuareg nomads in the distance. She watched them with fascination, their blue robes standing out against the golden sands. Destri was suspicious of anybody and everybody so they broke camp and headed away from the area, travelling five or six miles before daring to camp again. The nomads would have no care for the plight of climate refugees.

After weeks of arduous travel, the family finally reached the Mediterranean coast. The sight of the vast, blue sea filled them with a renewed sense of hope. However, their journey was far from over. They needed to find a way to cross the Mediterranean and reach Spain. Des had heard stories of people attempting the dangerous crossing, often falling victim to smugglers, or facing deadly conditions at sea. Determined to avoid such fates, they decided to take matters into their own hands. They'd sold the

Jeep for eighty thousand dinars[8]; the cash might be useful in Europe.

They needed a boat, but they couldn't spend their limited money on something which had only one purpose – to cross the Mediterranean. The boat would be valueless on the Spanish side as they'd have to abandon it. Also, only illegal migrants would have a boat for sale, and it would attract the authorities. Under cover of darkness, they found an old rowing boat tied to a pier. It seemed sound and oars were lying in the bottom. Could they row so far? Destri and Bright exchanged worried glances but knew they had no better option.

'We must do this,' Des whispered. 'For sake of children.'

The Mediterranean was deceptively calm as they set out, but the journey was fraught with danger. The small boat rocked precariously with each wave, and the exertion of rowing took its toll on Destri and Bright. Mariam and Edu huddled together, their eyes wide with fear.

Days turned into nights, and even Mariam took short turns rowing. Bright was concerned about Destri becoming exhausted, but the thought of a better life in the far north, Sweden or Norway, perhaps, kept them going. They encountered other boats, some filled with refugees like themselves. There were also coastguard vessels, and they stopped rowing, lying low in the boat to make it appear to be floating debris.

---

[8] About £400 or US$500

With no experience in rowing, they suffered horrific blisters, and their muscles ached continually. The journey was an immense challenge, the sea merciless, and the family battled exhaustion, dehydration, and fear but they rowed day and night, driven by the hope of a better future. On one occasion they'd caught sight of the coast in the north but were snared by a current which drove them backwards several miles, leaving Bright and the children in tears. The journey seemed endless, but their resolve never wavered.

After what felt like an eternity, the distant lights of the coast came back into view. Was it Spain? They knew they'd drifted east with the wind. It could be France. They'd heard that the French were firing upon migrant boats. The European countries were making a determined effort to protect their shores.

Nevertheless, tears of relief streamed down Bright's face as they approached the land. They had made it, but their journey was far from over. The family knew that the challenges of travelling north to Scandinavia awaited them, but for now, they allowed themselves a moment of hope.

In the darkness, they stepped onto the treacherous rocks in a tiny cove. Destri looked at his family with pride and determination. 'We did it,' he said softly. 'We survived.'

Mariam and Edu clung to their parents, their hearts filled with a mix of relief and uncertainty. They knew that the road ahead would be difficult, but they also knew that together, they could face whatever challenges came their way.

HEAT

Quickly, they pushed the boat back into the sea so that it would not give away that someone had arrived in this location. Stealthily, they then climbed a steep footpath out of the cove, crossed a coast road and walked a few miles into the countryside.

Dog-tired from their sea crossing, Destri unpacked the tent and erected it on wasteland shielded by trees, leaving the sides rolled up to allow any breeze to pass through the structure. Bright took out the last of their bread and dried meat. She knew they would need to buy food the next day. Would the dinars or cedis give them away? Care would be the watchword. It was stifling hot, but, for the first time, Destri felt that the family were relatively safe and the following day they'd begin the journey northwards, with little money and no form of transport.

HEAT

2034

23 Port Khalifa

Five landing vessels neared the coast. They'd each held position at a small offshore island and waited until the fleet was complete. All had arrived from different directions, and had their transducers switched off to prevent detection. This was an incognito expedition. No one knew they were there.

Each ship was seventy metres long with an aft superstructure and forward landing ramp. They were designed as landing craft so that they could be run ashore, and equipment unloaded directly onto the land, the engines being run to force the hull farther onto the beach as each weighty piece of plant disembarked.

The coast here, for three miles in each direction, comprised heavy gravel beaches, primarily glaciated rock; remnants of ice and snow remained from the previous winter. Cliffs ran behind the beach, close to the water at each extreme, but exposing more beach and low-lying land as the centre of the six-mile crescent was reached. The cliffs were in a bay-like configuration, sheltering the entire area.

A huge crane reached the landing ramp of boat four, but as it began to cross the free-floating platform, the now almost empty vessel began to slip seawards.

'Power, more power!' shouted one of the army majors. 'Quick, or we'll lose her!'

The last thing the construction team needed was for the largest crane to slip into salt water.

'Full power!' was the retort over the field radio.

Water churned behind the vessel, trying to drive it forward against the beach. The crane leaned to the left. Major Darius held his breath as the tracked undercarriage spun and dug into the landing platform which was buckling and also tipping leftwards.

They were going to lose it!

A bright yellow digger was rapidly approaching the crane, driving down into the shallows and turning towards the crane. Its bucket rising and moving forward, it contacted the operator's cab and began to push the crane to the right, attempting to steady the giant vehicle, while its own predicament worsened. Now sideways on to the beach, it too, was beginning to tilt. The driver pushed harder against the crane. Other vehicles had arrived, but Major Darius stopped them from driving down to assist. Men left their cabs and stood on the shingle, watching and hoping. Everyone knew the importance of the giant crane. Waiting for another to arrive from North Africa if they lost it, could take months.

Would the digger's pushing be sufficient? Still the ramp buckled. The crane's front tracks spun as gravel was encountered. Had the tilt been stopped?

Yes. The digger continued to push against the structure. Glass broke on that side and the bucket was denting the framework.

'Careful, careful!' shouted Major Darius into his radio.

Out of breath and doubtless still panicking, the driver responded, 'Can't be helped, sir, got to stop the tilt!'

'Okay, okay, almost clear,' sounded another voice – the crane driver.

The monster vehicle was now more on land than on the ramp. It rebounded to the vertical, all three sets of tracks at full power.

'Cut ship's power,' shouted the major.

The ship stopped its engine. The reaction was instant. It rebounded from the shore, the ramp twisted and ruined. This ship would not sail the oceans again without major repairs.

The crane, with its three independent tracked supports was safe and moving slowly, but inexorably up the gravel beach, rocks beneath it twisting, turning, and being ejected. Three workmen ran for cover as bucket-sized boulders flew through the air towards them.

'Care, Cepos! It's not a race!' called the major over the radio.

The front treadplates slowed and the expedition's largest vehicle eased itself more sedately onto the higher beach, clear of the possibility of any high tide, and eventually on to dry land.

'Well done all!' complimented the major. 'Quick thinking, Jabari. Your digger saved the day.'

The digger had, in fact, stalled. Water must have entered the engine. It was almost half submerged. Jabari shouted to others on the beach to get a line to the digger's front arm. Eventually, chains were attached. A bulldozer on the shore began to retreat, pulling the digger around to face the shore. With rocks flying everywhere from the slipping tracks of the dozer, it slowly made progress, and the digger was pulled to safety.

Each in turn, the five vessels deposited their loads, and a team of construction engineers martialled the equipment close to the cliffs. A dozen diggers of one variety or another; small, medium, large, and gigantic tipper trucks; the huge crane and two smaller versions. Five tractors and fifteen trailer loads of materials were parked to one side. Men were busy unloading portacabins and a working basecamp was quickly taking shape.

Once the landing craft had fulfilled their duties, the command was given for them to disperse. None departed the same way as any other. There was no way General Khalifa wanted his expeditionary force to be spotted from space. As individual ships, they might appear to be fishing vessels, unimportant and of no interest. As a fleet, they would attract attention. He didn't want his annexation of this small section of Antarctica to be drawn to the attention of busybodies in Europe or the US.

Major Darius parked his Land Rover beside a blue cabin, got out and joined others inside, where thick green tea was being shared. Phase one of the creation of Port Khalifa was in place. Now the real work could begin and more landing craft were due the following week.

24 Fireside Surprise

Jenny McRoberts, prime minister of Britain, was immersed in papers, photographs, schematics, and illustrations which almost completely covered the antique desk of her office in 10 Downing Street, the residence of the British prime minister.

She was quite clearly extremely busy and was finding the documentation somewhat challenging.

Sir Joseph McKinley, cabinet secretary, tapped hesitantly at the door, cracked it open and peered at the PM, who raised her gaze, looking over the top of her frameless spectacles at him and elevating her eyebrows inquisitorially. She'd asked not to be disturbed.

'So sorry, Prime Minister, but the foreign secretary would like a word, and he tells me it's urgent.'

'What is it?' snapped the PM, slumping back into the vintage leather Chesterfield-style office chair. It was her favourite and had reputedly been owned by Winston Churchill almost one hundred years previously. He'd supposedly brought it to Number Ten during the Second World War.

'He wouldn't say. Said it was sensitive,' said the cabinet secretary.

She huffed at the interruption. 'Okay, Joe. I should take a break anyway. Send Mr Andrews in and why not bring in some tea,' said the PM, rising and wandering over to the lounge area where she sat beside an open fire which crackled away pleasantly and gave off a slight aroma of burning birch. The office was air-conditioned, of course, but she loved the homeliness of the open fire. It meant that in just a few steps, she could leave the heat outside and the worries of state behind, even if only for a few minutes.

Mr Andrews was a tall, upright man with a headful of bushy silver locks, wearing a light-grey three-piece suit with a contrasting colourful tie. He entered the room, carrying a burgundy leather document case, strode over to the PM, said, 'Sorry to disturb,' and shook her hand.

'Sit down, Wally. I needed a break anyway. Tea is on the way,' she replied.

They sat, facing each other with the fire flickering away cheerfully. A low coffee table sat between them.

'What is it? We were going to meet later anyway, weren't we?'

'Yes, the Gibraltar matter, but I'm afraid this is a little out the blue and couldn't wait. You'll be getting an encrypted call from the US secretary of state.'

'*I will*? You'd better explain. Fire away.'

'I had a call from our man at NASA. They've spotted something unusual, and he was there when it was examined. They might have wanted to conceal it, but our man's presence made that impossible.'

'Now you're intriguing me. Don't tell me it's a UFO come to rescue us from the heat,' the PM said with a chuckle.

There was a rap on the door, it opened and a silver tray with teapot, hot water pot, a couple of cups and saucers, milk, sugar, teaspoons, and a selection of biscuits was brought in by a young intern. The intrigue would have to wait.

'Over here,' said the PM, waving him towards the coffee table.

The young man nervously carried the tray to where they were sitting and, not without a little rattling, settled it onto the table.

'Thank you,' said the PM. 'What's your name?'

'Anthony, ma'am,' he said nervously.

'Thank you, Anthony. That'll be all.'

He turned, bumped into a very solid visitor's chair which he hadn't noticed, and made his way hurriedly out of the office, clearly a bundle of nerves.

Walter laughed, 'His first time?'

The PM smiled and, as she poured the tea, said, 'Think it must have been. Joe has a couple of students on work experience. So, what's the problem, Wally?'

'Although the ISS is no longer in a low orbit,' he began, 'we still have access to a number of low-level surveillance satellites. We share the data and imaging with several allies. This particular satellite was a US military one and Johnson, our man in NASA, was only there by pure chance. Security was breached when one of the technicians showed the deputy NASA administrator the images while Johnson was with him. Johnson's regular visits probably didn't register as important to the technician. He might have imagined Johnson was part of NASA.'

'Come on, Wally, I don't want the long version. What did the images show?' asked the PM impatiently.

'The images were of a snow-covered coastline. I have copies here,' said the foreign secretary, opening his document folder and handing three A4[9] sized photographs to Mrs McRoberts.

'What am I looking at? Seems to be a harbour, small town, and some ships. What's the significance?'

'They shouldn't be there, Prime Minister. This is Antarctica. The port has appeared very suddenly,' Walter Andrews replied, handing over another photograph. 'This one shows the same area a couple of years ago.'

'What?!' the PM exclaimed, 'Someone has constructed an entire town on the Antarctic coast without anyone being aware of it. Who's responsible? The Russians?'

'We're not sure yet, ma'am. It would appear that it is none of our allies. It isn't only the port, either.'

The prime minister returned her empty cup to its saucer and refilled it from the pot, adding hot water to weaken it.

'Chinese? North Korean?' she asked.

'We don't know. That's why the US secretary of state will be calling you. He wants to contact all three of them, and other likely suspects, to find out. At first, they thought it might be us.'

'This is an area covered by the charter, is it?'

'Yes, ma'am. No one has applied for permission to build anything on this scale. It has been done clandestinely.'

Jenny McRoberts sifted through the images again and asked, 'That's a substantial ship tied up in the harbour, isn't it?'

---

[9] A4 is the standard letter-sized paper in the UK. 21cm x 29.7cm or 8.3 inches by 11.7 inches.

'A frigate, we think.'

'What did you mean about it not just being a port?'

'There seems to be an enormous amount of construction traffic running to and from the hills behind the port. It's possible that they're building some sort of underground installation. A refuge, maybe.'

'I see,' said the PM, dragging out the word thoughtfully. 'You know about the central refuge we're constructing with the US farther inland?'

'Not in detail. It's classified.'

'Yes. I suppose someone else is thinking along the same lines. A refuge from the growing heat.'

'Yes. The heat is worrying. Looks like the secret of how bad it will eventually become might soon break, and potentially hostile countries are already planning their own refuges,' said the foreign secretary.

'Indeed,' she said, pressing a button on a small gadget.

The cabinet secretary knocked and entered, 'Yes, Prime Minister?'

'Is it full or partial cabinet on Thursday?' asked the PM.

'It is the full cabinet, Prime Minister,' he said.

'That's all,' said the PM and Sir Joseph closed the door. 'When is the secretary of state calling?'

'I must let him know when you're "free" to talk,' said the foreign secretary.

'Okay. Give me thirty minutes to think this through then ask him to call me. I think we'll need to break the news to the cabinet on Thursday. In the

179

meantime, can you despatch a ship to pass by the port to gauge reaction? Maybe a non-military vessel that just *happens* to see the port when passing and calls in to find out what's going on. General curiosity. Know what I mean? Volunteer crew. Understand?'

'Yes, Prime Minister. Incognito. I'll speak to Charles,' the foreign secretary said, and they both stood.

'Thank you for coming, Wally. Very worrying indeed! Events are appearing to overtake us. We knew it would happen.'

'Yes, Prime Minister,' said the foreign secretary over his shoulder, as he opened the door to leave.

25 Le Bec de l'Aigle

Thirty-four people from central Uganda were coaxing the failing outboard motor of an inflatable vessel they'd purchased to cross the Mediterranean Sea in their quest to move northwards. They comprised ten families. Unlike the boats of mainly adults which had for more than a decade, been making the journey, these families were in fear of their lives, not because of some oppressive regime or ideological war but because their crops had failed and there was no government support. It wasn't always that government didn't want to help, but that they did not have the resources.

Many, back home, had used the last of their money to feed themselves, paying extortionate prices for second-rate food, but the families in this boat had realised the hopelessness of fighting the rising temperatures and food prices. They had clubbed together to travel northwards, routing through Chad and the Libyan Sahara to the Tunisian coast. Four days earlier, they'd set off across a calm Mediterranean for Spain.

The heat had been too much for any of them in Uganda. Regularly temperatures had soared to above fifty degrees. Bush fires had been rampant, killing the nomadic people and causing the wildlife to panic and run. Stampedes of African buffalo had destroyed crops and killed people, and it could only get worse. Vegetation was dying in the droughts and both animals and people were suffering.

An enormous fire had spread from Rwanda into the Queen Elizabeth National Park, destroying vast swathes of forest and bush. The death toll of animals was huge, and poorly equipped emergency forces were incapable of dealing with fires on such a scale. Smoke filled the air and was blowing towards Kampala where people who still lived in the city wore facemasks to protect themselves from the acrid atmosphere. The fire raised the death toll of people over seventy to huge proportions. It was no wonder the young and healthy had made the choice to flee northwards for their lives.

Spanish coastguard vessels had intercepted them and refused to allow them to reach the shore. Several attempts were made, but each time, the faster official boats had forced them to move back across the sea. On one occasion they'd been harried until they believed they'd have to land again farther west at the coastal city of Algiers, but the Algerians didn't want them either. There were tens of thousands accumulating along the North African coast looking for some way to head north.

When the coastguard gave up its harassment, the inflatable headed due north, but soon other coastguard vessels were steering them farther east and farther north. They guessed they had left the Spanish coast after thirteen days. Fuel was running low, the second to last jerrycan having been emptied into the failing engine that afternoon. Would they have more luck getting ashore in France?

The military port of Marseille was not a solution. It was bristling with naval ships and gunboats. Farther along the coast sheer cliffs plunged into the sea, but there seemed few boats or settlements.

It wasn't a hospitable place to try to land, but anything was better than spending more time in the inflatable where thirst and hunger were now adding to their misery.

They steered towards the coast, passing a huge, pointed structure like the beak of a gigantic bird. The map told them it was named "le Bec de l'Aigle". Just beyond was an area of beach with only a few dwellings. Dusk was falling, the failing outboard was cut, and the men aboard used paddles to ease the boat landwards silently. They'd made it. They were in Europe.

Fifty metres from shore, the boat was lit with the brightest of searchlights. A gunboat was rounding an outcrop along the coast and had them in its sights.

An amplified voice, in French, called for them to stop. In seconds, the grey military gunboat drew alongside but this wasn't to be a rescue. The gunboat took a line from the dinghy and turned out to sea. Making four or five knots, it quickly opened a few miles between it and the coast. Two hours later they cut the refugees' vessel loose, let the gap open to a few tens of metres and soldiers opened fire. Not for long – just for a few seconds. The shots were aimed at the waterline. They had not deliberately intended to hit the people, only the inflatable, but with the swell of the sea and opening distance, some were shot. In any event, the result would soon be the same. Was it better to drown or be shot?

Cries of despair and pain filled the air as the occupants clung to the rapidly deflating hull, screaming for help, crying out to be rescued, holding children above the rising water.

    The gunboat crew didn't have to put up with the wailing, whimpering, and sobbing for long. Soon, nothing but the mass of deflating plastic floated at the surface and the weight of the outboard would eventually drag it, forever, into the depths. Some on the gunboat took pleasure in their achievement but most, in their hearts, were in despair that the heating world had driven their nation into taking such awful action.

26 Industrialisation

Outside the panoramic canteen window, the monochromatic surface of the moon was as inscrutable, stark, and beautiful as ever. Shadows were beginning to stretch as the two-week-long lunar day approached its end. Inside Moonbase, the lunar day was irrelevant. Human astronauts followed their own clocks, running their days and nights on Greenwich Mean Time. The human body and mind were not designed to cope with fortnight-long days and nights.

Today, the canteen was hosting a meeting. Thirteen astronauts were assembling for a briefing, and they were just the vanguard of a much larger contingent which would be arriving over the coming weeks, hence the effort to create so much radiation-protected underground accommodation over the previous two years.

Commander Bert Lewis headed the meeting, sitting at the top of a block of dining tables used to simulate a conference facility, the plastic tabletops looking somewhat incongruous for such an event. Christine, Dave, Elena, and Lex were all there, plus the new arrivals; a team overseer, Julian Hide, and eight construction engineers, five women and three men. They mostly wore brightly coloured tracksuits or Bermuda short outfits which were normal for leisure in Moonbase.

Each in turn, prepared their lunches at the counter and sat ready to hear what the overseer of the new arrivals had to say.

'Okay, Julian, fill us in,' said the commander.

Julian Hide was tall for an astronaut, well over six feet, with neatly combed, dark hair, grey eyes, and skew-whiff nose but an overall pleasant face. He wore an orange flight suit and held a large computer tablet. He stood to address the others, gripping the tablet in his left hand and turning it to examine his notes. Thirteen pairs of eyes swivelled in his direction, anxious to learn what NASA had planned for them.

'Thanks, Bert,' Julian began. 'My engineers are already fully apprised of the situation but for security reasons, it was decided that my briefing would be more effective if it were given to everyone at the same time.' He turned towards the commander. 'These astronauts are all now permanently moon based?'

Bert nodded. 'Yes, they have all committed to remaining on the moon as long as the heat crisis continues. It has consequences. If ever they return to Earth, it could take years to fully readjust to Earth gravity.'

Julian swayed from foot to foot nervously, as one who was not used to addressing others so formally. 'Yes. Not an easy decision to make. All of my engineers have made the same commitment. At least we should all be safe. The heat on Earth, even in the most temperate regions, is becoming unbearable.'

He leaned forward onto the table, both arms straight, palms flat. He continued, 'A decision was recently made by NASA, ESA, UKSA, and Roscosmos, to bring forward the industrialisation of Copernicus. We know there is substantial frozen water in shaded areas of the crater, plus more locked up in the regolith. Look at the monitor.'

HEAT

Julian turned to the right, where a two-metre television monitor was fixed to the canteen wall. On it, at a touch of his tablet, was projected an illustration of a mining derrick surrounded by several dome structures.

'This is what we're here to build. SpaceX has robot ships en route to us right now containing materials and plant plus the components for the domes.'

'Why domes? Surely underground shelters are safer during flares, or do you intend to shut down operations during flare cycles?' asked Elena.

'I'll get to that,' said Julian. 'In fact, these domes are double hulled, and the insulation has been designed to protect from the flares.' He flicked his tablet and the image on the monitor changed to a schematic. 'As you can see here, there is a layer of metal-fibre insulation lining the inside of the domes. The gap between the two hulls will be filled with water our plants will provide, saving shipping weight. If live tests during flares show that the insulation is insufficient, a layer of regolith could be added to the outside. When mixed with water, it forms a kind of paste which can be spread over the domes' surfaces. Once it bakes dry it holds together quite well. It has to be applied quickly during the moon's day to be effective.'

Elena said, 'That should do it.'

'We hope so,' Julian agreed. 'In fact, we're pretty sure that the double hull and water shield will be sufficient. You might not have been aware of it, but some of your experiments on the surface have been designed to check the protection.' He projected the next image, but Christine interrupted.

'That's what that stupid lidded thing was for that I had to put in a brightly lit location. Wondered what it was,' she said.

'Probably. Anyway, this is the manufacturing plant which sits alongside the derrick. It will allow us to produce up to five tons of water per day.' The schematic was replaced by an aerial shot of the crater.

'Here' – he pointed at a complex of tanks – 'are the storage containers for liquid hydrogen and oxygen which we'll be producing.'

'That's a lot of fuel!' exclaimed Dave.

'It is, and that is the nature of the plan which requires security. The heat on Earth is increasing. There is a fear that it could make the planet almost uninhabitable if it continues.'

'Thought that might have been just a conspiracy theory,' interjected Elena.

'Wait a minute,' said Christine, 'what about nitrogen? We can't work in pure oxygen. It's dangerous. One spark and…' She threw her arms out in imitation of an explosion.

'I'm told that it's possible to extract nitrogen and trace gases from the regolith. You can be sure that scientists are working on that right now to perfect it.'

He took a drink of water and continued, somewhat more at ease, 'Well, governments are allowing it to be seen as a conspiracy theory, but in fact, there is a real danger that Earth could be too hot for normal life in just a few decades. What we are doing here is preparing for that eventuality.'

'I understand the importance of the water,' said Bert, 'but why store it as separate gases?'

'Fuel,' said Julian.

'Fuel for what?' asked the doctor.

'Sorry, that's still classified,' said Julian, his words striking everyone dumb.

After a very pregnant silence, Christine stated, 'We're preparing the moon for a substantial population to arrive. It's an evacuation!'

'You might think that,' said Julian, 'but it is rather more complicated and, I'm afraid, I cannot put you out of your misery because I am not fully in the picture myself.'

'Why?' asked Bert. 'I don't like secrecy, it smacks of military.'

'Simply, knowledge is on a "need to know" basis and government has decided that we don't need to know yet,' the overseer replied.

'Not very satisfactory,' murmured Christine.

'I'm sorry, Christine, isn't it?'

The Scot nodded.

'It's all any of us have got. We've been given a task and must get the manufacturing of the gases underway as soon as possible. Commander Lewis has also had a cyphered communication about it,' said Julian, sitting down.

'I have,' said Bert. 'I'm sorry, but everything we've seen or heard today about this expedition is classified. I trust you all understand.'

'Can we speculate?' asked Christine.

'You can,' said Julian, 'but only among ourselves and only because you are now permanent Moonbase personnel.'

∞∞∞∞∞∞∞∞∞∞

Later, Christine and Elena were suiting up in the airlock to prepare for more drilling and exploring of the nearby crater. The inevitable concerns about the situation on Earth were discussed.

'What do you think they're planning?' asked Elena.

'Don't know, but it seems strange that they should be concentrating the finished product in individual gas tanks. Why not simply as water,' replied Christine, stopping her checks of the suit to turn to look at her colleague.

'So that must mean it's for fuel.'

'Well, not necessarily, I suppose. The gases could be recombined to produce water, but it defies logic to do that.'

Elena held her helmet ready to assemble. 'There was one water tank, I noticed.'

'Logical, I suppose, but the whole industrial nature of the set-up screams fuel,' said Christine. 'Are you going to put that helmet on?'

'Well,' said Elena, placing the helmet back on its hook, 'once we're suited up, we can be overheard by others.'

'What's on your mind? Come on, spit it out!'

'We know how bad it is on Earth. There are lots of my family heading northwards from Spain. The heat is too much for older people, Christine. There's also a migration of people from Africa. They say that the French are using gunboats to patrol their southern coast and are turning boats away, threatening to fire on them.'

'And what's your point?' asked the Scot.

'I think it'll lead to violence. What will your country do if it's suddenly flooded with Italians, the French and us? Let alone hordes of Africans.'

'See what you mean.'

'It'll mean serious violence. Sure thing,' said the Spaniard.

'And that's making you think, what, about the gas tanks?'

'They're going to build a starship. We're thinking of abandoning the Earth,' Elena replied.

'Starships would be no good. The radiation would kill everyone before they passed Mars,' said Christine.

'Not if they kept Earth between the sun and the ship until they were far enough out.'

'Not possible. The fuel needed to maintain such a course would be horrendous and the shadow of Earth's magnetosphere wouldn't protect the ship for that long.'

'QED. That's why so much fuel is being mined. A starship.'

'But the nearest star,' said Christine, 'would take centuries to reach with current technology.'

'Ha. You can bet there are pretty good minds working on that problem right now.'

'You really think that?'

'I do,' said Elena. 'What else can they do if the world is too hot to support life?'

'Hmm. Possible, I suppose,' replied Christine. 'Come on. Finish suiting up. Let's get out there.'

'How do we get to be on the starship?'

'Not sure that I'd want to. Imagine the rest of your life in a spaceship. Not a nice thought.'

'Well, Moonbase is like a spaceship. Just not moving. Could be possible.'

'Not for me. Life wouldn't be worth living if I couldn't go back to the hills and lochs of Scotland. No thank you. At least on the moon I know I'm only a short journey from home. On a starship, well, doesn't bear thinking about. Too late to change your mind when you're passing Sirius at close to the speed of light!' She laughed at the thought. 'Come on, check my helmet.'

'But you've already committed to stay at Moonbase,' said Elena.

'Well, for a period. You think it's forever?' the Scot asked.

'I think it could be,' Elena replied.

They both stood in silence contemplating their thoughts.

'Dave here,' the speaker in the airlock said. 'You two going out or not?'

Elena pressed the intercom button. 'Yes, sorry, Dave. Just making some extra checks. Leaving shortly.'

The ancient surface of the moon beckoned them. Procedures complete, they stepped onto the regolith and summoned Artoo and Detoo from their kennel. The women and their mechanical hounds headed for the crater rim once more.

'Look north!' exclaimed Elena excitedly, lifting her arm and pointing to her left.

The Scot followed her directions, and the two astronauts watched a large ship approaching at a height of, they guessed, a mile or so. It was moving rapidly, spurts of gas coming from various locations along its side.

As it approached, the ship's shape became clearer. It wasn't streamlined. That could only mean one thing – it had been assembled in orbit, not launched from Earth. It comprised four orbs connected along its length. As they watched, it began to swivel into a more vertical orientation.

'It's heading for Copernicus. It's preparing to land,' said Christine.

They realised that they were seeing one of the freighters to which Julian had referred. This was one of the supply vessels for the new water and gas manufacturing plant.

'Didn't expect them so soon,' said Elena.

'No. This has obviously been planned for some time, perhaps even years.'

Still gradually losing altitude, the huge vessel passed overhead and soon disappeared behind a range of low hills in the distance.

'You realise it was pure luck you spotted it?' said Christine.

'Yes. No sound on the moon to alert us. I wonder if this is the first, or one of many which have already arrived,' mused Elena.

They both looked north to see if there were more, but after five minutes they trudged on towards the crater in which they were working.

27 Cabinet

'I declare this meeting of the full cabinet open,' said Jenny McRoberts. 'We have matters of the gravest importance to consider today and I cannot emphasise strongly enough how important it is that no leaks, hints, or suggestions escape this room. Do you all understand?'

There was a murmur of general agreement from all present. Everyone was aware that cabinet meetings were confidential and the PM's emphasis of it in her opening welcome was unusual and therefore taken most seriously.

'Senior ministers have been aware of what we will be considering for almost two years. Now we are telling the whole cabinet, it is vital that secrecy is maintained.'

Those who had no idea of the reason for her statement wondered what was to come. They didn't have to wait long.

The prime minister looked towards the home secretary. 'Jack, fill everyone in.'

'Yes, Prime Minister,' he said, opening a document folder and beginning, 'Over the last eighteen months, we've been gathering a lot of information on the heating of the planet. It has included learning about the effects on other countries, particularly central Africa, South America, and the Far East.

He extracted photographs from the folder and passed some in each direction. They quickly passed from hand to hand.

'What you are seeing is the result of devastating fires being caused by the increased heat of the sun. Scorched earth, trees turned to charcoal, dead and dying animals. This is not just taking place in Brazil and Central Africa, but also in many temperate areas. Parts of Mediterranean Europe are afire and have been for weeks. Greece and Turkey are in a desperate state, unable to control fires which are destroying centuries-old olive groves and vineyards. Whole towns have been burned to the ground, not just there, but also in Spain, Portugal, Italy, and France. Hundreds of thousands of deaths are being reported from around the world. The people most unable to cope with the heat and smoke of the fires are the elderly and infirm. There is an almost unnoticeable migration of people northwards. We only know about it because statistics from the European Union are starting to record a population shift from south to north.'

Never, since the Second World War, the Cuban missile crisis, and the nuclear strike in Ukraine, had there been so many concerned faces staring at each other around that historic table.

Jack Easton continued sombrely, 'The prime minister wants me to ensure that you are all fully in the picture, and this means that certain information we've had for a short time must be passed on.'

'It also explains the need for utmost secrecy. Brace yourselves,' added the PM.

The home secretary continued, 'The heat is *not* going to stop. Scientists tell us that it will continue to increase to the point where the surface of Earth will become uninhabitable. Very few will survive this mass extinction, and it will be very democratic because all countries will be affected. Nowhere on Earth will be safe.'

Shock ran across the faces of those who were learning this for the first time.

'Surely, some will be better placed?' asked the minister for pensions, 'Greenland, the north of Russia, Canada, et cetera.'

Jack shook his head. 'No. These areas might be survivable for longer than most, but we anticipate violent hordes of migrants fleeing dying countries, and I must include Britain in this, because our country will be a wasteland within ten to fifteen years if the scientists are right… and we think they are.'

'What is being done?' asked another minister.

'Well,' said the PM, 'that is another reason for secrecy. The plan is to create some refuges. One on the moon, one in the centre of Antarctica and two orbital colonies.'

'But they could only hold a few thousand!' exclaimed another. 'The world's population is billions!'

'Yes,' said the home secretary, 'Nine billion and change.'

'And we're only going to be able to save a few thousand?' asked the same minister.

'That appears to be the situation,' said the PM. 'There are already tens of thousands trying to move north or south from the equatorial regions and we know that some countries have already introduced measures to prevent it.'

'What measures?' asked the overseas development minister.

Sir Charles Browning, defence minister and former prime minister answered, 'We know, although it is not admitted through official channels, that France, Italy and Spain are preventing landings of migrant boats from North Africa.'

'How are they doing that?' asked the same minister.

'How do you think?' said Sir Charles, in a surprised tone of voice. 'They're sinking the boats!'

There were several calls of 'no' from around the table.

'Come on, people,' said the PM, 'Given the situation with the rising heat, it was obvious this would happen. We'd had rumours it was happening and now we have proof. It is happening in all countries with south facing coastlines. Sri Lanka is on the verge of war with India over the number of attacks being carried out on boats making the crossing.'

'Let no one be in any doubt,' said Sir Charles. 'All countries are likely to be in this situation soon. How is Scandinavia going to stop migrants from Mediterranean regions, or, for that matter, from Britain? We also know that Canada is making preparations to protect its southern borders. The US government is desperate to come to some sort of deal with them. There is even discussion in the EU about curtailing the free movement of people. At the moment, anyone from the southern European EU countries has a right to live anywhere in the EU. You can imagine how this will affect Sweden and Finland. Sweden is already thinking of applying restrictions.'

Silence fell over the meeting.

'Anyway,' said the home secretary, 'we have decided it is time to release this information to the cabinet but must try to prevent it reaching the general public.'

George Smith, the transport minister, asked, quietly, 'And how will people be selected to be considered for the refuges?'

'That's a hornets' nest none of us are yet ready to discuss,' said the home secretary.

'We will need to ensure a fair share of our population is included,' said Sir Charles, 'but how that will happen is not a priority. It is likely that only women of childbearing age will be shortlisted. We, in this room, need to be aware that it will be down to us to ensure it is done fairly.'

There was a buzz of conversation until the PM intervened, 'Before anyone starts thinking about how they might be affected personally, I want to make it *absolutely clear* that while we should help administer the situation, *none* of us should expect to outlive this crisis.'

'We have to agree not to try to save ourselves?' said George, his voice tense.

'The whole purpose of government, George, is to support and protect its people. Imagine the reaction of the population if they thought ministers would be first in line to be saved. Can I remind you that "One rule for us, and one rule for them," eventually brought down the Conservative government after the Covid crisis.'

Now, George Smith raised his voice. 'But this is life or death. We have as much right as any other citizen to look after ourselves and our families'

'*No, we do not!*' said the PM, speaking more loudly. 'Immediately – show of hands if you agree.'

George Smith and one or two others did not raise an arm, but the vast majority of the cabinet did.

'Joe, record that vote in the minutes,' the PM said. 'The three of you who did not agree have until the end of this meeting to change your vote. If you do not, then you will no longer be a member of this cabinet, and this entire discussion will remain under the Official Secrets Act. You *must not* talk about it.'

'Sorry,' said George, 'it's such a shock. Of course I vote with the Cabinet.'

The other rebels also relented.

'It's because it *is* a matter of life and death that we *must* take the moral high ground,' said the PM so emphatically that it stopped further discussion.

Stunned silence plagued the table.

'Second agenda item,' said the cabinet secretary, using the shocked silence to move the meeting onwards. 'The PM has come into some related news.'

'Yes,' the PM said, 'Intelligence has told us that a massive installation is being built on the Antarctic coast. I had a call with the US secretary of state about it the other day. The construction project is being undertaken by a country or countries unknown. It includes a commercial scale harbour, a town and, we believe, an underground refuge built into the hinterland.'

The cabinet secretary handed around photographs of the construction in its current state, and the coastline two years previously.

'Who's doing it?' asked the minster for the environment.

'If we knew that,' said the home secretary, 'we wouldn't be speaking about countries unknown, would we?'

'Calm down, please,' said the PM, taking a drink from her glass. 'We think it might be Libya. They've been buying up vessels, construction plant and sheep, cattle, poultry, and, surprisingly, pigs in large numbers, together with shiploads of grain and animal feed.'

'What are we going to do about it?' asked Beryl Charters, the chancellor of the exchequer.

'We have an undercover vessel heading to the port about now,' said the PM. 'That will tell us more. However, we have to consider whether or not to do *anything* about it. Do we have the right to stop any country from peacefully trying to save some of its population?'

'But they don't have any rights to Antarctica,' said the chancellor.

'Beryl, this is an existential problem for the whole world. Do any of us think we can justify exclusive rights to the only place on Earth which might offer some chance to save humankind?' said the PM. Beryl Charters nodded thoughtfully.

'You're talking about the end of the world,' said George Smith.

'More accurately the end of civilisation. The world will still be here,' said the home secretary. 'We believe it is that serious, though, and that is why secrecy is so important.'

'The public will be furious when they discover we've been lying to them. Buchanan's been claiming that all along. His followers could be even more violent than the last demonstration,' said Diana. 'I've been saying, all along, that we must come clean on this.'

'And we agreed not to,' said the PM. 'Next week, I want ideas for how we are going to take this matter forward. All of you, please, give it your thoughts. My closest advisers are already talking about a government of national unity. What do you think? I want your ideas.'

The prime minister stood, gathered her folders, and began to make her way towards the door, saying, 'Charles, Jack, Wally, Beryl… my office, please.'

28 Building Cash

With the increasing temperatures, some of the farms in Denmark were switching to more lucrative crops. Fields of wheat and barley were giving way to strawberries, raspberries, and other soft fruits. This changed labour patterns considerably as cropping wheat, barley and other cereals was nowhere near as labour intensive as fruit harvesting. Immigrants were aware of that and many, legal and illegal, were involved in the new industry.

The area around Sengeløse, just west of Copenhagen was fast becoming one of the most important soft fruit growing regions of that part of Europe. Destri, Bright and the kids cycled from their campsite a few kilometres south of Sengeløse to a farm owned by Johan Erikson. They only had one chain for security and Destri linked the rear wheels of each of the bikes together and attached them to a fence beside the entrance to that day's field. Strawberries.

It was hot, damned hot. As soon as they'd dismounted and secured the bikes, all four of them went to an area inside the field where a shower was provided to cool them down. They were wearing just T-shirts, shorts and flipflops and stood on the two-metre square drainage panel. Destri hit the silver button, and cool water began to drench them. Not that cold initially, but after a minute or so it ran very cool. They just stood and enjoyed it. After three minutes it cut out.

'Come on then. Let's get earning,' said Destri and they made their way to a caravan.

As they approached, a window was slid open and they were asked, 'Names?'

'I is Destri, wife Bright, adult daughter Mariam and son, Edu.'

'Children's ages?'

'Mariam seventeen and Edu fourteen,' said Destri.

'Fourteen-year-old can only work five hours,' said the voice inside the caravan office.

'We know that. We regular,' said Bright.

'You're logged in, punnets and boxes over there.' A hand waved in the direction of an open-sided marquee. The window slid shut and the cooler air Destri had felt on his face stopped instantly.

In the marquee, they collected a stack of cardboard outer cases and several dozen punnets then surveyed the field. There were already several pickers at work, making their way up the rows of low strawberry plants.

'Let's go to that row on the right, no one in there,' said Destri.

It was backbreaking work. Strawberries could only be picked if they were ripe or just about ripe; the latter meant that there could be some green flashes on the fruit. Each one had to be briefly inspected then twisted and removed from the plant and placed gently in the punnet. Bruised fruit would not be tolerated. Work began, and in over forty-five degrees it was exhausting, and they were soon covered in sweat. However, the pay was good. Strawberries were a new crop for this part of Denmark – the climate change had made it lucrative – and there was no shortage of migrant labour.

Gradually, the family filled punnets, then stacked them two deep in the cardboard outers. Once an outer was full, forty-eight punnets, they were carried to the marquee. Inside, the case was weighed and had to be within the required range. The tallyman then provided a plastic token to the picker.

By lunchtime, the family was exhausted, particularly Bright and Edu. Also, every hour or so, each of them would take a walk to the shower to cool down. The heat was such that the water evaporating from your body was a real boon.

Lunch had been made by Bright and contained cooked sausages, some bread rolls, cheese, and salad. They ate for thirty minutes, rested for another ten, visited the shower to drench themselves again and then it should have been back to the field.

Bright put a hand on Destri's arm, 'Look. He back again,' she said.

Mariam turned to look.

'You kids go back to picking. We'll catch you soon,' said Bright, waving them to go.

A large blond man who resembled Thor was leaning on the gate. A smaller, but no less intimidating dark-haired, swarthy fellow stood beside him.

'What we going to do, Des?' asked Bright.

'Come on,' said Des, taking Bright's hand, and they walked over to the men, who changed their posture. Standing ready to fight if needs be.

'What you want now, man?' asked Destri.

'Same as yesterday. Half your earnings,' the giant said.

'No way,' said Destri. 'That was a one-off 'cos you said you'd turn us in. Not paying no more.'

'Difficult to pick with a broken arm, nigger!' the smaller man said.

'You threatnin vilence now?' asked Destri.

'Tell you what. You pay half and you'll never see us again,' said the giant.

'Until the next time,' said Destri.

'No. Final payment. We won't bother you again,' said the giant.

'Got no money on me now,' said Destri.

'How can we trust you?' asked Bright.

'We'll be back later. Cash your tokens today,' said the smaller man.

They turned and walked away. Destri was shaking. He hated confrontation.

'Let's go back to pick for a while then leave after hour,' said Bright.

'You wearing money belt?'

'Am.'

'Need get tent. Other stuff in bag we buried too,' said Destri.

'We cycle quick to wood and then get bus over bridge,' said Bright.

'Need to get tickets for bikes and us,' said Destri.

'Unless we go long way round. They say there no checks on bridge. Bridge best. Just family on holiday.'

HEAT

'I s'pose so. Okay. Pick for forty minutes. I'll take tokens to office and we head to tent. Put half cash in money belt with rest,' said Destri.

'I'll do dat in the toilet.'

'Okay, let's get back to picking.'

'Shower visit first,' said Bright.

'Too right,' Destri said and the two of them stood under the shower again before going to catch up with the kids in one of the rows of strawberry plants.

∞∞∞∞∞∞∞∞∞∞

At about three o'clock, the family finished their picking, handed in their last trays of strawberries, and collected their tokens.

'You three head for the shower. I'll cash the tokens,' said Destri. He walked up to the caravan and knocked on the sliding window.

'Can I cash in now, please?' he asked.

The woman inside was munching on a snack. She swallowed and said, 'But it's only just three.'

'Got pointment with doc in Sengeløse so must go early. Full day tomorrow though.'

'Alright. Just this once.'

Destri handed over a bag full of blue tokens. 'There's a hunerd and twenny in there.'

The woman emptied the bag and stacked them in piles of twenty. 'Correct,' she said. She turned to a safe behind her and removed some cash then counted it out on the countertop where Destri could see and handed it over.

'See yous tomorrow,' he said.

'Right,' said she.

The porta toilets were located beside the shower. Destri met Bright, gave her half the cash, and went to the shower where he soaked himself. God, it was hot. Hotter than back in Ghana.

Bright emerged from the blue cabinet, and they unchained the bicycles.

'No sign of them guys,' said Destri.

'No, and I looked up and down the road while you sorting cash. They not lurking out of sight, don't think,' said Bright.

'Now, listen carefully, Edu, Mariam. If those guys from last night try to stop us, you just cycle fast as can to the tent and wait. Okay?'

'Okay, Da,' they both replied.

They mounted their bikes and, despite the heat, headed at top speed for the woodland where their tent was concealed.

Fifteen minutes later, Destri and Bright swung around the bend which led to the forest track and slammed on the brakes. Mariam and Edu were standing astride their cycles and the two men were facing them, standing side by side, blocking the entrance to the track.

'You weren't trying to make a getaway, nigger, were you?' asked the smaller man, holding a baseball bat in his hand and slapping it down upon his other palm.

Destri accelerated on his bike, passed between the two children, and rode straight at Tiny. It took the man with the bat a couple of seconds to realise what was happening then a pair of handlebars hit him in the stomach followed by a two-hundred-pound Destri

Esturu, who ploughed into him, grabbing the bat as they fell. Destri was up in a shot, swinging the bat in a full circle and crashing it into Tiny's head. The man was out for the count.

Back on his feet, Destri squared up to Thor and started to shuffle towards him. The big blond backed off but dug into his trousers and pulled out a machete.

'Come on then, nigger!' he shouted.

Despite appearing confident, Destri was a bundle of nerves. He never was a fighter. He always tried to compromise rather than confront. He approached the giant slowly, swinging the bat back and forth across his chest, thinking about how to go for an attack but still avoid the machete.

He didn't need to worry. The giant's head suddenly pitched to one side, and he crumpled to the ground. Mariam had hit him with the broken top half of a fence post. Now there were two bleeding bodies lying in the track.

'Help me,' Destri said, 'let's get 'em into woods.'

'How, Des?' said Bright. 'They too heavy.'

'I'll pull big one, you and Mariam pull the other,' said Destri. 'Edu, get bikes into wood and hidden from view. Quick. Come on. Get moving!'

Destri's words brought them all to life and they jumped into action, dragging the two men about forty metres into the wood along the footpath then pulling them off to one side. Soon the two were lying in a hollow, out of sight of anyone on the path.

'Think the small one's dead,' said Bright, holding her fingers to his neck.

Destri checked. 'Yes, think you right. Edu, run to tent and get the blue rope. Quick. Fast as you can.'

The boy, using his initiative, jumped on his bike, and pedalled along the pathway. He was back in less than a couple of minutes.

'Bright. Your scarf,' said Destri.

His wife pulled a plain scarf from her bag and passed it to her husband. He put it around the giant's head, opening his mouth so that it was between his teeth, tied it securely at the back and measured out two metre-long lengths of rope, cutting them off the coil with the machete.

One length, he tied around the giant's legs at his knees and pulled it really tight. The second rope he used to tie the hands together.

Next, he searched both of the bodies. There were over two thousand kroner. He passed the cash to Bright.

'Put with rest of cash in belt. I've 'nough for our 'mediate needs,' he said.

Bright fiddled around under her shirt and soon had the extra kroner in the money belt.

'What we going to do, Des? This is murder,' she said.

'Wheel bikes to camp. We got to pack up and go before these two goons found,' said Destri.

'Is he really dead?' asked Edu.

'Yes, son. Was him or us. Had to do it,' said Destri, patting the boy on the shoulders. 'Now, quick, to the tent!'

HEAT

As darkness fell, the four bikes were stored in the luggage section at the bottom of the bus with the tent and they were sitting in the air-conditioned comfort of the coach travelling over the Øresundsbron towards Sweden. They were good at hiding and would soon be out of Malmo and heading farther north.

HEAT

29 Hideaway

'You anything planned for the weekend?' I asked Gren on Thursday evening, as I arrived in the kitchen after leaving the car to garage itself.

Our children, Geoffrey and Caroline were playing in the garden as Gren chopped onions and peppers for the evening meal. 'What have you got in mind?' he asked.

'I've found a little hideaway cottage for us. It's called Fetlar and located in a nature reserve.'

'Hideaway?'

'Somewhere which might be cool, if you get my meaning. Discovered it on my last trip to the new telescope at SaxaVord on Shetland. I was asking Professor Davies about properties in the area, and he mentioned an isolated cottage in the Hermaness Nature Reserve which had been owned by a friend of his who recently died. Sixty-one degrees north so as close to the Arctic Circle as we can get within Britain. I've done some research on it.'

Gren had finished slicing the peppers and had begun to cut the chicken breasts into bite-sized pieces.

'That will still be too hot though, won't it?' asked Gren as he stood over the chopping board with the knife raised like a conductor's baton.

'Eventually,' I said, and threw the details onto the countertop. 'It has solar panels, a small wind turbine, storage batteries and would fulfil our needs until the sun shrugs off its madness or, well, until the end.' I didn't enjoy saying the final word.

'How much space?'

'Enough just for us really, somewhere to escape to for the odd break in the interim and permanently when needs must. The kids could sleep in the sitting room if they came with us occasionally. I'd want the children to know where we'll be as I'm still hoping we might be able to find them a place in one of the refuges. I'll be too old to go with them. My childbearing days are over, Gren. It's unlikely any woman too old to give birth will be selected, except some medical specialists. Even my astrophysicist knowledge won't suffice. I doubt I could keep up with modern thinking on it anyway. I already rely on others for interpretation of modern theories.'

Gren put down the knife, washed his hands, and came over to hug me. 'Government ministers have been told they will not be selected either, only young scientists are likely to be among those saved.'

'Really? Is that a rule?'

'Yes. The PM told us at the last cabinet meeting. They intend to provide suicide pills for us.'

'You're joking!'

'No. That's what the health minister said when I was chatting to her at lunch,' Gren said.

'I worry about the children. Most will be orphaned deliberately by the selection process. Many won't cope.'

'So you see this cottage, Felspar is it, as a final refuge for the two of us?'

'Fetlar. Yes, I do. We could build extra rooms if the kids must come with us.'

'You're thinking of Sandra and Malcolm and their family too?'

'No, Gren. Maybe Cas and Geoff, but that would be it. The hideaway is not likely to support more than four of us.' I felt tears building.

Gren held me tighter and kissed me.

'You want to take a look at this place?' he asked.

'I do. I can get Sandra and Malcolm to look after Geoff and Cas for the weekend and we can investigate. You up for that? I'll run them down to Beaulieu in the morning. They'll love a weekend in the woodland with their stepsister and their nieces.'

'The very north of Shetland. We'll be isolating ourselves from doctors, hospitals and so on. Is that a good idea?' Gren said, squeezing me again then returning to the chicken.

'Doctors and hospitals will already be becoming scarce or unable to operate effectively,' I replied, taking a bottle of a cheap Chardonnay from the refrigerator, cracking it, and pouring two glasses. 'At least we'd be safe. I hate the thought of hordes of migrants, fighting their way north. The last thing I'd be wanting us to do in the end days is shooting groups of invading migrants. Shetland would seem the safest as most people making their way north will have their sights set on northern mainland Europe by the time the heat becomes unbearable. We could still be living relatively comfortably in isolation if we can bolster the power system at the house. We'll need to look at it with that in mind.'

'And food?'

'We'll get some chickens and grow some vegetables. We can live on that once trade ceases – well, safe trade, anyway,' I said sadly, perching myself on one of the bar stools beside the breakfast bar. 'It has a barn apparently. You'd need to lay in some wine from that supplier you know. Some really good stuff for the end days.'

'Okay, speak to Sandra and Malcolm and see if they can babysit. Have you checked flights?'

'Yes. If we can leave at four tomorrow, there's a flight to Aberdeen with a connection to Lerwick.'

'And then?'

'A caravanette and we drive north. There's a place in Lerwick which has some four-wheel-drive motor homes,' I said, sipping the wonderfully chilled wine. 'The access track to the house isn't paved according to Professor Davies.'

'You have done your homework.'

'I'll call Sandra. You can get off tomorrow afternoon?'

'Yes. No problem,' Gren said as he shovelled the onions into a hot pan with a selection of herbs. They began to sizzle and give off the wonderful aroma of spiced onions cooking.

I phoned my daughter, and she was only too pleased to take the kids for the weekend. Gren continued cooking, and I was finally feeling the benefits of the air-conditioning after my journey home.

The next morning, I took the A31 Portsmouth road from Guildford down to the New Forest and my daughter's house in woodland west of Beaulieu. It was roasting outside, and I'd had to leave the car for twenty minutes preconditioning before we departed, just to make the interior bearable.

HEAT

My daughter and son-in-law's house was beautiful. Set right on the edge of the famous New Forest, it provided easy access for her to the Montagu Arms Hotel where she was the head chef. Malcolm, her husband, worked from home as a copywriter. It was lovely to see them, and they were only too happy to look after my young children. Their twins, Patricia and Linda, were a few months older than Geoffrey, and were jumping for joy at the surprise visit of their grandmother and the auntie and uncle who were younger than they were.

'Can we go and play in the woods?' asked Caroline excitedly.

'Put your hats on,' I shouted, seeing that Patricia and Linda were wearing white, floppy hats for shade.

'Yes,' said Malcolm, 'but don't go out of sight of the house.' The four children were already disappearing from the garden.

I stayed for a light early lunch, and we discussed the dreadful heat. I couldn't be completely honest about the climate problem, but I'm sure they sensed my concern.

It was unlikely I could do anything to save them from the crisis which was to come. Even being a Michelin-starred chef wasn't enough to be accepted in one of the refuges. Nor would my son, Wilson's footballing talent save him. The whole situation was such a catastrophe.

I drove back with a cloud of gloom hanging over me. Perhaps Shetland could be the answer, but only for Gren and me.

We stayed the night in the refurbished Queens Hotel. What a strange place. Originally a collection of houses, shops, and offices, part of the buildings stood in the water and our room looked out over the sea on the outside of the harbour; an interesting experience and the restaurant offered several lobster recipes. Wonderful. The only drawback was the lack of air-conditioning. Lerwick, in common with most of the world, was suffering record summer temperatures.

The next morning, we took a cab the short distance to Wulver Motorhomes. The all-electric Mercedes we rented was perfect for our purposes. It had everything we might need for our trip from Lerwick to Hermaness using the network of ferries between the islands of the archipelago and it boasted all-wheel drive for our visit to the nature reserve. There was a comfortable double berth in the rear, surprisingly sophisticated cooking facilities, and a small bathroom with loo.

There was the usual battle over who was to drive, and I won, but had to agree to let Gren drive the return trip. Our first stop was a supermarket where we bought enough food to see us through three days, leaving a little spare, then we set off. Good roads and the enjoyment of a couple of ferries. It was wonderful to feel the breeze on my face with the heat of the sun beating down.

The journey to Haroldswick passed relatively quickly. We had soup and a sandwich at the quaintly named Victoria's Vintage Tea Rooms and took the tiny road towards Hermaness. I'd been here before to visit the new telescope at the now-closed SaxaVord

Air Force Station, but this time we were skirting the western side of the firth.

As we approached Shorehaven and the nature reserve, we'd been told to keep an eye open for a tiny signboard 'Fetlar'. It was hand-painted and nailed to the top of a fence post standing at the entrance to a dirt track. Another hand-painted sign said 'PRIVATE' in red letters on a white background.

Now, we were driving a farm track, basically two wheel tracks with a central grass mound, the longer fronds of which could be heard caressing the underside of the campervan occasionally. That grass was also growing in the wheel tracks showed that it was rarely used, and it was littered with potholes, though none too severe for us to drive over. After about a mile, we drove around a hill and could see two stone buildings in the distance overlooking the most wonderful coastal scenery.

'This place *can't* be real,' said Gren, as we came to a halt in the turning area beside the isolated buildings. On our left was a fenced area which had obviously, in the recent past, been somewhere that grew vegetables or perhaps enclosed a few animals. It would be perfect for a small garden and chicken compound. Backing on to it were the remains of a steading or barn. It was roughly constructed, and roofed with extremely rusty corrugated iron sheeting. The doorway was wide, about two metres and, if there ever had been a door, it was long gone and only the door jamb and a hanging hinge remained. Forty or fifty metres beyond the steading, a modern glossy white wind turbine stood. It was unmoving despite the steady breeze. Beneath it stood a concrete building about ten metres square. I guessed that would hold the storage batteries.

'Hope the house is in better condition than the barn,' I said and laughed.

We left the Mercedes and walked around to the front of the second building: the house. Again, it was constructed of rough stone blocks but had been pointed with cement and even harled and whitewashed in places. The rear, the section we could first see, had a small sixty-centimetre window with frosted glass and, to its right, an incongruously modern uPVC framed window with one large pane and two smaller panes above. It appeared to have brown curtains, and we could see nothing inside.

'Grim,' said Gren disapprovingly.

As we circled the structure, we saw that the gable end sported a chimney which seemed to have been rebuilt recently and properly harled. We reached the corner and turned along the front of the cottage. My goodness, the view was stupendous. The house overlooked an area where the cliffs were less high and, in the middle, there was a small river and well-used path leading down to a spur from the firth and a tiny cove.

'Wow,' I said.

Gren was trying to see inside the main picture window, but, again, there were dowdy curtains. 'Have you got the keys?' he asked.

I tossed them to him but couldn't take my eyes off the vista in front of me.

There was the sound of an opening door, so I joined him, and we peered into the gloomy hallway. He flicked a light switch, but nothing happened. Using the torch on his cell phone, he continued into the hall. The modern door on the left opened easily and led into a lounge area with two grubby easy chairs, one threadbare, a sideboard which was much the worse for wear, its top scarred with marks from numerous cups and plates which had lifted the veneer, and a Formica table and chairs beside the window.

Gren strode forward and pulled the curtains open. One slid along an ancient runner, but the other fell to the floor. The view over the dale and path to the cove was stunning.

'It has its benefits,' said Gren, admiring the scene. I came alongside him and encircled his shoulders.

'Let's check out the rest,' I said, as I turned on my own phone's light and opened the opposite door. This was the kitchen and, it too had a view over the cliffs on one side and towards the wind turbine and steading on the other. Behind that was a bathroom in need of modernisation and the final room, with views out of the rear of the house was a reasonably sized bedroom.

'What do you think?' I asked.

'Needs some work,' Gren replied, 'but it could be perfect for what we have in mind.'

'I think so too,' I said, and we hugged.

'Will tradesmen come out to do work, do you think?'

'At a price.'

'Have you got the power information booklet there?' asked Gren.

'In the Mercedes. I'll get it,' I said and quickly returned to the motorhome to fetch the solicitor's folder.

I returned to find Gren standing outside looking at the roof. 'Wouldn't have thought these would give much power,' he said, assessing the solar panels.

'There's more over there,' I said, pointing to a south-facing framework almost hidden behind the power room and wind turbine.

'Yes, hadn't noticed those.'

I read the instruction notes. 'It seems the whole thing is automatic. You have to unlock the windvanes and turn on the master switch inside the battery room. They collect power from both the generator and the solar panels. The batteries can store up to four days winter requirements if there's a lull in the wind.' I handed him the relevant document.

'I'll turn it on,' he said, taking the keys to the battery room and I followed.

Although roughly built from concrete blocks on the outside, the door was made of steel. Once opened, the inside was surprisingly clean and modern, with plastered walls painted white, and the equipment appeared as good as new.

I stood in the doorway and read the agent's description, 'The installation was completed just two years ago, it says here,' I said. 'The solicitor says the owner died shortly after the work was finished. It's been used but should be in perfect working order.'

Gren shone his cell phone light on the operating manual which hung from a hook beside a bank of batteries. 'This handwritten note says that the system is set to a fifteen percent charge, so we should have power if I turn it on.'

'What about the turbine?'

He flicked through the pages, 'No. I think we should get it serviced before use. It needs unlocking in order to rotate. I don't think I should turn it on just for our viewing. This is the master switch for the power system.'

He pointed at a standard, large, isolating switch and snapped it down. The room was suddenly lit by LED lights in the ceiling. 'Bingo!' he said.

We returned to the house and inspected the interior more carefully, switching all the appliances on and off to ensure they were working.

'It does all seem fine,' he said.

'What do you think?'

'A place to see out our final years? Yes,' I said.

'That makes us seem old. You're not forty yet and I'm hardly on my last legs,' said Gren.

'Depends how long we live here. The isolation offers us protection and as long as we have power, air-conditioning will help us survive. There's just the one small air-con unit in the kitchen. We'd need to install them in every room and the battery room, or it'll overheat. It'll cost, and we'll need spares for everything.'

'But you agree it is a solution for us?' I asked anxiously.

'Yes. The best solution I can imagine at the moment.'

We hugged.

∞∞∞∞∞∞∞∞∞∞

That afternoon, despite the heat, we wandered down the path to the cove. It was low tide, and a small gravelly beach presented itself to us. We walked up and down it, holding hands and stopping occasionally to look up at the cliffs which stood about thirty to forty metres either side of the entrance to the inlet. Seabirds cawed at us and swirled around the vertical areas which were being used for nesting.

'Look! Puffins!' I cried.

Although the tide was out, substantial waves were crashing against the beach. These were not the more violent waves experienced on outer exposed shores on Shetland because the fjord of Burra Firth was sheltered by the land on each side.

'We could get a boat,' said Gren.

'Don't like that idea. Too many dangers.'

'Could use it to look after a few lobster pots. Only go out during relatively calm times. How do you fancy lobster or crab on the daily menu?'

'I like the thought of that very much. Do you think it's possible?' I asked, smiling.

'I'll do some research.'

'It's perfect, isn't it?'

'Considering the circumstances, as perfect as we might hope for.'

I pulled on his arm, and we started up the path. Dusk was falling. On the incline, the heat was even more oppressive, and we were both sweating profusely as we reached the house.

'Let's finish the measuring-up, cook a couple of those ready meals and stay the night in the van,' I said.

'There's an EV charging cable in the power room. I'll connect it and turn the van's air-conditioning on an hour before we decide to turn in,' said Gren. 'Otherwise, it'll be roasting.'

HEAT

30 Excavation

General Khalifa stood on the bridge of *The Gaddafi*; the two-hundred-metre luxury yacht the president of Libya had the pleasure of commanding. Initially, he'd sent the vessel down to Cape Town and once it had arrived, he flew to the South African city incognito. Once there, a helicopter was used to fly the Libyan leader to the yacht which had already set sail on the several thousand-kilometre journey to Port Khalifa which was being constructed on the coast of Antarctica.

On the bridge, the crew were spick and span in their pure white uniforms. Captain Mohammed with his gold braid insignia and matching cap stood hands on hips staring forwards towards the horizon. The general stood beside him surveying the apparently endless extent of the Southern Ocean. The captain swayed with the movement of the ship in a natural way learned from many years at sea. The general held on to a grab handle on the front console to keep himself steady. He wasn't a frequent sailor and, when he was at sea, it was usually in the less turbulent waters of the Mediterranean.

'How long?' he asked.

'Should be on the horizon any minute, sir.'

'Is the sea usually this rough here,' asked Khalifa as a particularly violent wave shook the ship and he had to hang with both hands to the brass handle.

'This is relatively calm, sir. I've not been in these waters myself previously, but the ship's mate has, and he has been remarking how quiet the sea is this week.'

'Wouldn't like to see it in a storm.'

'The mate is probably exaggerating, sir,' said the captain. Then to the nearby sailor he said, 'Five degrees to starboard.'

The yacht turned slightly to the right and the captain pointed to the horizon, 'Land ahoy, sir.'

The windscreen wipers battled to keep the forward vision clear. The general still couldn't see anything but raised a pair of binoculars and eventually acknowledged that there was an end in sight to the awful ocean. The beautiful white craft cut through the grey-green surface of the sea, its foamy wake cascading aft. On the rear deck, the khaki Leonardo SW-4 helicopter was secured with steel cables. Khalafi wondered whether or not it might be a good idea to fly to the port. It would add an unexpected edge to his arrival.

'Can you call my pilot to the bridge?'

'Certainly, sir. Number two, call the pilot,' said the captain. 'You're thinking of flying ahead, sir?'

'Possibly.'

'I couldn't advise that, sir. In this weather, the chopper could easily be unbalanced before you got airborne.'

'We'll ask the pilot,' said the general, not wishing to be put off once an idea was in his mind.

A short man in military fatigues opened the door to the bridge, allowing a violent squall of air to buffet the occupants.

'You wanted me, sir?' he asked.

'Yes, Asenath. How do you feel about flying us ahead? What's the distance, Captain?'

'About twenty-five kilometres,' said the captain.

Asenath looked at the sliver of land on the horizon, then both ways, taking in the force of the wind and waves. 'It would not be without risk, sir,' he said nervously.

General Khalifa prided himself in his reading of individuals. He realised that the pilot was showing bravado. Saying 'not without risk' could well mean that it was actually quite dangerous.

'Okay, Asenath. We'll leave it for now. Thank you.'

The pilot saluted and headed towards the door.

'Hold that door tight as you open it. The wind is now from starboard,' shouted the captain.

'Will do, sir,' the pilot said, keeping a firm grip on the door as he forced it open, slipped through, and allowed it to slam behind him.

'Yes,' said the general, 'probably best to stay aboard.'

'Shall I radio ahead?'

'No, Captain. They're not expecting us. Let's leave it that way.'

'What about weapons, sir? Might they think we're hostile?' asked the captain nervously.

'Hmm, possibly. Okay, just send an identifying signal, but don't tell them it's my yacht or that I'm aboard.'

'Certainly, General.'

HEAT

The Gaddafi eased itself gently against the harbour wall. Sailors in their whites jumped ashore, heavy ropes followed them, and the yacht was soon secured.

Other boats of all shapes and sizes were moored in the W-shaped harbour. Some were small military vessels, bristling with light weapons, but on the far side a heavily-armed destroyer class ship sat patiently, moored in such a way that it could be heading out into the ocean in a matter of minutes. Two substantial gunships were tied up alongside it.

At the central dock, a container ship and two grain vessels were being unloaded. They were buzzing with activity. Ship-to-shore cranes shifted the containers, placing them surprisingly delicately onto the backs of trucks which set off either towards the rising ground or along the roads to east and west. Marine towers with bucket elevators were stripping the bulk vessel of its cargo; again the lorries drove away towards the rising ground in sparse convoys.

Two Range Rovers and a couple of Jeeps containing soldiers sped along the harbour road, rapidly approaching *The Gaddafi*. Khalifa looked down at them from inside the bridge. He could see two senior officers in the Range Rovers and a number of other ranks in the Jeeps. Had they realised who it was? Of course they had. The name of the yacht would have given the game away.

He turned to the captain and said, 'Bring the senior officers to see me,' he said, and left the bridge through the central rear door which led away into the main body of the yacht.

Khalifa's stateroom was magnificent. It was at the rear of the ship with windows facing both port and starboard as well as onto a leisure deck and plunge pool to the rear. The pool hadn't seen any use on this trip across the Southern Ocean; in fact, it had been partially drained to avoid it overflowing if the weather became severe. Inside, the general relaxed into a comfortable green, Ercol Noto swivel chair behind an enormous rosewood desk sporting a traditional green and brass banker's desk lamp, an over-complicated desk tidy, and green leather-cornered blotter. A document comprising several pages lay in its exact centre.

The deck was carpeted in a floral design. Two more Ercol easy chairs faced the desk. In the starboard corner stood a small bar with three tall stools. Central within the port and rear space stood a rosewood dining table and six matching Windsor chairs with attached green leather cushions. The whole room was sumptuous and screamed class.

A corridor ran most of the length of the port side of the superstructure but ended with a doorway which entered the stateroom.

A sharp rap came on the door.

Khalifa swivelled lazily to face it. He waited.

He once lived in Oxford and had watched an old comedy television programme in which the chief executive had a method of making visitors feel anxious and uncomfortable. Each time someone visited, the executive said to himself, as Khalifa now did, 'One, two, three, four, make them wait outside the door; five, six, seven, eight, always pays to make them wait.'[10]

He shouted, 'Come!'

The captain entered with a general and two majors in tow.

'General Ahmed and Majors Darius and Bashir, sir,' announced the captain.

'You can go, Captain,' said Khalifa, watching the pristine white uniform disappear through the private door into the corridor which led to the bridge.

He looked at the military men. All three stood to attention, holding salutes. Khalifa casually waved his hand to his brow and then indicated the seats. 'At ease. Sit,' he said.

Ahmed and Darius took the comfortable chairs and Bashir walked to the dining table and carried a Windsor chair back to line up alongside the others.

'We weren't notified that you were arriving, sir,' said Ahmed.

'No. The opportunity arose so I took it. The harbour looks impressive and a hive of activity,' said Khalifa. 'Give me a progress report, Mohammed.'

'Yes, sir. The harbour is now fully functional, and the main facility is coming along well. The two outer towns to east and west are under construction and many homes are now ready for occupation. Warehouses are full of animal feed, and livestock will be arriving in a couple of weeks,' said General Ahmed.

---

[10] From 'The Fall and Rise of Reginald Perrin'

'I'm looking forward to a guided tour, General. Major Darius, I believe you are responsible for the excavations. How is that progressing?'

'We're a week or two behind schedule, sir. There was a major landslip in one part of the tunnel complex which delayed us, but we're catching up rapidly. I'd love to show you around when you're ready.'

'Yes. Yes, we'll do that. Maybe tomorrow. General, there was a cable querying some of the livestock. Is that now resolved?'

'Yes, sir. We were surprised to find pigs on the manifest and thought it might have been an error by the shippers. I queried it and they confirmed it was on your instructions.'

'It was,' Khalifa said more introspectively. 'This is an existential situation. Pigs are easy and quick to breed. We can't allow some outdated religious dogma to perhaps cause the demise of our entire race. We are fighting for survival here. We need all the livestock we can support. Sheep, goats, cattle and, yes, the lowly pig. When I lived in England I grew to love roast pork. I'm sure you will too.'

The three looked uncomfortably at each other.

'But what about the ordinary people, sir? There could be problems,' said Ahmed.

'The time is gone when we allowed beliefs to rule our minds. Today we must concentrate on survival. The people will do as they are told.'

'Yes, sir.'

'Major Bashir, how is security?'

'We have observation posts and vessels all along the coast. We avoid contact with any other Antarctic colonies. When there has been contact, we have gently persuaded them to leave our waters. There was an Argentinian vessel which became rather too inquisitive. We sank it.'

'Any repercussions?'

'Not so far, sir. We cannot conceal the harbour either, but the houses and apartments being built are camouflaged with green roofs.'

'Thank you, Major. We will, of course, be discovered sooner or later.'

Bashir replied, 'We'll be ready, sir. There's another frigate en route. Two plus the destroyer should be capable of seeing off all but the most concerted threat. We also have more armed patrol vessels due, but no fixed time yet. The destroyer is kept in a state of readiness and can leave the harbour within about twenty minutes if there is danger.'

'Very good, Major. I'll see you tomorrow afternoon and we'll run through the entire fleet requirement. Major Darius, pick me up at ten and you can give me a tour of the installation,' said Khalifa, then added, 'Dismissed. General Ahmed, please join the captain and me for dinner. Shall we say seven?'

'Thank you, sir,' Ahmed said, and followed the majors out of the stateroom.

∞∞∞∞∞∞∞∞∞∞

The next morning, Major Darius arrived at the yacht fifteen minutes early. He knew General Khalifa was particular about times. There would be no need to report that he was there and there was no way he would have arrived late; it would be more than his job was worth.

On the dot of ten, Khalifa, accompanied by a colonel, briskly descended the steps to the harbour wall. The sun shone brightly, but its watery radiance lacked warmth in these southern latitudes, even though it was some ten degrees above normal temperature for the time of year. It was a relief to be out of the sweltering heat they had been enduring in Tripoli.

Colonel Omar was Khalifa's personal assistant, looking after his diary as well as keeping notes of meetings, commands, and suggestions which might need to be recalled at later meetings or in telephone conversations. He was a small man, South Asian in appearance, and about forty, with a dark moustache and horn-rimmed spectacles. He carried a leather document case, tablet, recording device, and clipboard for making notes. He was extremely efficient.

Khalifa saluted the major and introduced Omar. 'Okay, Darius, take us to the construction. All three sat across the width of the squat Jeep, Omar in the middle. A sergeant took the controls and set off along the harbour wall.

'Sir,' said Darius, 'which was the latest report you've seen?'

Khalifa looked to Omar, who studied his tablet and announced, 'Sixth of the month.'

'Thank you, sir. Since then, we've made a lot of progress, mainly towards the east. Sergeant, stop a moment,' said Darius.

The Jeep slowed to a halt.

Darius continued, 'If you look over to the left, do you see the ridge which runs away inland, sir?'

'I do.'

'Well, we're now well into that rock. It comprises sedimentary rocks, mainly sandstone and limestone, but also shale. It's easy to excavate, and, in fact, we've just had to call a halt while we await the next shipment of supporting girders. We've also hit coal seams, which might be useful in the future for energy once all of this is over.

'Looking to the right, sir, we're encountering underlying gneiss which is a problem. It's much harder to tunnel through so progress in the livestock areas is a little slower and we've been considering switching some of the effort to the east and south. You'll see. Sergeant, drive on.'

The general liked Darius' straightforward approach.

The terrain was lost to view as the Jeep entered a substantial port town which was bustling with activity.

'What's the population of the town, now?' asked Khalifa.

'I'll find out for you, sir. At the beginning of the month, Port Khalifa held two thousand, but it's growing rapidly as all the subsidiary industries and commercial ventures become established,' said Darius.

'Impressive,' said the general. 'I see you have a bulk grain carrier in the harbour. Where is that being stored?'

'You'll see, sir. Some underground bunkers for grain and fodder are already in use.'

'Excellent.' Khalifa had known Darius was efficient and what he was hearing so far continued to impress him.

The Jeep progressed through the town, which had been laid out with wide straight avenues, named in the style of New York – First Street, Second Street, First Avenue et cetera. The terrain was now beginning to rise as they moved away from the ocean towards the hinterland. The highway was wide, equivalent to four lanes each side. This was nothing to do with the volume of traffic, but the vehicles' actual sizes. A mile or two out of the port, the Jeep had to cross into the opposite carriageway to overtake an enormous transporter supporting a dozen curved tunnel roofs.

'Those are heading for the area I mentioned earlier, sir,' commented the major.

Straight as an arrow, the highway headed towards the rising hills. Shortly, the entrance to a tunnel appeared in the distance. On each side were huge industrial complexes: warehouses, some factory units, and open spaces covered with containers or metal fabrications for the tunnels. Khalifa had seen all of this in photographs and videos, but he could not fail to be impressed by the sheer scale of the construction. Libya's financial reserves, built up through the oil industry over almost a century, were being drained by the investment in this Antarctic development. It was costing billions of dollars with no end in sight, and all being undertaken at breakneck speed.

The Jeep plunged into the hillside opening, over fifty metres high and a hundred wide. It reminded him of Gaddafi's giant bridge to nowhere. That had been enormous, but ultimately a total waste of money and resources. This, however, had to be one of the largest tunnels in the world, had a real purpose and was part of something extremely worthwhile. LED lights provided illumination no greater than weak moonlight, such was the expanse of the space.

'Take us to East One,' said Darius to the driver.

'What have you been doing with the spoil?' asked Khalifa.

'Some of it has provided aggregate for road building and harbour walls but most has been transported out of the crescent bay area and dumped. The volume is, as you can imagine, sir, enormous. I'll show you photographs of the spoil dumps later,' said Darius.

'Very good,' said Khalifa.

Ahead, they approached a six-way roundabout. The vehicle swung almost all the way around and started down a slightly lower and narrower tunnel, though still allowing for smaller loads of the prefabricated roof sections to be transported.

'We're now heading towards the main eastern complex, sir. This will be primarily domestic – houses, retail, services and so on. One section, East Sixteen, is already occupied by thirty families who are assessing the facilities to allow us to make improvements to the designs.'

'So, they're living totally underground?' asked the general.

'Most of the time. A bus takes the children to the schools in Port Khalifa each day. It will be a while before they have their own school. The space is there, but we felt it wouldn't be a good idea to put it into use until necessary.'

'Until necessary?'

'Yes, sir, until conditions outside make living underground during the day essential.'

'Right. I see. Any adverse reactions,' said Khalifa.

'Well, some, sir. Dr Wadi tells me that some of the adults who are spending most of their time underground are experiencing a few mental health problems. He thinks it is the lack of seeing the sky, the sea and what little greenery there is around the port. Even the lack of wind and rain is taking its toll. He has promised to keep me informed and I will include it in my monthly report to you.'

'Very good, Darius. Where are we heading now?'

'I thought you might find the first area with shops and residential properties worth seeing. We'll be there shortly. About another kilometre.'

The Jeep proceeded along the tunnel, the dimensions of which were continually reducing until it was similar to a two-lane tunnel on any motorway in any country. Junctions ran off left and right. Khalifa looked down each as they passed. Several were lined with the fronts of dwellings, doors and windows looking out onto the underground streets like any normal village. They had small, fenced areas to their fronts, that might become gardens or patios. None of them appeared to be occupied. Darius saw the direction of his gaze.

'These are unoccupied areas at the moment, sir. We need to put in infrastructure and time the occupancy with the arrival of industries and shops,' he said.

'Yes. You've done very well from what I've seen.'

'Sir, may I ask how bad things are back home?'

'It's not good, Darius. We're experiencing more days over fifty Celsius and fifty-five is not unusual. The toll on the elderly is extreme and we can't really offer salvation here, either. This complex must be primarily for young healthy families. I know it sounds harsh, but we must be realistic. From what we understand in other nations, we are one of the few who've had such foresight,' said the general. 'That is all in confidence, Major.'

'Of course, sir. I'm surprised we haven't been visited by the US and other so-called Western Nations.'

'We will be. It is our intention to make ourselves too dangerous to be worth bothering with. Hence the growing navy which Bashir is bringing together for us. We believe we are already too well established here for anyone to try to evict us.'

'Yes, sir. We've been speculating along those lines when we've had command meetings. We're approaching East Sixteen now.'

The Jeep turned off the main highway. In the distance the highway's surface had not been completed, much of it was flooded, and huge tunnelling excavators were pushing forward into the hills.

'Water problem?' asked Khalifa.

'Yes, sir, but we're turning it to advantage. It will eventually be fed into our water silos. We also allow some wet areas as a visual amenity. Shortly you'll see a pond in the E16 town square.'

On the current roadway, the same style of residences could be seen on either side. Real gardens sat in front of many of the properties, with grass, shrubs, and flowers. Khalifa noticed that the roof illumination was far brighter in this tunnel.

'Is this level of lighting going to be the norm for these estates?'

'Yes, sir. The first nuclear plant is now up to speed and power is unlikely to be a problem in the near future. Dr Wadi insisted that variable light would be important. It peaks during the day and drops to a glow at night. Twelve hours pure daylight, two hours of dimming illumination for sunrise and sunset and eight hours of low-level light.'

The Jeep turned into an enormous space hewn out of the rock, the roof being over thirty metres high, the overall dimensions some one hundred metres square. On two sides were shops, several occupied, many still empty, and some social buildings like a mosque, town hall, youth centre and more. In the centre was a park-like area with a pond and several trees standing over five metres which would, one day, add maturity to the scene. Children played in the park area either on their own, in groups, or with parents. If it hadn't been in a cavern, it would not have looked out of place in any small modern town or large village.

'Will the trees and shrubs develop?' asked the general.

'Yes, sir. It has not been without cost. We found a good supply of soil along the coast and that has provided a deep foundation, but that brought with it other problems: irrigation and drainage. We now have an excellent clean and wastewater systems which are being built into all new residential areas, so trees and shrubs should survive well.'

'And light?'

'Yes, sir. Amazing what these new LEDs can provide. There is little difference between our artificial lighting and the spectrum of sunlight, although we're avoiding harmful rays. It'll be a long time before we'll know if the trees will do well, but so far, so good.'

The general looked upwards at the roof supports. 'Are those spars sufficient?'

'Oh yes, sir. The rock here is very stable.'

'Right.'

'I've arranged for a few families to be in the town hall with a finger buffet. Would you like to meet them, sir?' asked Darius.

'Thank you. I most certainly would,' said Khalifa.

The Jeep was parked and the three of them disembarked, leaving the sergeant with the vehicle. The general turned towards the park area and walked into it, following a crazy-paving route to the pond. Koi carp swam over to him, expecting to be fed. He watched them for a minute or two, then returned to the major and colonel.

'Very impressive,' he said. 'Looks as if it's been there for years.'

'Yes, sir, we've tried to make it seem as near a realistic environment as we could.'

'Lead on.'

The three men crossed the road, climbed a few steps, and entered the town hall. Arabic in design, it was similar to any town hall in any community in Libya. The main large space had windows to the front, which showed the park area. Simulated windows on the other three sides depicted trees and fields in the distance, branches being blown by a light breeze. It was very realistic. To one side, a few tables had been pushed together with an excellent buffet spread. Half a dozen families were standing around with tea or coffee cups, the children with orange juice or milk.

Everyone turned to see who had entered and, of course, they all recognised their president. They had been expecting a VIP, but no one had imagined it might be the country's leader. He strode quickly over to the nearest group.

'How are you settling in?' he asked.

One of the men replied nervously, 'Very well Mr President. It is actually better here than it was where we lived in Al Maqrun.'

'You'll be missing trips into Benghazi, though?' said Khalifa, with a laugh.

'Well, Mr President, we may miss the larger shops, but not the traffic, dust and heat!'

'No, I suppose not. You have children?'

'Yes, the two boys and girl over there,' he replied, waving towards a group of children who were playing with building blocks and other toys.

'Do they miss the outdoors?'

'Not so far. They spend a lot of time on the village green and we have a five-a-side football stadium too.'

'Very good.' Khalifa turned to another family. 'How are you getting along?'

Several similar conversations followed. They all partook of the buffet and later left the town hall to return to Port Khalifa for the general's meeting with Major Bashir. En route they stopped at a series of huge caverns. Several were open, but the major had the driver stop in front of one which was sealed with an enormous, shuttered doorway.

'Would you like a quick look inside, sir?' he asked.

They stepped down onto the road surface. Darius called some workmen who had watched the Jeep coming to a halt. 'Open it for us, please,' Darius said.

A button was pressed, and the huge portal concertinaed open. The cavern stretched away before them. One side was full of grain.

'Wheat?' asked Khalifa.

'Yes, sir, and barley. There are several other stores which have increasing stocks of other foodstuffs and fodder,' said the major.

'Excellent,' said Khalifa.

'Sir, is it true that the Americans and Russians are building an installation like this on the moon?' Darius asked.

'We believe they are.'

'Imagine getting rid of the excavated material up there, through airlocks and things, sir.'

'Yes. Amazing how this heat has concentrated the minds of the spacefaring nations,' said Khalifa.

The Jeep continued its journey back to the port, eventually passing into brilliant sunlight under a pure blue sky.

∞∞∞∞∞∞∞∞∞∞

General Ahmed and Major Bashir arrived on time and in their best uniforms when they boarded the yacht. Colonel Omar was already sitting in a side chair when General Khalifa strode into the room and took his seat behind the magnificent rosewood desk. All three subordinates jumped to their feet until Khalifa waved them down.

'Sir, how did you find your visit to the excavations?' asked Ahmed.

'Excellent. It is far more than excavations; it is a veritable underground city. You've done well. It will not be long before busybody nations discover our port and that is what I wanted to talk to you about,' said Khalifa.

There was a knock on the door and a white-uniformed naval officer brought in a tray of coffee and tea for the president and his visitors.

'Thank you, Mo. We'll help ourselves,' he said, and the officer swiftly departed.

'Have you had any visitors yet? I mean the inquisitive kind,' asked Khalifa.

'Just one Rio registered fishing vessel,' said Bashir.

'And what did you do?'

'We pursued and sank it, sir.'

'Brazilian? I thought it was Argentinian,'

'Yes, it was, sir, but registered in Rio.'

'When was this?'

Colonel Omar spoke up. 'General Ahmed reported that to us, sir, twenty days ago.'

'Have there been any repercussions?' asked Khalifa.

'There have been no press reports in Brazilian or Argentinian news media, sir. These are dangerous waters, and it is quite possible that the loss has not yet been realised,' said Omar.

'We haven't had any other craft anywhere near the port, sir,' said Bashir. 'I must admit that your yacht's approach gave us some concern.'

Khalifa laughed. 'I guess it did. Yes, it would have set off alarms.'

'We were just about to investigate when we received Captain Mohammed's signal,' said Bashir.

'Very good. Well,' said Khalifa sitting more upright in his chair in a businesslike manner. 'The reason for this meeting is to discuss how we will react. It cannot be long before a major player discovers what we are doing here. They'll likely decide to try to put a stop to it or, as is my plan, they'll accept it as a fait accompli and will do nothing.'

'It would be difficult for any nation to prevent our efforts to preserve our own people from what is inevitable, sir,' said Ahmed.

'Indeed, Ahmed. If our scientists are correct and Antarctica is the only possible refuge for the human race from this tribulation, then it must be right that we be allowed some Antarctic rights,' said Khalifa.

'That seems a fair appraisal, sir,' said Ahmed.

'So,' continued Khalifa, 'it is important that we deal with any future visitors very carefully indeed. This is the plan.'

HEAT

31 Tourism

The emergency room of Hospital Regional Universitario de Málaga was packed full of people, some standing, but many slumped in seats and even more lying on the floor with relations or friends standing over them. Many of those friends were using provided litre spray bottles to give respite to the unconscious. The heat was oppressive, and heatstroke had afflicted thousands of visitors to the south of Spain. Most were holidaymakers from Germany, Britain, and Scandinavian countries – completely unsuited to the temperatures that week which hovered between fifty and fifty-five Celsius.

The accident and emergency department was incapable of coping. People were lying outside in the shade provided by the awning of the concrete monolith of a hospital. Voices were raised and there was shouting as a couple of policemen stood in the doorway, turning everyone away. The scene was becoming ugly and could only deteriorate. The government knew that this was happening in some countries in Africa, but for it to occur in a modern European country didn't seem possible.

Suddenly, a Land Rover arrived towing a bowser. It parked beside the entrance area. Two men jumped out and ran around to the rear. They grabbed hoses and began to spray the people with cold water; not a jet of water, but a fine misty spray. More individuals arrived and, without doubt, it was having an effect. Some prone tourists were sitting up and being comforted by their friends or relations as they began to recover.

HEAT

It was the same all over Spain, even up in the hills. The heat was relentless. Many visitors were trying to change their plans to fly home early. Others were screaming at the hotel receptionists that the air-conditioning wasn't effective enough and still more were complaining that their hotels had no air-conditioning at all, and that sleep was impossible.

The beaches were emptying of people. The sand was causing burns to uncovered feet, adding to the numbers who were dashing to pharmacies and hospitals for treatment.

The mayor was tearing her hair out in desperation as the city's main industry was verging on collapse. News of the crowds at hospitals was now making headlines in other countries – countries from where Spain's greatest numbers of visitors arrived. Holidays were being cancelled.

Of course, it wasn't just Spain which was suffering. North African countries, the Middle East, and all the Mediterranean nations were in the same predicament. It was the extra few degrees of heat that week which had turned the media's attention to Spain's southern coast.

Adding to the misery, forest and scrub fires were raging throughout the heat-stricken regions and acrid smoke filled the sky. The air was growing, not only too hot to breathe, but was starting to cause respiratory illnesses.

Mediterranean tourism could not survive such heat. It was only the month of June. Could it be even hotter in the peak season of July and August? The mayor was giving orders left, right and centre for bowsers of water to be moved around the city, spraying groups of people. It was going to grow into an economic disaster.

HEAT

32 Southern Ocean

Gansbaai, or Goose Bay harbour is one of many fishing ports on the South African coast. It is neither remarkable nor particularly busy. Its main industries have gradually morphed from straightforward fishing to specialist operators taking people out to view whales and great white sharks.

Equally unremarkable, the fishing vessel *Mary Louise*, which bore the registration mark FH for Falmouth, a Cornish town with a seagoing heritage, sat in the harbour, having unloaded its catch to the local canning factory.

What was remarkable, however, was the fact that a crew of three naval officers and five British Commandos had arrived incognito. The senior officer commandeered the vessel from Captain Pearce, brought a promise of financial reward to him and his crew, and took over the ship. The original crew, handsomely compensated, were sworn to secrecy and were to experience six weeks paid vacation.

Once Captain Gregory Mead RN had been briefed on all the ship's quirks and idiosyncrasies, they set off on a direct route towards an area of the Antarctic coast which, for some reason, had become of interest to the British Ministry of Defence. The journey would be nearly three thousand miles, and the orders were to make 'all speed'.

The *Mary Louise* had been chosen as, firstly it was in the right place, and secondly, it was capable of close to forty knots. Given a fair wind, the fishing vessel would achieve its destination in four or five days.

HEAT

It took some time, but eventually the crew became familiar with the vessel's peculiarities. The Southern Ocean was also behaving itself and the Antarctic coast came into view only a few hours later than expected. They turned parallel to the coast and proceeded at a gentler velocity as the captain wanted to arrive after dawn had broken.

'Target location off the port bow, sir,' said the second lieutenant.

'Okay, Mayne. Half speed. Turn to approach,' said the captain.

No one seeing any of the crew would have any inkling that they were military. All wore typical fishing-crew attire and were instructed not to salute or use any military language once they were in sight of the object of the defence ministry's interest.

They were approaching steadily now, five knots and taking a direct course towards the harbour entrance.

'There's a gunboat approaching, Captain,' said the lieutenant.

'Drop to three knots.'

'Three knots now. It's signalling to come alongside.'

'Cut speed to minimum for stability. Hide all weapons. Tell the crew.'

'Done,' the other said then dashed outside to speak to the crew.

The battleship-grey gunboat circled the *Mary Louise* then came alongside from the rear.

'Ted, throw a line,' shouted the lieutenant.

HEAT

The two vessels continued towards the port, now joined. Ted, one of the Commandos, threw down a ladder. A man in a blue uniform with a little gold braid on his shoulders grabbed the bottom rung and began to climb. Behind him, four uniformed men stood with what looked like Kalashnikov assault rifles.

The boarder reached the deck and asked politely, in good English, 'Permission to come aboard?'

Ted Marston waved him aboard. Captain Mead made his way down from the bridge and offered his hand, 'I'm Mead, captain of this vessel. We were surprised to find this port here. Wasn't here a couple of years ago when we last passed by.'

'I'm Lieutenant Farag. The port is a restricted area,' he said.

'Restricted? Why?' asked Marston.

'Antarctic survey,' said the gold-braided boarder.

'Didn't know the port was here. Can we dock and give the men time ashore?'

'I'll stay aboard and guide you in,' said the lieutenant. He then shouted down to the gunboat, 'Cast off and follow us in.'

One of the gunboat individuals with a weapon saluted, shouted, 'Sir!' and the others began undoing the ropes.

∞∞∞∞∞∞∞∞∞∞∞

Major Bashir knocked on General Ahmed's office door and entered. 'Sir, there's a fishing vessel which has just triggered the coastal approach radar. It'll be in sight of us shortly,' he said.

'What have you done?'

'I've briefed Farag to intercept with GB2.'

'He's fully aware of the protocol General Khalifa provided?'

'Yes sir. He's got a good head on his shoulders.'

'Right, keep me apprised.'

∞∞∞∞∞∞∞∞

The *Mary Louise* passed the breakwater and pulled into the central harbour spur. As it tied up, a Jeep approached. Major Bashir jumped out and waited for Farag to climb down to the quay.

'Fishing boat, curious about the port, sir. Said they were last here two years ago and there was nothing,' reported Farag.

'Very well,' said the major, looking up to the boat and seeing the captain climbing down the now-installed gangway.

'I'm Captain Mead,' the man said, approaching the pair and offering his hand.

'Major Bashir. I manage the port,' said the other after the handshake.

'It would be good to allow the men some shore time,' Mead said.

'This is not a tourist attraction, but they might visit the inn over there,' the major said, directing the captain's gaze to a building at the end of the jetty. 'There is also a supermarket adjacent, but the rest of the port is off limits. Will you make that clear?'

'I will but the port seems much more than a research station. There's a lot of heavy equipment and the town appears substantial. Which country built it?' asked Mead.

'Inform your crew of the shore rules, then I'll take you to the commanding officer. He'll answer your questions, if he can,' said Bashir.

Mead called up to the lieutenant, 'Mayne! Tell the men they can have access to the inn and shop at the end of the jetty. The rest of the port is restricted. Ensure two remain on board.'

'Will do, Cap'n,' Mayne shouted back.

'Right, Major, ready to go.'

'Farag. Set up a guard,' said Bashir.

'Sir,' said Farag with a salute.

Mead and Bashir jumped into the Jeep, and it sped off towards the town. In a minute, it arrived at a modern two-storey office block and parked.

'Come with me.'

The soldiers at the office block carried no weapons, which put Mead at ease. Inside, they climbed a staircase and Bashir rapped upon one of the doors off the upstairs corridor.

'Come!' was the call inside in Arabic.

Mead was ushered into the utilitarian air-conditioned office which was furnished with visitor chairs, filing cabinets, free-standing cabinets or wardrobes and a large teak desk. Behind it sat General Ahmed, large and imposing, in a smart uniform. Bashir introduced the captain.

The general stood and reached across the desk to shake Mead's hand. 'Please sit,' he said.

Mead sat in one of the visitor's chairs.

'So, Captain Mead, what are you doing in these waters? We don't get very many visitors as you might imagine,' said the general.

'We were passing by. We usually put down the nets about fifty miles east of here and take the catch to Buenos Aires or Rio. It's good fishing down here.'

'We could be interested in your catch, Captain. We'd match the Argentinian price.'

'That sounds a good deal, General. Less travel time. What's going on here? The gunboat officer said it's a research base, but it looks much larger than that to me. We're curious.'

'I would not want you to be allowing your crew to spread misinformation in Rio or Buenos Aires. Can I have your word that what I tell you is for your ears only? Otherwise, it would be better for you to go now, and we'll not be buying your catch,' said the general, looking intensely into Mead's eyes as he spoke.

'I can agree to that.'

'This port has been built by the Libyan Government of National Unity,' said the general.

'You're a long way from home.'

'Our leader, President Khalifa, ordered the construction of this port and town to provide accommodation for the Libyan people if this climate crisis continues to worsen.'

'So, it's an official set-up?'

'It is, but we're concerned that rumours do not spread about us preparing for even greater heat. It could cause problems elsewhere in the world. You British are also building a refuge in the centre of the continent.'

'I didn't know that,' stuttered Mead. 'Are you sure?'

'See,' he snapped. 'We all have our secrets. Yes, we're sure.'

'You think it is going to get even hotter? Cape Town was unbearable. Over forty-five degrees.'

'That is what our scientists tell us,' said Ahmed. 'You see why it is… shall we say, "sensitive".'

'Yes, indeed. I'll keep the secret.'

'It will be good if you do. A supply of fresh fish would be a great advantage to us and profitable for you,' said the general, standing up to indicate the end of the meeting.

'Shall we say two days for my men, then we'll depart?' asked Mead.

'I'll arrange a supply of wine, spirits and beer in the Inn. The shop sells no alcohol,' said the General.

'I hadn't thought of that.'

'The inn is there for just that purpose. You will not find any local people in there. It's just for the tourists!' the general said and laughed.

'Good to have met you,' said Mead, standing and shaking hands with Ahmed once more.

'Yes. Bashir will return you to your ship. Please ensure the rules are followed. It would not be good if they were flouted, Captain.'

'We'll be careful, General.'

'Bashir, send Ebrahim in, please.'

'Yes, sir,' the major said, saluting and then leaving with Captain Mead.

As they left, Bashir called in through an open door that the admin assistant was needed. A small man with wire-rimmed spectacles rushed through to the general's office as Bashir and the captain left the building.

'Sir?' asked Ebrahim.

'Is that all recorded?' asked General Ahmed.

'Yes, sir.'

'Send it to the president's office.'

'Yes, sir,' the small man said and dashed back to his own room.

33 Summit

Organising a summit for the leaders of the countries of the UN Security Council was always difficult. That it was to be in Downing Street gave Sir Joseph a considerable headache but, finally, he'd managed to get each of the leaders to agree.

Cabinet Office Briefing Room A, the famous COBRA, was as a rule used for domestic meetings but on this occasion, it was believed to be the best and most secure location. Downing Street was under siege by climate protestors who wanted action taken to reduce global warming. They believed that governments had been lying about the reduction in emissions of carbon dioxide as the heat grew. Governments knew the true cause, but it was still considered far too dangerous to risk telling the general populace that the world was possibly going to end, and it was likely that everyone would be experiencing hell in the not-too-distant future.

Presidents Fichefeux and Zhang spoke good English, but President Gorlov did not. He carried an IBM translator which, by then, was almost perfect, even picking up nuances in the conversations.

Jenny McRoberts welcomed them all to Britain, the door was shut, and the only people present were the five leaders.

The PM opened proceedings. 'We all know why we're here,' she said. 'We sent a clandestine vessel to Antarctica to visit the mysterious base which has been growing over the last two years.'

'Libyans,' said Zhang.

'Indeed,' McRoberts replied. 'They have called the town and harbour, Port Khalifa, which is not surprising. Khalifa always did like to promote himself.'

'I was surprised they didn't try to hide what they were doing,' said President Barker.

'Yes,' said Zhang, 'they've obviously decided that the truth would come out eventually, so honesty was the best policy. The Argentinians believe that one of their ships was sunk a few months ago. It was probably them. The world's ending and they want a part of the only place which might remain habitable.'

McRoberts said, 'I don't think they would have been honest until it had reached the state of development it is now at. The latest satellite images show a destroyer and two frigates in the harbour. It would need a fair-sized task force to evict them.'

President Fichefeux asked, 'What are we going to do about it?'

'I don't see how we can do anything,' said the mechanical voice of President Gorlov's translating device. 'Does any country have the right to stop another from trying to do their best for their own citizens?'

'Good point,' said President Barker.

'Look,' said the PM, clasping her hands together as if praying, 'we're all working on refuges. Russia, China, and the Japanese are building a refuge on Komsomolets Island which is eighty degrees north. France, the US, and ourselves are building ours in the middle of Antarctica. Surely, any other country with sufficient forethought and resources should be able to construct their own refuges elsewhere in Antarctica.'

'Yes,' said Fichefeux. 'We've heard that South Africa is working on their own plan for the Antarctica coast.'

'So,' said Barker, 'we do nothing.'

'War helps no one,' said Zhang, and Gorlov nodded.

'We're cooperating fully with each other,' said Gorlov. 'Let's just let them get on with it. Antarctica is a pristine environment but preserving it at the cost of stopping human lives from being saved is ridiculous.'

'I agree,' said the US president.

'Okay,' McRoberts said, 'let's move on. The migration problem.'

'No choice,' said Fichefeux. 'We can't allow it. Food resources are limited. None of us can allow uncontrolled migration.'

'It's true that you're sinking migrant boats?' asked Gorlov.

'We don't have a choice. We can't cope with the influx. Spain's doing the same, and Italy. We think Greece and Turkey long ago lost any qualms about it,' said the French president.

'It's dreadful, but you're right,' said Barker. 'The much-extended Trump wall has helped to secure our southern border, but boats are bypassing it. We, too, have been sinking boats attempting to land along the Gulf Coast and California.'

'It'll become a flood,' said Fichefeux.

'We know. What else can we do? There'll be riots when food runs short in our own countries, and the migrants will be blamed. There could be civil war,' said Gorlov. 'We too are seeing our southern neighbours moving northwards and have stepped up security.'

'Strangely, we're seeing dropping numbers of migrants,' said the PM. 'They seem to have realised that the north of Britain will not be cool enough. They're sticking to mainland Europe.'

'Yes,' said Fichefeux. 'There is a steady, but continual rise in the number of EU citizens making their way towards Finland and Sweden. Norway has warned migrants not to cross the Swedish border.'

'How do we tell people it's the end of the world?' asked Barker.

There was a chorus of, 'We don't.'

'They'll realise eventually,' said the PM. 'Would honesty be the best policy?'

'I don't think so,' said Zhang. 'People who know they are going to die do not always behave in a rational manner.'

'That's true,' said Gorlov.

'Some of the press is aware and we've slapped D-Notices[11] on the story, so they can't use it, but we have no idea how long they will hold,' said the PM.

'Social media is already full of conspiracy stories about it,' said the French president.

---

[11] A request to news editors not to publish items for reasons of national security.

'Yes, but there are so many different versions of what is happening that the public are likely to ignore them,' said the PM.

'Let's wait until Jenny's "eventually" arrives,' said the US president. 'No general release yet. Agreed.'

There were no dissenters.

HEAT

2037

34 Heatwave

Gren and I were skipping channels on the Sky network one night and came across an Arabic news station. The scene was of a Middle Eastern city which was later identified as Tehran. We couldn't understand the narration, but intently followed the subtitles.

The temperatures reached 50°C in parts of the country and hundreds, perhaps thousands are seeking treatment for heatstroke.

The scene cut to a hospital which was packed with people. Queues were developing outside, and the military were trying to keep order.

A growing heatwave has been smothering Iran, causing, once again, the authorities to close many facilities. All government institutions are to close until the temperature falls.

Temperatures ranged from 42°C to 47°C in Tehran, the capital, according to the ministry for the interior.

Banks, many offices and most public institutions will be closing until further notice to protect people's health. Also, a power crisis is likely and only hospitals and medical institutions will be allowed to run air-conditioning without a special licence. We understand that licences are being granted to care homes and other buildings where elderly people are housed.

Some anonymous looking places were shown on the screen.

HEAT

A spokesperson for the government claimed that over two thousand people had sought medical help. Many had been admitted to hospital and over three hundred had died, mostly elderly.

The National Meteorological Organisation has said that temperatures exceeding 50°C were recorded in eight provinces yesterday with the highest 54.7°C in Balochistan province in the southeast near the Afghanistan border.

They also announced that the temperatures were not expected to fall for three days and, even then, the air will stay very hot. People are being advised to remain indoors until sunset and only venture out then with drinking water to avoid dehydration.

The NMO also claimed that heatwaves are becoming more severe and prolonged owing to the global climate crisis, which has been caused primarily by the burning of fossil fuels.

I turned the channel off. 'Fossil fuels. How can they still be blaming this on fossil fuels,' I said.

'Maybe they don't accept Sol's misbehaviour. Strange country Iran, with some odd beliefs,' said Gren.

'But I know that they've been given all the data.'

'Probably just misreporting then, or the authorities know the truth and, like us, are keeping schtum about it.'

I looked at him and said, 'You realise we're in for this same sort of heat in just a year or two?'

'Yes, frightening. Any more news on the refuges?'

'I'm going to Reykjavik again Tuesday week. I'll know more then. Can we get up to Fetlar this weekend?'

'Should think so. Angie[12] sent me an email saying the new air-conditioning units have arrived, plus the extra bank of solar panels. They're being fitted to the framework and connected to the system this week.'

'Décor?'

'All done. Chimney sealed. New kitchen fitted. Waiting for cooker. He says the new bed, lounge furniture and dining suite has arrived and been stored in the barn. If we're going up for the weekend, I'll tell him to leave the trailer by the house and we'll clear out the dross.'

'Sounds great. Can't wait to christen the bed!'

Gren laughed. 'He also said he's found a nice clinker-built boat for three hundred and fifty pounds. Shall I say yes?'

'And we'll be able to push that in and out of the sea ourselves?'

'Should think so. It's only three and a half metres long. I'll need to get oars and stuff.'

'I wonder if we should get the two extra rooms built for the children. The chance of them being selected for a refuge is so slight,' I said.

'I'd rather not just yet. Let's see what happens first. Extra rooms are a huge expense and it's well over the budget already. Don't want to leave us destitute.'

'We're not that tight, really?' I asked.

---

[12] Angie with a hard g, often used instead of Angus.

'No, there's plenty in reserve so far.'
'Okay. Let's see. I'm busy the next couple of days. Can you book flights and a car?'
'Sure thing.'

35 Appeal

James Buchanan sat quietly in an empty meeting room in the House of Commons within the Palace of Westminster. He'd been promised a meeting with the home secretary and had been waiting for over half an hour. He'd made good use of the time though, telephoning and WhatsApping the EW group members. The next protest was to be in Parliament Square. Once again, the Home Office had denied permission. All that did was add to the suspicion that information was being kept from the general public.

His wait had reached fifty minutes before the door suddenly opened and Jack Easton, the home secretary and two assistants marched into the room and sat on the opposite side of the table to the eco-warrior. James felt like it was an interview panel for some super-duper job.

'Good morning, Mr Buchanan. Sorry for the delay. What did you want to say?' said the home secretary.

'You don't mind us recording this?' asked one of the assistants who had already pressed play on a recorder and stood it on the table between them. Deciding the question was rhetorical, James didn't bother responding.

'We have another demonstration planned for this weekend, but I thought we'd give you the opportunity to come clean,' he said, leaning back in the chair.

'What do you mean by "come clean",' asked the home secretary.

'Government is clearly lying to us about the climate crisis. We've been talking to experts who have told us that if the reduction in emissions you are claiming is true, then global temperatures should already be falling. In fact, they are rising, and rising faster than ever. I took the temperature outside on my way into parliament and it is currently forty-three degrees Celsius. How do you explain that?'

'There's a lag between reducing emissions and the effect on the climate,' Mr Easton said.

James laughed. 'You can't be serious,' he said. 'People are annoyed at what you call "the lag". Just look around the world. Some of the worst hurricanes and typhoons ever. That one in Florida killed over two hundred people. The typhoon in Bangladesh killed a similar number and over a thousand died in the floods which followed. The northern coast of Australia was hit by hurricane force winds too, and, by all accounts, not a single house was left standing on Martinique last month. This is all unprecedented. There must be some other force at work. Tell us about it. *Come clean!*' He hadn't meant to raise his voice, but lost control at the end of his statement.

'Mr Buchanan. Scientists are telling us that the lag is longer than expected. Frankly, global warming had been far worse than we realised. We certainly should have acted faster in the teens and twenties, but we have made huge strides on converting to renewable energy. You just need to be patient. The greenhouse gases need to be cleared out of the upper atmosphere and that's taking far longer than anyone anticipated.'

James sat more upright and folded his arms defensively. 'It's not good enough. You're trying to get the media to hide the extent of the problem. Crops are failing in Central Africa and South America. There's going to be famine and mass migration. What are you doing about that?'

'We are trying to mitigate the problems. Cooling shelters are being set up in southern Europe, Africa, and Central America plus the Far East too. We have increased aid to areas struggling with growing crops. There is only so much we can do, and your protests are not helping,' said the home secretary.

'Is it true that the French and Greeks are sinking migrant boats in the Atlantic?' asked James, hoping to gauge the reaction to the question.

'Our policy hasn't changed. We return illegal immigrants to their own countries unless there is a genuine asylum claim. We can't control other countries' policies, but I would caution you not to believe every rumour you see on social media,' said the home secretary.

'So, you admit nothing?'

'There is nothing to admit. I agreed to see you in the hope that you could tame down your demonstrations. Several have led to violence and looting. How does smashing shop windows and burning peoples' cars help your case?'

'There are always some bad eggs. We do our best to control the crowds, but the fact of the matter is that we believe you're lying to us about the climate and nothing you've told me today offers any explanation. Don't say we didn't give you the opportunity.'

'I'm sorry you feel that way.'

'You know, home secretary, if something worse is happening to the climate, people have a right to know. They have the right to adjust their lives. People are far better in a crisis than you might imagine, but you won't trust us and distrust breeds revolution.'

'Are you threatening revolution, Mr Buchanan?'

'Your government needs to wake up and come clean. I have nothing further to say,' said James.

'In that case, this meeting is over,' said the home secretary. One of the assistants picked up the recorder and the three of them left the room.

James was dumbfounded. He sat still for a few moments, raging inwardly, then a security officer entered the room. 'I've been asked to show you out, sir. Please come with me,' he said.

Outside, a temperature of almost forty-four C was waiting to hit James as he walked into Parliament Square to meet with key followers.

In the other camp, the home secretary went straight to Number Ten and, once again, told the PM that the government needed to take a different approach. It was time to tell the truth.

The PM said, 'No.'

36 Maize

'It can't be scorching, it's under continual spraying,' Mikel said as he examined the maize leaves Helga had brought him. They were almost completely brown with just a central green area.

'But it is, chief,' said Helga, a tall, well-built Black woman of about forty-five years of age.

The office was in a concrete-built structure, a regional HQ for Eduard Farming Co. Mikel, a tall, rangy Black man in his thirties, was responsible for the company's farms on the east side of the Kafue National Park, about a hundred miles from Lusaka, Zambia. Inside the building, an ancient air-con machine was rattling and wheezing as it struggled to keep the temperature below thirty-five. Outside it was approaching fifty. He was sweating like the proverbial pig, his jet-black skin sparkling in the flickering illumination of an old and failing fluorescent light fitting. The walls were plastered with maps of the region, flow charts, Eduard Farming corporate posters, and a year planner.

'Somone must have turned off the irrigation!' raged Mikel, convinced someone must be to blame.

'No. Checked myself. Been running continually during hot spells.'

'It can't be!'

'Come, see for yourself.'

'I can't go checking every farm!'

'We can't be only farm losing crop,' Helga insisted.

HEAT

Mikel went quiet. It was true he'd had reports from other company farms, but no one had shown him anything as bad as this.

'I'll maybe do a tour,' he said, still full of anger. 'Get back to your farm and keep a better eye on the irrigation.'

'It *not* my fault!' she retorted and left, slamming the office door behind her.

He telephoned head office. 'Put me through to Mr Mbewe, please.'

A pleasant-sounding male voice said, 'Cheelo Mbewe.'

'Cheelo, it's Mikel. We've some crop problems. Maize leaves are being scorched by the heat, even with the irrigation running full blast.'

'You too?'

'It's not just us then, boss?'

'No, it's general. I suggest you get out to each of the farms and emphasise the importance of continual spraying while this heatwave continues.'

'The supervisors insist it is all being kept running.'

'Yes, but in this heat, it is important to ensure there is no slacking. Get out and check.'

'Okay, will do, boss. Bye.'

Mikel slumped back in his chair, swivelled around, took a fresh bottle of water from the office fridge, and downed it in one swig. He didn't want to go on a farm tour. Hours in the Land Rover in the awful heat. At least it had no roof. There'd be some air movement as he drove, but the dust. Oh yes, the dust, but it had to be done. Must follow orders.

HEAT

∞∞∞∞∞∞∞∞∞∞∞

Later that morning, Mikel was bumping along roads visiting the farms under his management. At the first, he came around a low hill and was alert that he'd see the farm very shortly. They weren't aware that he was on the way, so this was the perfect opportunity to discover if the irrigation was operating. He'd ordered all low altitude farms to turn it on continuously when the latest heatwave began. The only problem was that it no longer seemed to be a heatwave. The increasing temperature was continual. There was talk that it would never stop.

There it was; the farm came into view and, right enough, spraying could be seen over all fields. He pulled into a collection of huts on the edge of the largest field.

'Mikel, sir. Didn't know yous coming today,' said a hefty man emerging from one of the buildings. He was in shorts, no shirt, and a pair of trainers without socks on his feet.

'Surprise visit. How's the crop?'

'Not good. Leaves turn brown. Stems wilt. Due cut in two weeks, but suspect lose some of it.'

Mikel climbed out of the vehicle and the two men walked into the field. The cascading mist of water was welcome after his thirty-mile journey on the dusty roads. They stopped and the warm spray soaked them to the skin. Mikel examined leaves. True enough, many of the upper leaves were scorching despite the water.

'And it's been on twenty-four seven?'

'Abslutly.'

'All fields?'
'Yes. No ceptions.'
'You're sure?'
'Postive.'

Mikel shared a beer with the supervisor then drove off to the next farm on the list. En route he stopped off in a village to buy some cold water and fruit to eat. He got talking to the shopkeeper and learned that the heat was taking its toll on the people. Fifteen had died in the village and surrounds from heatstroke in the past month.

The shopkeeper told him, 'Think world is coming to an end. Can't go on like this. Youngsters leaving for the north and the elders dropping like flies. World ending for sure.'

Mikel drove on.

37 Starship

This meeting in Reykjavik was larger than any previously. We'd all gathered the night before for a meal together, drinks, and a chance to socialise. I was in attendance together with Dr Linsey Delve of UKSA and the British science minister, Sir David Brenner. Other participants were similar officials and scientists from a number of other countries. By far the largest contingents were from NASA and Roscosmos who were critically involved with the refuges on the moon and in orbit. The idea here was for us to learn how the planning stage had been progressing.

The next morning, we assembled in a theatre-style meeting room with a dozen NASA and Roscosmos scientists sitting on the stage in front of us; a large screen stood behind them.

Harry Kinsman, head of NASA, stood and moved along to one side of the group where a dais had been set up. He cleared his throat and took a sip of water.

'Good morning, honoured guests. We have called you here as part of the first meeting of the Refuge Management Committee.'

He shuffled some papers and continued. 'As you are aware, work is already underway on the Antarctica Refuge and the Moon Refuge. The Russians and Chinese are also working together on the Komsomolets Island Refuge. We now have plans to share with you for the orbital refuge and the Starship Refuge.' He flicked a handset and an artist's impression appeared on the screen.

'This is the Starship Refuge. It is similar to this' – Harry changed the image – 'which is the orbital refuge.'

The refuges were huge metallic disc-shaped objects, like frisbees.

'Who'd have thought we'd be building flying saucers ourselves?' he joked. 'Each revolves in order to provide almost one g of gravity for the outer areas. So, down is towards the outside edge, people will walk around the inside of the circumference of the refuge. As you climb towards the hub, gravity will reduce and, as you can see, the hub is hemispherical on both sides, protruding up and down from the disc like a ball. This is the control and administration centre. The circumference of the refuge is two thousand five hundred metres, providing up to four thousand apartments on the outer rim and leisure areas towards the hub. This should be adequate space for the two thousand people who will be housed on board and their growth in numbers over time. That expansion will be strictly controlled. For instance, no female will be allowed to have a second child with the same partner. We must avoid genetic problems. We don't know how long it will be before they can return to Earth. We're not advocating a sexual free-for-all, nor wanting to break up any relationships. Additional children will be by artificial insemination.'

Harry clicked his handset, and a cutaway appeared.

'Living accommodation occupies the outer ten metres of the refuge. The other almost four hundred metres of the radius is mainly the hydroponic cultivation area and storage of food and drink. There are also many leisure areas: basketball courts, lecture and movie theatres, et cetera.'

'No animals?' a voice shouted out from the audience.

'No. It was recently decided that the space available would be insufficient and that animals were an inefficient method of producing food. Perfectly acceptable meat substitutes can be produced using hydroponics so perhaps this is the time to stop killing animals for food. The vegetarians will be pleased. There will, however, be animals on the moon and in the Antarctica Refuges.'

'Going back to the Starship Refuge' – Harry returned to the first slide – 'the main difference is that the orbital refuge does not need to be powered. It will sit in a geosynchronous orbit in the shade of Earth's magnetosphere which stretches far beyond the moon's orbit.'

'Why do the flares affect the moon, then?' was a call from the audience. I huffed to myself at such an ignorant question from what was supposed to be an elite group.

Harry answered in an irritated tone of voice. 'The moon is not always aligned with the sun and the Earth, only during eclipses.' More enthusiastically, he added, 'Now, back to the refuges. The orbital refuge does have power, of course.' He switched back to the relevant image and pointed at modules around the circumference. 'These modules produce the power which is needed to control and adjust its orbit if there is any drifting. A fuel supply is being kept in a nearby orbit to reduce the chance of any accidents. In fact, we're considering using nitrogen for thrusters now that we know we can extract it from the moon's regolith. The fuel supply is estimated to last many decades if adjustments are as small as predicted.'

He switched back to the Starship Refuge image once more. 'The Starship Refuge does need to be powered, of course. The shape is not vastly different from the orbital refuge, but, as you can see, the hub is different. It extends forward to a point, which contains the control centre and bridge, and, on the other side of the refuge, this extended blunt cylinder houses the ion drives. These are designed to produce between one and ten percent of a gravity which will push the ship close to light speed surprisingly quickly which is why we've chosen Kepler-452 B as the destination. Once we get close to light speed, distance is no longer a factor because time dilation reduces its effect. Travelling a thousand light years takes little longer than travelling five light years as experienced by those on board. Thank Einstein for that.' He chuckled.

'Why was Kepler-452 selected?' someone asked.

'We now know that its planet B has an oxygen and nitrogen atmosphere similar to Earth, with enough water vapour to indicate oceans.'

'What about temperature?' another called out.

'Its orbit around Kepler-452 indicates that it should be similar to Earth's and as the star is smaller than the sun, we're trusting to science that it will neither be too hot nor too cold. You can be sure that we're trying to measure the temperature, but it's not a simple task. There's evidence that there might be at least one ice cap, and that is promising.'

'How do they get to the surface of planet B when they arrive in orbit?' I asked.

'Good question,' said Harry. 'In addition to a handful of craft which can land and return to the refuge if conditions are unsuitable; you see these bumps which pepper the underside of the refuge? These are escape capsules. They can be set for automatic descent into the atmosphere. There will be five hundred of them carrying up to twelve passengers totalling far more than necessary for the expected total number of residents. The number arriving should be similar to the number setting off.'

'Why would you expect the number arriving to not have increased?' called another voice.

'Indeed. As with the orbital refuge, procreation on the Starship Refuge will be controlled to prevent any substantial increase in the population. The first generation will be permitted only enough children to provide a second generation of the same size. More will be permitted if there are deaths on board. Naturally, the first generation to be born on board will increase the total numbers and they will only fall back when the original population reaches old age. The limit leaving will probably be two thousand and we're allowing for growth to four thousand maximum during the journey, but it will be carefully controlled. We mustn't let it run away.'

'How long before departure?' I asked.

'We believe we'll be launching the crew in 2046 and departing for Kepler-452 as soon as the starship is fully loaded. Most of the large components are being launched using the SpaceX Falcon Heavy and smaller components and the crew will be launched in adapted SpaceX Starships.'

'How do the ships which can return if conditions are unsuitable, blast off from the planet?' someone asked.

'There are a small number of tankers which can be landed by remote control to provide return power for the launch modules,' said Harry.

'When does selection begin and how will it be conducted?' asked Sir David Brenner. This question was accompanied by a low-level buzz of conversation.

Harry dipped into one of his many folders and pulled out a document. 'Current thinking is that the Kepler crew should comprise one-quarter teenagers, one-quarter aged between twenty and twenty-five, one-quarter aged between twenty-five and thirty and the remainder between thirty and thirty-five. No one over thirty-five will be eligible.'

'Qualifications?' I asked.

'Number one priority is health. No one suffering from any illness or disease will be included.'

'The disabled are not being considered then?' asked a delegate in a wheelchair.

'That is *not* the case,' said Harry emphatically, 'but the disability must not be one that can be passed on or inherited during reproduction. A limb missing owing to an accident will not bar someone from selection, but, say, those with cystic fibrosis or haemophilia will not be valid for selection. This population must breed, and the total number is so few that we cannot risk introducing a genetic problem which might wreck the long-term plan.'

'And race or colour?' asked another.

'Well, some races are more susceptible to certain diseases, but if those diseases cannot be detected in the young and cannot be proven to be inherited, there is no reason to omit anyone based on their skin colour or race,' said Harry.

'That's good to hear,' said the questioner. 'Thought you might be trying to create a master race!'

Several delegates laughed. 'I suppose we are, but only based on health and mental ability,' said Harry.

'And what are the tests for mental ability,' someone asked. I was interested in this question as both of our children were extremely clever and we had been pushing them academically for this very reason.

'One simple factor which will rule out the majority is that a series of intelligence tests will be carried out. Only those with IQs exceeding 130 will be considered. I'm told that these tests will be conducted in multiple sittings which will ensure that people will not be ruled out if they perform badly, say in word tests, or shape tests, as long as their average exceeds 130 over the entire series.'

My concerns went deeper than this, so I enquired, 'What about subjects: languages, mathematics, science and so on?'

'A good point, Dr Arnold. I should mention that you are listed on one of the selection committees, so you should have quite a say in the selection process. Those who've excelled in mathematics, physics, biology, botany, and medicine will carry a higher tariff than other subjects. This group, after all, are the future of humankind. The starship selectees will also have to tackle unknown bacteria and viruses when they get to Kepler-452.'

'And who will do the menial tasks?' asked Sir David.

'I guess there'll be sharing of those.'

'How will corruption and favouritism be avoided?' asked another delegate.

'As I understand it,' said Harry, 'candidates will only be identified by a number. No one will know who has been selected until the numbers are matched by names. It will be strictly monitored.'

Gosh, it was confirmed then. I was one of the selection panel. Was that good or bad for my children? Even if selection was anonymous, if one or other or both of my children ended up in a refuge, would anyone believe there had not been corruption?

Questions, answers, and discussions went on for a further two hours before we broke for lunch.

∞∞∞∞∞∞∞∞∞∞

When I got home, I told Gren about my being chosen for the starship selection committee.

He looked at me glumly. 'Surely that isn't a good thing.'

'How do you mean?'

'We're hoping to get Geoff and Cas into one of the refuges. Won't your involvement rule them out?' he asked anxiously.

'Apparently not. The odds make it very unlikely that anyone on the committee will have their own children selected, but it's not a barrier. No one will know who the candidates are. Tests and medical examinations will be anonymous. We'll be selecting based on data. Numbers fifty-two, seventy-eight and one hundred and twelve will be selected and no one will know who they are until the selection certificates are issued and names replace the numbers.'

'Oh. Hope it's both rather than one of them. Better neither than just one.'

'Can't do anything to prevent that. The chance that it will be both of them is infinitesimally slight. As it is expected that the ship will depart around 2046, the selection process will be finished by 2040, and the subsequent six years will involve four years of specialist education and two years training.'

Gren said, 'Geoff loves maths.'

'He's good at physics too,' I added, 'and Cas's love of biology is in the right vein. We'll need to encourage them.'

'Careful, Beth. Parental encouragement can often be a turn-off for kids.'

'We'll need to take care then,' I acknowledged.

Later we were lying in bed and Gren turned towards me, took my hand, and said, 'We'll need to think about ourselves too, you know. None of us will get out of this crisis alive. We should be thinking about how we can extend our lives.'

'Not if the quality isn't there,' I said sadly. 'No point in extending life if it isn't worth living. Fetlar is about the best answer we can really hope for. How're the improvements progressing?'

'Well. Let's head up there again next week. Much should be complete, and we can see what needs refining.'

'Yes, I could do with a short break. The selection process will be very intensive when it begins,' I said.

'Let's keep our thinking caps on.'

'Life's too short and I've a better idea,' I said, and draped my legs over his.

38 St Antonin-du-Var

Var was being devastated.

Never in the history of this beautiful region of France had such a forest fire been encountered. It wasn't just the woodland that was burning, but the scrub alongside fields, the vines themselves, and homes.

Alain Lob stood in the roasting heat, sweating in his red firefighting suit and yellow helmet. He watched as another of the converted DC-10s flew overhead and dropped its cargo of water onto the raging inferno on the south side of the hill. Helicopters were more precise, but the use of the larger aircraft was essential as the time it took to reload and reach the fire was more important than accuracy, however, it was clearly a losing battle.

'Keep them coming,' he said into his radio.

'Number four on the way, Commander,' was the tinny reply.

'Did we get an answer on the extra flights?'

'Yes, one more should be here shortly, but that's it. There's a new fire just north of Marseilles and the remainder will be heading there, sir.'

'Damn it! It's crazy. We're losing the battle. Out,' he said, switching channels. 'Get me the prefect in St Antonin-du-Var. Quick.'

Another huge plane skimmed over the vineyards to his left, rose on the approach to the hill and a tenth load of water was released.

'Allard here. Who's that?' came over the radio.

'Commander Lob. We're losing the battle. If the fire crosses the hill, it'll be upon you in minutes.'

'It's here now. My men are evacuating everyone who hasn't already left. Houses are on fire on the south of the village.'

'Don't let anyone delay. Seriously, we can't stop it.'

Alain could visualise the scene on the other side of the hill. People panicking, trying to take belongings with them as they left ancestral homes.

Philippe Allard, prefect of police, pulled his patrol car to the side of the road. An elderly couple were carrying furniture and boxes to a dilapidated old Citroen van standing in the driveway.

He shouted to them. 'For God's sake, Henri, what the hell are you doing. Go!'

'We've got a while. Trying to take important things,' the grey-haired hobbling man retorted.

'And they're more important than your lives? Seriously, get out. *NOW!*' He leaned out of the car, looking behind the vehicle. 'Look, the Dubois place is on fire! You can't wait.'

Flames were rampant around the Dubois bungalow and flaming debris was flying through the air, settling on the Laurents' roof.

'Look! Your roof is burning,' the prefect shouted. 'For fuck's sake go!'

The woman looked behind her and upwards. She looked as if she was going back into the house. 'Don't go back in, Louise,' shouted the old man, suddenly appreciating the threat.

It happened so quickly. A flaming branch fell into the hedge along the roadside, and it caught fire instantly. The old woman came out with a cardboard box, running towards the van. Her husband saw the debris raining around them. The box was burning, then the woman's dress. She screamed and the old man ran towards her, beating out the fire as she fell to the pavement.

Alain was out of his car in a flash, fire extinguisher in hand and rushed to the rescue, spraying the retardant over the squirming crying figure. The two men pulled her to her feet between them.

The hedge continued to burn, a strong wind fanning the flames throughout its length. The entrance to the garden was through an archway covered in the same hedge material. They were cut off from the road.

Alain ran through the flames and turned the remainder of his extinguisher onto the trellis. 'Quick, get out!' he shouted.

He looked back and saw that both the elderly people's clothes were alight. He ran back into the garden and started to roll them backwards and forwards on the ground. Henri's clothes were quickly out, but Louise was still afire and screaming as the flames burned her hair and arms as she tried to fight them off.

Outside, in the road, the Citroen exploded into flames. Alain tried to pull the woman out through the arch, but she'd lost consciousness. He turned to the man, saw despair in his face, and called for him to run out of the garden, but he stood, stock still, watching his Louise being consumed as the fire took its dreadful hold. He didn't run outwards, but threw himself on top of her, as if to protect her, but it achieved nothing other than setting his own clothes burning again.

'Henri! Leave her! Run!' shouted Alain, realising that it was now hopeless, and he was in fear for his own life. Flames were in the road, branches and fiery paper were being whipped along by the growing strength of the wind.

He looked at his car, then at the couple again. There was nothing he could do for them. The old man's face turned towards him in hopelessness. Alain jumped into the vehicle, hit the accelerator, and raced up the street, barely keeping pace with the speed of the advancing inferno. Tears ran down his face.

He sped out of the village as fast as he could, heading east. He needed to get to Lorgues. The fire was heading that way, and he must warn them. His burned hands gripped the steering wheel as he raced away from his now destroyed home village of Saint Antonin-du-Var. He wondered how many had died. How many foolhardy individuals hadn't heeded the seriousness of the evacuation warning and had died trying to save possessions.

What price those possessions now?

39 Coast

I heard the front door open and Gren dashed into the lounge, grabbed the TV remote, and turned it on. He asked, 'Haven't you been watching the news?'

'No, what's happened?' I'd been curled up on the settee with *Astronomy Now*. I turned to watch the television and tossed the magazine onto the coffee table.

'The Venice barrier broke!' he said.

'No!'

The screen was showing an aerial view of water inundating the Italian city.

Five years previously, dams had been built at the two southernmost openings to the Mediterranean and a giant lock had been constructed between Faro di San Nicolo and Faro di Punta Sabbioni through which cruise liners and other vessels could pass. Sea levels had risen to the point where historic buildings in Venice were in danger of collapse. The dams were a huge success, stopping public areas like Piazzetta San Marco suffering almost continual flooding at high tide. Another benefit was that the new locks had discouraged fleeting visits by giant cruise liners, something the residents had long been objecting to, but it still permitted those who wanted to visit for more than a few hours to enter – at a price.

Now it was clear that the lower dam near the shipyard of Cantiere Mose had been breached and the whole lagoon had been flooded with billions of gallons of seawater.

HEAT

The images clearly showed many of the famous buildings with water halfway up their ground floors and the piazzas totally submerged.

'How dreadful,' I said as the enormity sank in.

'It's not the first either,' said Gren. 'The spring tides have broken through dykes along the Dutch coast. Huge areas are flooding, and the dead are in the thousands already. The Thames Barrier was ineffective today, too. The sea circumnavigated it and the authorities are trying to block off the tide.'

'Even Canute failed in that endeavour,' I said, then realised it was in bad taste.

The newscaster continued, 'We're getting reports from all around Britain. Burnham-on-Crouch has been evacuated. Boston, Spalding, and parts of Peterborough are also underwater. Greenwich has been inundated by the Thames backing up and the whole of the Thames Estuary is flooded. Millions of homes are affected.'

'I suppose it can only get worse,' I said.

'I think the media is concentrating on Venice to calm people in the UK. It's the beginning of the end of coastal habitation. Parts of New York, and other coastal cities will be hit by this spring tide,' said Gren.

We watched the scenes in amazement. 'Can they save Venice, do you think?'

'Probably easier than saving our coastal towns,' said Gren. 'At least they have a dam they can repair. Much of Lincolnshire and the Wash, can't be protected. Too open.'

'We really should think about anything more we need to do at Fetlar,' I said.

'We've had the turbine serviced and installed a third bank of solar panels. I've had a contractor do some more work on the power room. The quality air-conditioning units will be fitted any day, and Angus says the air-conditioned chicken coop is almost ready. The garden is well planted and he's rigging up automatic spraying of the crop from the river. Oh, and the boat's arrived. He's building a shed for the oars and ropes, et cetera.'

'I'm worried about being invaded by hordes of people looking for somewhere similar to live.'

'There's no reason they'll come to Shetland. It will be as bad there as anywhere outside the Arctic Circle.'

'We don't want to get caught up with migrants. There'll be violence. There isn't room for everyone in the Arctic Circle and what about food? Where's the food going to come from if everyone heads north?' I asked.

'You're right but Fetlar is still the answer,' Gren reassured me. 'All the improvements we've made would not be expected at the end of our farm track. Why would anyone seek it out? Nothing to pique their curiosity. I dare say we can both handle guns, but I don't fancy living somewhere where we're forever under attack. It would be like a homestead in the Wild West.'

'Yes, I suppose you're right. Fetlar really must be the answer,' I said.

'We'll both be doing our best.'

The Venice news item ended and the news moved on to sport.

I stood up. 'There're some Indian ready meals in the fridge. Fancy those tonight? The kids'll be home soon.'

'If we can't get them into a proper refuge, they'll have to come to Fetlar too. That means building those extra rooms.'

'Their IQs pass the test. Caroline's well over 140, and Geoff's 133,' I said.

'They'll still need good exam results. IQ won't do on its own and it will still be a lottery.'

'Yes, but I'm worried about trying to push them too hard.'

'We must take care,' Gren said.

We heard the door open and there was laughter as our children bundled into the house from their extra science classes.

'I'll get dinner ready. Kids!' I shouted, 'Indian okay?'

'With bhajis!' Geoffrey called back.

'I'll see,' I said, rising and walking through to the kitchen.

Gren followed me and said, 'I'll crack a bottle of Frascati.'

∞∞∞∞∞∞∞∞∞∞

The following weekend, with the football season finished, Wilson and his family were coming for dinner and to stay the night at our home in Guildford. Their five-year-old daughter, Emma, would share Caroline's room. Gren was cooking his speciality, stroganoff.

When the doorbell rang, I dashed through to open it. Wee Emma, a beautiful child rushed into my arms, delighted to see her granny. The moment she'd released me, Wilson, now such a strong, fit, and healthy-looking Black man, lifted me off the floor and crushed me to him.

'Dad! So lovely to see you,' he said. Wilson had never changed to calling me Mum after Mindslip and, however incongruous it might now appear, still saw me as his father. As father and son, we'd so often gone to the Tottenham Hotspur stadium to watch our favourite team. We could never have dreamed that one day he might not just play for them, but captain them to the Premiership. Mindslip had changed Wilson into a young lad living in Rwanda. His skin colour was not the only change, he'd also discovered that he had incredible footballing prowess.

Finally, Angela gave me a hug. Like many professional footballers, Wilson had married a trophy wife, a white super model with flowing blonde hair. It was clear that they were in love. Emma's glowing, golden-brown skin colour and blonde curly locks were the perfect combination of the two of them.

Dinner was terrific as Gren is such a good cook. Afterwards we sent the kids off to bed and sat in the lounge sipping brandy and liqueurs.

'Been taking your advice, Dad,' Wilson said to me.

'How's that?' I asked.

'Leaving Tottenham.'

'What? They'll be lost without you.'

'No one's indispensable and if we're going to move north, it would be good to do it while I'm still a good player. I was thirty this year. Only a handful of years left at the top of the game,' he said with some sadness.

'You look in your prime,' I said.

'Probably still am, but making a move now means I can pick and choose. I'm out of contract. Spurs have offered millions to ensure I stay but I've got a better deal,' he said and gave me a wicked smile.

'Don't tell me you're going to the scum[13],' I said in horror.

'No, much better than them: Tromsø Idrettslag.'

'Who? Never heard of them.'

'They're in a town called Tromsø, Norway, and we've bought a lovely house in a place called Vågnes, about twenty-five miles from the stadium,' he said and laughed.

'Sorry, never heard of either,' I said.

'It's three degrees *inside* the Arctic Circle!'

Now I realised. He'd sacrificed his megabucks career at Tottenham to give his family the best chance of survival in Norway.

'How wonderful,' I said and rushed over to the sofa to hug him.

'I'd been nagging him to do something,' said Angela. 'He didn't seem to be listening, then a few weeks ago we were flying to Tromsø airport. Tromsø Idrettslag couldn't believe their luck, one of the best players in Europe for peanuts.'

Gren laughed and said, 'That's fantastic. Beth's been so worried about what might happen to you.'

---

[13] A reference to Arsenal used by many Spurs fans.

'It's really going to be bad, isn't it, Dad? I've not done this for nothing, have I?' Wilson asked anxiously.

'It is. Strictly between the four of us, it could be the end of the world as we know it,' I said.

Angela added, 'When you let us know what you were doing on Shetland, I told Wils that he *must* do something, and he finally took note.'

'Had to wait for my contract to end. There's no way Tromsø Idrettslag could have bought me. Will we be safe there?'

'To be honest, probably not. This house you've bought. Does it have any land?' I asked.

'About a hectare,' he replied.

Gren said, 'In that case, install a good quality wind turbine and battery storage facility. Double insulate everything. I know you won't get much sun, but put up a bank of, say, forty or fifty solar panels and connect them into the system too.'

'No proper daylight in Vågnes from late November to the end of January,' said Angela. 'There's two or three hours of a sort of twilight apparently.'

'Top solar panels will still generate some power from that, but the wind will keep you in power through the worst,' said Gren. 'Don't stint on the cost. Your lives will depend on it.'

'Protect yourselves too. Are polar bears a problem up there? Get a licence for a high-powered rifle and shotgun,' I said. 'If we're right about the sun, you might have to live most of your lives indoors, even at that latitude. Lay in plenty of stores.'

'You're serious, aren't you?' said Wilson.

'Deadly,' I said. 'I'm so glad you've made this move. When do you get into the house?'

'End of the month,' said Angela.

Gren added, 'Buy the best quality air-conditioning units for *every* room and two or three spares as well. That's why you'll need a good power supply.'

'Really?' asked Wilson.

'Really!' said Gren, topping up the liqueurs.

'Don't worry,' said Angela, 'I'll ensure he does.'

'Oh, something else,' said Wilson, 'one of our new neighbours is an old friend of yours.'

'Old friend?'

'Yes, the doctor Sir Mark Weston. He said to say hello to you. He lives a short distance away.'

'How did you meet him?' I asked. Mark had been the doctor involved in the plan to return people's minds to their original bodies after Mindslip, but the government banned the process and slapped a top secret label on it.

'At the club, when I was introduced to the board.'

'How is he?' I asked. He had been planning to transfer my wife, Caroline, from an old greyhound into a younger animal until they'd perfected the animal to human transfer, but Caroline died before it could happen. 'I haven't seen him since 2019.'

'Well, that's very odd really,' said Wilson. 'Not sure how he knows you from then. He's only about twenty-five now.'

HEAT

My blood turned to ice.

'What's wrong?' asked Gren. 'You've gone as white as a sheet.'

I recovered my composure a little. 'Are you sure? In his twenties? Did you meet Julia?'

'Yes, she's in her twenties too,' said Angela. 'We got on fine.'

I was shocked. I couldn't say anything. I was, literally, struck dumb with shock.

'What's up, Beth?' asked Gren. 'Are you okay?'

'Yes. Let me think. This is serious,' I said.

All three of them looked at me in puzzlement. I had to think clearly about this. I guessed what had happened, but it was part of a state secret. Did that matter this long after Mindslip? Could I swear my family to secrecy? Should I report this to the authorities? If so, which authorities? Norway? What good would that do? No point telling Charles Browning. What could he do about this happening in Norway? I'd warned the government that the procedure would be driven underground if it was banned. It obviously had been.

'Come on, Beth. What's going on?' asked Gren with real concern.

Wilson reached over and took my hand. 'What's up, Dad?'

'Did this man attack you?' asked Gren, getting angry.

'No. Nothing like that. I need to swear you all to secrecy,' I said.

'No problem,' said Wilson.

'I mean it,' I said. 'None of you can ever talk about it if I tell you. It's an official secret from 2019. Do you all promise?'

'Of course,' said Gren, and the others nodded.

'Come on, Dad. I'm intrigued. Seemed like he was a nice guy,' said Wilson.

'Well, he might be, but he should be in his late fifties, not his twenties. He had designed a system whereby a mind could be put back into its original body. The government realised that it could lead to immortality for a favoured few and banned it. Once Mark had perfected the system, he secretly offered to transfer your mother into a younger greyhound as an interim measure, hoping to put her back into a human body later, but she died before he could perform the transfer,' I explained.

'So, what has so shocked you?' asked Gren.

'That he should be late fifties. Isn't it obvious? He's transferred himself and Lady Julia into younger people. He's trying to make himself immortal,' I said.

'Wow. Amazing,' said Wilson.

'And now the sun's misbehaviour is spoiling his parade,' said Gren.

'Yes. I do know that he had been planning to store a mind in its digital form. I wonder if he did that.'

'And every now and then, he downloads it into a younger body,' said Angela.

'You realise it could mean that there are multiple versions of him. It was mind copying, not mind transfer. Whatever, it was pronounced illegal by all governments at the time and classified top secret.'

'I wonder where he found the younger bodies,' said Gren.

'Yes,' I said. 'Very worrying. There was a rumour that he had set up in business, transferring old and dying billionaires into new younger bodies. It was never proven though. Wilson, Angela, be very wary of him and keep him clear of your children. Keep him at arm's length.'

'We will,' said Angela.

'And there's me thinking Mindslip was cast into history. Maybe it isn't after all.'

HEAT

40 Progress

Over thirty space-suited mechanics toiled over the bright yellow machine components. The first of three giant tunnelling machines were being constructed. It had to be built outside the new underground habitat because it was far too massive to enter the caverns already created. The second and third excavators could be built inside one of the larger pressurised spaces the first one was designed to excavate.

The work was not without its dangers; in fact, the construction of the enormous machine offered additional hazards as large mechanical sections were manhandled and then bolted, screwed or welded into place. Even the bright yellow panels which hid most of the machine from view were cumbersome and difficult to manoeuvre. They only covered areas of the excavator which needed to be protected from regolith or people. Nothing was added for aesthetic reasons; no one wanted to waste fuel transporting anything with no other purpose than to look good or promote the manufacturer's logo.

By the time excavator one was fully assembled and tested, two astronauts had died. One fell from the upper part of the starboard caterpillar track and her helmet cracked open. The safety team rushed to her aid but were too late to prevent death by decompression. The second fatal accident was foolhardiness. The engineer reached into a section of the electric motor without switching it off. It was something he'd done many times before – on Earth – but here on the lunar surface, gravity was a third of that on his home planet. When he pulled on the frame to adjust his position, his whole body lurched forward, and his arm was pulled into the mechanism. The strength of the snagged suit prevented all efforts to rescue him, and he'd bled to death within it before the safety team were able to switch off and extract him.

So, two more graves had to be dug in the lunar regolith to the east of the habitat. There were already twelve and there would, no doubt, be more over the coming months. An engineer who was also a chaplain conducted a short service for the dozen or so astronauts who could attend the interment.

Big Bertha, as the giant excavator was named on its completion, began its work the following week. Like an exposed mole which was trying to bury itself, the rear of the machine used integral jacks to lift it to an angle of thirty degrees so that the twenty-metre corkscrew drill on the front could point downwards and commence its task.

An hour later, the jacks at Bertha's rear retreated under their carapace, and the machine gradually disappeared beneath the lunar surface, ejecting jets of regolith which slowly fell to the surface when their kinetic energy was exhausted. One benefit of working without atmosphere was that there were no clouds of dust hanging around to get into machinery and cause mechanical failures.

The low gravity on the moon allowed enormous caverns to be constructed free of the usual tangles of girders and frameworks necessary for such work on the mother planet. On Earth, there would have had to be reinforced columns and the whole of the cavern ceiling would probably have had to be constructed from metal or concrete. The moon was a difficult and dangerous place to work, but it had its advantages. As Bertha began to create a tunnel to the next planned cavern, the parts for two more machines were brought into the first space so that their construction could be begun as soon as the entrance was sealed. These excavators would never again emerge into sunlight.

'That's them both in cavern one,' said Commander Lewis, observing operations inside the cavern with the doctor and an engineer.

Engineer, Lucy Silver, replied, 'Right. I'll give the go-ahead for the construction team to begin work on the entrance airlock. We've already brought pipes into the right-hand side of the cavern and when we've sealed the external doorway, your guys can begin to pressurise.'

'The spoil conveyors have their own locking system?' asked the doctor, who'd come along with Lewis to view the construction work.

'Yes, it's dumped in one of several hoppers which are sealed, depressurised, then the content dumped outside, so not a true airlock. There are four diggers outside loading giant tipper trucks, which are full time on removing it to designated craters,' said Silver.

'Right. Wondered about that.'

'Much of it will be re-used for roads between future settlements, I'm told,' said Silver.

'It'll be good to work without suits,' Lewis said, turning and following Silver towards the bright sunlight streaming into cavern one.

HEAT

'I'll leave you guys to it,' said the doctor, turning the other way towards an airlock into a completed part of the cavern network.

Outside, more yellow construction vehicles were arriving, carrying the components for the biggest airlock ever created – twenty metres in diameter and with an internal length of more than forty metres. When it was complete, it would be able to handle the cylindrical containers from Earth which would be carrying everything the refuge would require to allow life to exist on the moon.

∞∞∞∞∞∞∞∞∞∞

Elsewhere, the mass production of oxygen, hydrogen, nitrogen, other trace gases and water was underway. Pipelines were buried in shallow trenches between Copernicus crater and Moonbase. The gases were combined into breathable air which, like water, was stored in metal-lined silos hollowed out from the rock. This prevented impurities from the regolith from tainting the supply.

At the other end of the system, sewage was being pumped into caverns which had been specially designed to use bacteria to turn the waste into usable nutrients which would be stored for use in the hydroponics caverns to assist in food production. It might not have smelled too good, but it was very nutritious and the odour would dissipate once the bacteria were working correctly. It would take time.

∞∞∞∞∞∞∞∞∞∞

That day, Commander Bert Lewis was on an inspection trip with Dr Jason Ingersoll. They travelled the three miles along corridors from Moonbase to one of the new development areas. There, they jumped out of the four-seater electric Jeep.

Ingersoll, who had only just arrived on the moon, looked admiringly around at the vaulted arches of that section of the moon refuge. He couldn't believe the size of what he was seeing, nor the speed in which it had been constructed.

Before them was an oversized metal airtight doorway, some twenty metres wide and a similar height. It needed to admit container trucks and plant. It didn't need to be an airlock as its only purpose was to keep air in. It would never be opened if the tunnel and cavern network remained pressurised. Depressurising any of it would be an exceptional procedure. It could, of course, happen by accident, but that would be unlikely too. The door was the final safeguard.

Beside it, painted green, was another airtight door, human sized this time. Lewis punched the green button, and it opened inwards to admit them, as did every airtight door leading into sealed caverns. They were designed to hold air in if a rare accidental depressurisation occurred in the cavern network outside.

The two men were now in a room, about ten metres square and three high, with a couple of desks, computer terminals, and video monitors. The walls to left and right were covered in beautiful images of earthly country scenes. Trees, fields, clouds peppering blue sky – and it was all in motion. The walls were like giant television monitors, projecting extended gifs showing life back on the home planet.

Psychologists had insisted these be installed in every working area for the mental wellbeing of the astronaut workers. They would also be integral to the orbiting and spaceship refuges.

The wall opposite the airtight door had glazed windows and a central glass door. This gave a view into the enormous cavern beyond. What they saw beggared belief.

The huge space stretched more than two hundred metres into the distance and another hundred metres to left and right – an almost square space two hundred metres per side. The ceiling here was sky blue. Ingersoll wondered how long it had taken to paint. The distant walls were images of hardwood trees like oak, beech, and horse chestnut. From the large airtight door to their left, low dividing walls, about 1.3 metres high ran the length of the cavern. Built into them were troughs. The one immediately on the left was full of food and a herd of cows was peacefully munching on the content.

'Wow,' said Ingersoll. 'I knew what I'd be seeing, but to actually encounter it is amazing.'

'It is now stocked to twenty-five percent,' said Lewis.

'Yes. Wonderful. How are they getting on in the reduced gravity?'

A woman in a boiler suit was walking towards the office. She was of stout build, short with a round face and curly black hair, the epitome of a farmer, which is what she was.

'Ask Beatrice Ardent. I think you know her. She's the manager of Dairy One, as we call this farm,' said Lewis.

The door opened, she walked over to Ingersoll and said, with a strong French accent, 'Jason. Pleased to see you arrived safely.' They shook hands.

'Nice to see you, Beatrice. How's the gravity affecting them?' he asked.

'Well, it's almost six weeks now and while milk production fell with the chaos of the freefall journey, and strangeness of the cavern, we're pleased that it is now almost up to normal,' she said. 'Come see.'

The three of them left the office and walked towards the closest group of Holstein cows. Beatrice said, 'These ten were the last to arrive. That's why we're keeping them to one side.' She waved an arm towards an electric fence which isolated the group from the main herd. 'We've ten arriving each week and should have a full complement by the end of the year.'

'I can't see the bulls,' said Jason.

'They're in another cavern with other male livestock,' she said.

'And you've plenty of foodstuffs?'

'Yes, but Commander Lewis will tell you more about that. There's no rationing.'

Bert said, 'We have an adequate supply, an emergency backup and, of course, the intention is to grow what we need when the floors of those caverns have sufficient soil. Waste is being mixed with regolith. It seems to be working okay in one small area where we've been experimenting with grasses. I'll show you when we've finished here.'

'Excellent,' said Jason. 'Beatrice, does the milking parlour work all right now?'

'Yes, the low gravity adjustments you suggested seem to have done the trick. We're monitoring carefully,' she replied.

'I'll be back later, and you can run through the stats with me,' said Jason.

'Fine, but not just after lunch. We've another ten arriving.'

'No problem.'

41 New Forest

Sandra's stand-in was cooking the dinners on Tuesday night, one of the Michelin-starred chef's two evenings off. It meant that she was able to head home from the Montagu Arms in Beaulieu early in the evening. Their house was only a few miles along the B3055 road towards Brockenhurst.

The sun was dipping low in the west, painting the sky hues of crimson, golden yellow and pink when she joined Malcolm in the garden with a vodka and tonic poured over a mountain of ice. With the sun nearing the horizon, the heat was somewhat mitigated but was still a roasting forty degrees.

The garden was in a pretty location and very secluded. Almost constant irrigation had kept the lawn green and the herbaceous borders looking magnificent. It was fortunate that, in Britain, the heat was bringing with it, an increasingly wet climate, so most western European nations were not suffering from drought as well as heat. The atmosphere was sucking up water from the Atlantic and dumping it in large volumes when it approached western Europe. When it wasn't raining, Malcolm devoted his free time to pruning, planting, and dead-heading at that time of year. Theirs was one of the few houses actually inside the New Forest, a much loved and protected area on the south coast of England. The children were too hot to play and sat in an intimate shaded grove within the garden. Patricia was drawing something on a sketchpad and Linda played with a handheld computer game which emitted tinny sounding voices, music, and sound effects. They wore the bare minimum of shorts and T-shirts. Occasionally they'd jump up, kick off their flipflops, abandon their interests and run, laughing, through the water spray which was currently moistening part of the lawn.

'Watch you don't slip!' shouted their father.

For Malcolm, Sandra, and their family, this was a sanctuary, a place to escape the chaos of modern life.

Malcolm wandered inside, then shortly emerged, wiping his hands on a dishcloth and shouted to the children, 'Dinner's almost ready!' He looked to the south and noticed a breeze picking up. That would be pleasant. Was it too hot to eat outside? They often did that before the relentless warming of the climate. Maybe it would be okay. 'Pat, Linda, get some knives and forks. We'll eat in the garden tonight'

'Ooh! Yes!' shouted Patricia excitedly.

'What's for dinner?' Sandra called. 'Smells like a pie of some description.'

'Cornish pasties,' Malcolm replied, heading back inside. 'I've done some broccoli and new potatoes to go with it.'

'Herbs and butter?' asked Sandra.

'Stop telling me how to prepare meals!' he shouted back and then laughed.

As the glow of the sunset began to fade, they gathered around the table, sharing stories and laughter. The breeze seemed stronger, and it could be heard whistling through the trees.

'That's odd,' said Malcolm.

'What?' the others all asked almost in unison.

'The sunset,' he said.

'Yes, lovely,' remarked Sandra.

HEAT

'No...' He looked concerned. 'Look, it's moved around to the southwest. It's all wrong.'

'I can smell smoke,' said Sandra.

Malcolm made his way to the bottom of the garden where there was a more open view to the south. Sandra followed him.

'I think it's a fire!' she said.

The sky had been clear, now smoke was blotting out the sky and the smell of smoke was growing stronger. It was coming their way.

Malcolm ran back to the table, still bearing the debris of their dinner, grabbed his phone, and called a friend. 'George, it's Malc. Can you see that smoke?'

Sandra came over to him looking anxious.

'He's gone outside to check,' said Malcolm, then put his ear back to the smartphone. 'How bad? Where?' A pause. 'North of you? That's nearer us.'

Sandra's phone pinged. She opened the message and read in horror. *Emergency alert: Evacuation order in effect for the New Forest east of Brockenhurst. Please leave immediately.* Her heart raced as she read the message. She rushed over to Malcolm and showed him the screen. His phone pinged too, and he cut off his call to George with a curt, 'Gotta go!' then said to Sandra, 'I've got the same alert. We need to go.'

'Immediately?'

'Yes, damn it! There's an evacuation order!" he said, his voice trembling.

'Okay, let's gather the kids,' Sandra said, her voice steady despite the urgency. "We need to act fast."

They rounded up the children. 'Kids, we have to leave right now. There's a fire nearby,' Malcolm explained, trying to keep his tone calm.

'Is it going to be okay?' Linda asked, her big blue eyes wide with fear.

'Of course, sweetheart. We just need to get to safety,' Sandra assured her, kneeling down to meet her gaze. 'We'll be back before you know it.'

They moved quickly, packing essentials into the car. Food, drinks, and important documents. Sandra grabbed the photo albums, her heart aching at the thought of leaving their home behind. So many houses had been lost in Britain that year through forest fires, but never before had the New Forest been affected so seriously.

As they jumped into the car, the air grew thick with smoke, and the distant sound of crackling flames echoed through the trees. Malcolm turned on the radio, and the sound of New Forest FM burst out. A song ended and a voice told them that the fire was advancing rapidly from the south and people were to head for Brockenhurst. It was burning out of control, east of Beaulieu, had apparently leapt Hatchet Pond, and the wind was fanning it northwards from Beaulieu Heath which was more scrubland than forest.

'That's immediately south of us,' said Sandra.

'Let's go!' he urged, sliding into the driver's seat. Sandra and the kids followed, and as Malcolm pressed the start button, a sense of urgency washed over them.

The road from the house was about three-quarters of a mile long before they would reach the

HEAT

B3055. It was narrow and winding, flanked by hardwood trees. As they drove, a distinct glow could be seen approaching from the left. Smoke was drifting across the road. The usually inviting landscape now appeared ominous and threatening.

'Look!' Patricia shouted from the back seat, pointing out of the window. 'The sky's on fire!'

Sandra turned to see a glow in the distance, flames licking at the edges of the forest. Panic surged through her. 'Keep driving, Malcolm! We need to get out of here, and quick!'

As they navigated the winding lane, visibility decreased. Smoke swirled around them, and the heat was palpable, the fire's fierceness combining with the dreadful heatwave. Malcolm kept his focus on the road, but Sandra could see the worry etched on his face.

'Where're we going?' asked Linda, her voice small and tearful.

'Brockenhurst. It's only a few miles. They'll have resources and shelter,' Malcolm replied, trying to sound reassuring.

Suddenly, the car jolted as they hit a bump. 'What was that?' Sandra asked, her heart racing.

'Just that damn pothole,' Malcolm said, but his grip on the steering wheel tightened. 'Been meaning to get onto the council about it.'

Now they were encountering fallen burned twigs and small branches and smoking debris littered the road. 'We need to be careful,' Malcolm said, slowing down. 'The fire must be getting closer.'

The radio crackled with updates, warning of mandatory evacuations and advising residents to avoid certain routes. 'We can't go back,' Sandra said, her voice firm. 'We have to keep moving forward.'

As they rounded a bend, the sight before them made their hearts drop. Flames danced along the edges of the road, and thick smoke billowed upward like a monstrous cloud blotting out the moon and stars. The fire had spread rapidly, consuming everything in its path. Some deer leapt across the road in front of them, heading away from the flames.

The road forked. The left junction was the road to Brockenhurst. He started to turn then stopped.

'Malcolm, we can't go that way!' Sandra shouted, panic rising in her chest.

'I know!' he replied, his mind racing. 'Trouble is that the road north is nothing more than a track. Let's see if we can get through here first.'

He accelerated along the Brockenhurst road, but it was becoming increasingly treacherous. The flames flickered closer, and the heat intensified. The family's hearts pounded, fear gripping them tightly.

They rounded a bend. Their route was blocked. A tree had fallen across the road. Too big to move or drive over.

'Quick, turn around!' Sandra cried.

Malcolm did the fastest three-point-turn he had ever undertaken and then he floored the electric car causing it to whine under the sudden acceleration.

'Look!' Sandra pointed. 'There's the junction!'

They were back to the track they'd seen earlier. Malcolm squinted through the smoke. 'It might lead us away from the fire. Could be rough. Everyone hold on!'

He veered onto the bumpy and uneven dirt track, the car rattling and bouncing as they sped away from the main road, the flames now a terrifying backdrop. The trees around them were eerily devoid of life, the usual sounds of the forest replaced by the ominous crackle of fire.

As they drove deeper into the woods, the smoke began to clear slightly, a few deer and a fox ran across the track in front of them, and they spotted a small parking area ahead. 'Let's stop there,' Malcolm suggested, hoping to catch their breath and regroup.

They pulled into the clearing. Malcolm kept the motor on for the air-con. They stepped out, their lungs burning from the smoke and took a moment to collect their thoughts and look around at the towering ash, beech and oak trees that surrounded them.

'Are we safe here?' Patricia asked, her voice trembling.

'Not really. Just wanted to get a feel for the fire's progress behind us,' Malcolm replied, scanning the area, and looking back at the fire which was still heading their way. 'We need to keep moving.'

Sandra passed around water bottles, and they got back into the car and its welcome air-conditioned coolness.'

Sandra's phone buzzed and she read a message from friends in Beaulieu offering a place to stay if they could make it to town. 'Bill and Maude offering accommodation,' she said, showing the message to Malcolm who only glanced at it for a second.

'No way we can get to Beaulieu,' he said, determination in his eyes. 'Let's push on this way.'

Malcolm navigated the dirt road carefully. The air was still thick with smoke, but they could see patches of night sky peeking through. They drove for almost fifteen minutes which seemed far longer, the tension palpable.

Suddenly, they came to a crossroads. The dirt track continued straight on, northwards, but a somewhat better paved road crossed it.

'Which way?' asked Malcolm.

'Shush! What's that noise?' asked Sandra.

'Sounds like sirens,' said Linda.

The hi-lo wailing was approaching from the west. All of a sudden, a fire engine, with lights blazing went straight across their path. A second engine stopped and a couple of firefighters in their buff-coloured outfits and yellow helmets jumped down and walked over to them. Malcolm lowered his window.

'Where are you heading,' one of the men asked gruffly.

'Just trying to get away from the fire. Seems to be behind us,' said Malcolm.

'Right. When we've moved off to follow the other engine, turn left and keep driving until you hit the main A337. Then turn right and go to Brockenhurst College. There's a relief centre being set up there.' He ran back to the fire engine, and it tore off to the right.

Malcolm turned left and put his foot to the floor.

But their relief was short-lived. The fire seemed to be getting closer on their left.

HEAT

'I can see flames!' shouted Patricia.

'Stay calm, everyone,' Malcolm said, gripping the steering wheel tightly. 'We'll find a way through.'

As they sped westward, the fire getting closer all the time, the local radio station crackled with updates. The fire was spreading rapidly, and authorities were urging everyone to evacuate the forest and head north or west. Sandra's heart raced as she scanned the woodland. More flames were visible ahead and some seemed to be leaping from the left of the road to the right, a terrifying reminder of their proximity to danger. Malcolm accelerated, and the vehicle leapt forward.

They seemed to be past the worst of it then, ahead, a burning birch tree had fallen across the road. They were trapped again. Sandra shouted, *'Stop!'*

The tyres squealed as the car came to a shuddering halt. Malcolm looked in the rear mirror.

'We can't go back, it's worse behind us. I'm going to drive through it,' he said and accelerated towards the burning barrier, hoping beyond hope that there were no larger trees felled ahead.

There was a crash, the car bounced over the narrow trunk, cutting its way through the fiery branches, bounced again, and a clear road appeared before them. A larger tree was tottering in front and to the left. It began to fall, but, driving flat out, the car pushed through the descending branches, and they were past the worst. It crashed down behind them, a barrier which could never be crossed. There was no option other than going forward now.

With sighs of relief, and listening to the sound of crying from the children, they reached the main road, took the right turn at the junction and within five minutes they passed through the metal gateway into the college grounds. There was a group of low, brick buildings, cars, an ambulance, a hot-dog van, and lots of people milling around.

'Stay close!' Sandra instructed, holding Linda's hand while Malcolm took Pat's.

They approached the entrance and were met by a vicar and some volunteers who welcomed them and recorded their names. 'You're safe now,' one woman said, handing them bottles of water. 'We have food, shelter and air-conditioning inside.'

Tears of relief filled Sandra's eyes as they stepped into the cool interior. The chaos of the outside world faded away, replaced by the comforting hum of voices and the smell of food cooking. The cricket and football pitches surrounding the college buildings would break the oncoming fire.

Inside the college sports' hall, the atmosphere was a mix of fear and hope. Families huddled together, sharing stories of their escapes. Sandra and Malcolm found a corner in which to sit, their children nestled between them.

'Are we going to lose our house?' Patricia asked, her voice tearful.

'We don't know yet, love,' Malcolm replied, wrapping an arm around her. 'But we're safe, and that's what matters right now.'

Sandra's phone rang. 'Hello,' she said.

HEAT

'Oh, you're alright? It's Mum. Gren and I have been watching it on the news. Malcolm and the children okay?'

'Oh, Mum, we're all fine. It was scary, we nearly got trapped on the way to Brockenhurst. We're in the college buildings there now – it's a relief centre. I'll call you again later. Malcolm's trying to find out about the house. We left in such a hurry.'

'Okay, speak again soon. Let us know any news.'

'Will do, Mum,' Sandra said, cutting the call.

As the night wore on, they listened to updates about the fire. The community came together, sharing resources and support. Sandra felt a sense of camaraderie among the other families, each one with their own story of survival.

Eventually, they were taken into another building with camp beds set up for families to rest. 'Let's get some sleep,' Sandra suggested, exhaustion weighing heavily on her. 'We'll figure everything out in the morning.'

As they settled into the cots, the sound of the radio provided a backdrop of reassurance. The fire was still raging, but the community was rallying together, and help was on the way.

∞∞∞∞∞∞∞∞∞∞

The next morning, sunlight streamed through the windows of the sleep area, casting a warm glow over the room. Sandra awoke to the sound of voices and the smell of coffee brewing. She stretched and looked around, grateful to see her family safe and together.

Malcolm was already up, speaking with a volunteer. 'They're gathering information on the extent of the burned area,' he said when he saw her.

'What about our home?' Sandra asked, her heart heavy with uncertainty.

'We'll figure it out,' Malcolm replied, determination in his eyes. 'Right now, we need to focus on breakfast and getting our things together ready to head home or to a hotel or something.'

'I've an idea,' Sandra said. They all looked at her. She pressed a couple of buttons on her phone and put it on loudspeaker.

The telephone rang three times then a voice answered, 'You've got the Fletcher family. We're out. Leave a message or call back later.'

They cheered, Linda and Patricia looking at their parents in a puzzled manner. Why were they cheering at an answerphone message.

'The landline answerphone's working! It's in the lounge. The house must be safe,' Sandra said excitedly. 'The only reason we kept it was because our mobile phone signal was so bad indoors. Now it's told us the house is safe after all!'

The children realised what it meant and jumped for joy.

Malcolm stood up. 'I'll go and find out the best way to drive home. We'll probably have to drive north to Lyndhurst and down to Beaulieu that way if the road's clear. I'm sure the police will have signs out.'

Later, armed with as much information as possible on which roads to use, they ventured outside. The heat was worse than ever, over forty-five degrees.

Malcolm sent them back inside while he opened all the car doors, turned on the motor and fired up the air-con. As soon as the inside temperature matched the outside, he closed the doors, leaving the air-con running, went inside for the others and they made a dash to the car.

The journey home through the burned and blackened forest was depressing, its former beauty destroyed. The car's tracking must have been knocked way off kilter by driving over the birch tree as the steering was wobbling and would need a repair, but their priority was getting back home.

Almost miraculously, the house and garden were completely unscathed. They thanked providence.

They'd been lucky – incredibly lucky.

HEAT

2040

42 Family Holiday

This time, when we arrived in Lerwick, we got a cab from the airport to a local garage where we had long-term parking and collected our Range Rover. All-electric and all-wheel drive, it was the perfect vehicle for our remote home.

Geoffrey and Caroline were excited, as they always were when we travelled together. We'd told them about our retreat, but they'd never actually visited Fetlar, mainly because it only had one bedroom, so was unsuited to a family. If I hadn't had the two letters in my suitcase, we'd have had to build an extension to the house to allow the children to come with us when we made the permanent move. The letters I'd secreted in my luggage made that no longer necessary. We decided to keep the name Fetlar, as it meant 'Garden of Shetland', although, to be honest, it was a reference to one of the smaller islands in the archipelago. Somehow it still seemed appropriate.

The children were both teenagers now. Geoffrey fourteen, well-built and athletic, had inherited his father's good looks, with a tangle of ebony hair and jutting jaw. His sport was rugby, and he was pretty good at it. Caroline, sixteen, reminded me of the Japanese girl I'd seen in the mirror when Mindslip struck. She was taller than me, slim, and moved with great poise. She loved gymnastics. Although Caroline's oriental features were not quite as prominent as mine, her jet-black hair fell below her waist and augmented her growing beauty. They were both well-adjusted kids. Geoffrey had already passed A-level maths three years early, and had a bent towards physics, and Caroline was being specially tutored to university level in biology and botany. It cost an arm and a leg but had paid dividends. Had we directed their learning into those directions? You bet we had! We knew what would be needed to be selected for a refuge, and we'd just heard that both had been chosen for the starship project... although they didn't know it yet. Those were the letters I'd hidden in my case. They were both million to one successes and their selection was one of the reasons for this family break at Fetlar.

We'd hoped for places in Antarctica or on the moon, but beggars can't be choosers, and it had taken every ounce of ingenuity Gren and I possessed to get them into any refuge at all. It was impossible to cheat the system, so it was all their own work, but we'd known the best subjects for them to study and had pushed them in those directions. Now, we knew the endless hours of studying we'd coerced them into had all been worthwhile. When they learned about the starship, we guessed there would be ructions. It would, after all, be both good and bad news for them. Good that they were to be saved, but bad that they'd soon be leaving Earth and spending the rest of their lives in outer space. We'd leave the news until the final day.

As we pulled into the parking area behind the cottage, we saw an ancient Land Rover Defender standing next to the steading. Its back door was open with a rake, fork, shovel, and sack barrow leaning against it. A middle-aged man, called Angus, was stripped to the waist, moving sacks from the garden area into the steading. He waved as we approached, and his border collie dog ran over to greet us. Geoffrey loved it, immediately bending down to play.

We were struck by the heat as we disembarked and walked over to him. Gren said, 'Hot today. These are the two tearaways we've been telling you about.' He looked around and said, 'Geoff and Caroline, say hello to Angie, who's been keeping our vegetables from burning to a crisp.'

Angus was drenched in sweat. He wiped his hands on his jeans and shook hands with the two teenagers. Behind him, waterjets were pulse-spraying the crop.

'Irrigation system's working okay, Angie?' asked Gren.

'Aye, it's no bad.' He pointed over to the chicken coop and said, 'Had to put some steel mesh under t' henhouse, there were signs of predators trying t'dig under. Cost a bit and had to get Hamish to give me a hand.'

'Thanks. I'll catch you later to settle up. Need to show these two youngsters around before we lose the light.'

'Aye, evenings are closing in,' Angus replied and continued to heft the sacks of recently lifted potatoes into the steading.

'Come on, guys,' I said cheerily, and they followed me around the front of the cottage. 'Like the view?'

HEAT

'Lovely,' said Caroline. Geoffrey just gave an affirmative grunt which was typical of him.

Over the years, we'd had the property double-insulated on the inside, redecorated and furnished to our taste. The whole place was now light and airy. As I entered, I hit the air-con switch. There was silence for about thirty seconds then the gentle, soft whooshing sound of cool air circulating began.

The lounge had two easy chairs and a comfortable couch, plus a table with four chairs, but this was a modern replacement for the original Formica and plastic versions the previous owner had owned. Our bedroom was beautiful. Cool pastel colours, built-in wardrobe and dressing table, plus a king-sized double bed. The old bathroom had been gutted and replaced with a wet room comprising a walk-in shower and the usual facilities. The kitchen had also been stripped and equipped with the best labour-saving devices.

'Where are *we* sleeping?' grumbled Geoffrey.

'That's all planned,' said Gren. 'You and I will be on camp beds in the lounge and the girls will share the bedroom. Come with me, Geoff, we'll get the beds out of the power room.'

'Power room?' he asked, following Gren through the hallway.

'Yes,' I heard Gren say, 'we have a power room which stores the electricity generated by the wind turbine and solar panels. Come on, I'll show you how it works.'

'Better have a look too,' I said to Caroline. 'It's your dad's project. He likes to make it sound complex, but it's actually a breeze to operate.' We followed the boys outside into the hot dry atmosphere and along to the concrete battery room, shutting the house door to ensure the air-con was not being wasted.

'Why's that lorry parked there?' asked my daughter, looking to where a truck trailer unit was parked alongside the battery room.

'That's our refrigerator,' I said. 'We can store anything which might go off in there and the rear half of it is a deep freeze. It runs off the power we generate.'

'Refrigerator? It's huge!' exclaimed Geoffrey.

'The freezer is eight cubic metres, and the chilled area is twelve. It'll keep us in supplies throughout the winter,' said Gren. I ignored the white lie. This was not just a winter supply but would allow us to remain isolated from the rest of the world, as far as possible and for as long as possible.

In the power room, Gren unlocked the turbine brake, and we heard the whine it always made when starting up. We all stepped outside and watched it begin to gather speed in the breeze. It was almost silent once it was running, just the gentle whooshing sound of the blades cutting through the air.

That evening, the breeze cooled the atmosphere a little and Gren and Geoffrey fired up the barbecue. Beefburgers, hot dogs, onions, gherkins, and sauces were the order of the day. The full moon cast a steady pale light over the cliffs and cove, sparkling on the waves, as we sat in folding garden chairs to enjoy the feast and view.

HEAT

As we were all pretty shattered from the journey. Gren and Geoffrey soon put sleeping bags onto the two camp beds in the lounge and Caroline joined me in the double. We hadn't shared a bed since she was about six, and the air-con even permitted us to cuddle for a while until sleep overtook us. I made the most of the closeness, knowing what our news would likely mean for the future for us and them.

∞∞∞∞∞∞∞∞∞∞

Next morning, we were all refreshed and full of life. Bacon, sausages, eggs, and fried bread sizzled on the stove and, men in shorts and Caroline and me still in nighties, we all ate our fill.

'Can we go down to the beach?' asked Geoffrey.

'My thoughts exactly,' said Gren, 'and it should be calm enough to have a row.'

'We've got a boat?!' squealed Caroline.

'Sure have,' he said.

'It'll be hot out there,' I said. 'Shorts and Ts, I think. And don't forget your hats.'

In minutes, hurriedly dressed in the absolute minimum, we left the house and were hit by a blast of hot air, which reminded us unpleasantly of the very reason for us buying Fetlar. Gren and I had been to the tropics on vacations several times, but this was hotter still. Not as humid, but a dry, searing desert heat. Fortunately, Shetland still had rain so the grass was lush. Low-pressure fronts brought conveyor belts of clouds which drenched the grass and our crop field with warm rain sucked up from the heating Atlantic. Today, however, there was blue sky and little breeze.

The children ran on ahead, keen to start an adventure. Gren and I linked hands and followed on. Behind us, the turbine was revolving very lazily indeed. It didn't matter, the solar panels would take up the slack.

'They're not kids anymore,' Gren mused.

'No, Cas is a young woman now,' I said as we watched them disappearing down the steeply sloping path to the cove.

'She's as beautiful as you were when I first saw you that day in Guildford Townhall.'

'I was still trying to come to terms with my sex change then,' I said. 'I was with Sandra the day we met, remember it well.'

'They both did so well in their exams. I'm so proud.'

'Yes,' I agreed. 'They won't have realised yet, but it's probably what has secured their futures and maybe saved their lives. Glad we pushed them.'

'It is certain, isn't it?' asked Gren anxiously. 'There can't be any last-minute change in the selection?'

'Oh, yes. I have the official confirmations. One each. They'll be leaving for Alaska in two weeks for training. There will be some medical tests and vomit comet flights, but we know they have nothing wrong with them. It's breaking my heart that we'll be so far from them while they're training, Gren.'

'Yes, me too, but they'll be safe and, even better, they'll be together. I was so worried that one wouldn't be selected.'

'As safe as they can be in an experimental starship heading to God knows where, at God knows what speed, for God knows what length of time,' I said. 'They'll remember this break at Fetlar forever when they come to realise that they're to be doomed to spending the rest of their lives in a spaceship.'

'We've done our best for them,' said Gren, squeezing my hand tightly.

'I so regret being unable to do anything for Sandra and Wilson,' I said. My older children from the time before Mindslip had no special knowledge or skills to justify saving them. Sandra was a top chef and Wilson a professional footballer, but what value was that to the future of humankind. Wilson and his family had moved to the far north of Norway, inside the Arctic Circle and I'd been pushing Sandra to do something similar, but so far, she and her family were battling it out in the south of England.

'We knew they'd no special attributes to get them into a refuge,' said Gren.

'I know. It's just not enough to be lovely human beings,' I said, tears welling up in my eyes. And poor Emma, Pat, and Linda. They didn't deserve this.' It didn't help my sadness thinking about their soon to be truncated lives.

'No one did,' Gren said. 'You know, I really tried to figure out a way for them to come with us, but it just doesn't work. We'd need to more than double-up the power generation, build several more rooms and other things too. It's just not possible. I've already spent most of our savings and we're just staying afloat.'

HEAT

'I know, darling. There's only so much we can do. I've told Sandra and Malcolm what we've set up and I'm hoping they'll plan something similar,' I said.

'But not where? We agreed the exact location would be our secret.'

'No, just Shetland, but not the location.'

A call came from the beach. 'Come on you two landlubbers, we're waiting to set sail!' shouted Geoffrey. We could hear Caroline cheering us on and laughing.

'We're lucky it's so calm,' I said, snapping myself out of my sad mood.

'Yes, let's make the most of it,' said Gren and we hurried along the final few metres of footpath, sweat breaking out on our brows, and almost everywhere else. We'd need to change when we got back to the house.

'We're coming!' I shouted.

Gren and Geoffrey heaved against the boat, and it slid down the gravel and into the gently lapping waves. I brought the oars from the wooden hut where we stored them beside a stash of ropes and other nautical bits and pieces.

'What are those rope things?' asked Caroline.

'What these?' I asked, lifting one of the lobster pots.

'Yes.'

'They're pots for catching lobsters and crabs. Angie obtained some for us and must've brought them over since our last visit.'

'Can we use them?'

'Gren! Cas is asking if you can try to get a lobster or two?' I shouted to the boys.

'No bait.'

'What about one of those cod fillets I took out for dinner?' I asked.

'That might do it? Geoff, run up and bring one of the fish fillets, Mum has defrosting in the kitchen,' said Gren.

The boy was off in a flash, running up the cove path as if there was no heat or slope at all.

'And don't forget to shut the door!' Gren shouted after him. I arrived with the oars and a blue float. Caroline brought one of the pots.

'Why's it have this lump of metal attached. It's heavy,' she grumbled.

'Has to be weighted down to the bottom,' said Gren, tying the float to the handle of the pot and throwing the whole assembly into the boat. 'Lobsters and crabs are bottom dwellers.'

Amazingly, Geoffrey was back in just a couple of minutes. The cod was put into a holder in the pot. Gren and the kids jumped into the boat, and he began to row. The little craft was too small for all four of us. I waved from the shore.

'Has it got a name?' asked Geoffrey.

'The boat? No.'

'Oh, it must have a name,' insisted Caroline.

'Okay,' Gren said, heaving on the oars. 'What do you want to call it?'

'Boaty McBoatface!' exclaimed Geoffrey.

HEAT

'Not a chance!' Gren said. 'Think of something which has meaning for the family, and we'll paint it on the back.'

'I'll paint it,' cried Caroline. 'I saw some paint in the power room.'

'Okay, I'll think of a name,' said Geoffrey.

'We'll all have to agree on it. Including Mum,' said Gren.

∞∞∞∞∞∞∞∞∞∞

The week flew by. On the third day we retrieved the lobster pot and were delighted to find two lobsters which made a meal for the four of us that night. There was also a small lobster and two small crabs which we returned to the sea. The heat had dropped a little, only forty-one Celsius outside that day and we were all drenched by warm rain as we made our way up the cove path with our catch.

The wind was rising so we beached and tied up 'Greyhound', the name neatly painted on the rear by our daughter. Caroline, of course, was named after my pre-Mindslip wife who'd become a greyhound when Betelgeuse showered Earth with its radiation that fateful day nearly twenty-one years ago. I was pleased they'd chosen such an appropriate name and guessed Gren had had a hand in the suggestion. Once the paint dried, we poured some cava over the hull as an official naming ceremony.

Before we knew it, the ten-day break was over, and we tucked into Gren's signature beef stroganoff on the last evening. We allowed the children a glass of wine, watered down for Geoffrey, with the meal and treated them more as adults than we ever had before.

As we finished our rice pudding with raspberries from our vegetable patch, Geoffrey wanted to jump up to play with one of his computer games, but Gren quickly grabbed him by the arm and said, 'Wait. Stay seated please, son. We've an important announcement to make.' Both children looked to their father, but we'd agreed that it would be me who would break the news.

'We need to tell you about something which will affect all of our futures,' I said, and their eyes turned towards me.

'You know about the rising heat but we're not sure that you are aware of the consequences,' I began.

I didn't expect Caroline to interrupt but she jumped straight in with an immediate, 'We're all going to die!'

'Who told you that?' I asked, shocked at the plain way that she made her announcement. Gren and I knew that such rumours had been circulating for a year or so. Government denials had been so effective that the memes and conspiracy theories had remained fragmented. Caroline, however, had presented this one as fact.

'Everyone knows, Mum. It's been one of those facts that no one will talk about for months now. Is that what you wanted to tell us? Geoff knows as well,' she said in an incredibly adult manner. Geoffrey nodded at the mention of his name but said nothing.

'Well,' I said, 'it is partly about that, but there are possibilities.' Both looked at me intensely on the word 'possibilities'.

'What sort of 'possibilities' can there be to dying?' scoffed Caroline in a resigned way.

'You're aware that your dad and I have been pushing you to concentrate on your education and we tried to guide you into science subjects?'

'And it was all for nothing!' exclaimed Geoffrey, sitting back in his chair and folding his arms defensively. 'Everyone's been saying it's all going to end for months now.'

'Your education is where the possibilities lie,' I continued. 'It was *not* for nothing. We're unsure whether it was because of our pressure on you, but you chose science subjects. Cas has excelled in biology and botany, and you have found a love of mathematics and physics. You also have very high IQs – 140 and 133 and they are very important for what I have to tell you.'

'She probably cheated,' Geoffrey whispered under his breath. Caroline punched him in the arm.

'You can't cheat IQ tests,' said Gren.

The suspicion in their eyes seemed to lessen as they came to realise that there was more to this than a simple message of preparing to meet thy doom.

'Those subjects were not just relevant but are the *most* relevant to saving humankind and you've excelled in them,' I said, sipping from my wine glass.

'The truth is that it looks as if the heat might be going to continue to increase until it will be almost impossible to live on Earth's surface. That much is true, but it is not a certainty. The scientific jury is out,' I said.

'Your mother is telling you the truth,' said Gren.

'However, we have much more to impart to you both, so kindly hold your questions until I finish.'

This was so difficult, but I wanted to ensure I did not skip important points. I went on, 'I've been intimately involved with a multi-government project seeking a solution to the problem.'

Now I could see real interest in their expressions. They knew that as the official astronomer, I moved in exalted scientific circles. 'We don't know why the sun is misbehaving. Some think it will continue to heat for decades to come which would mean that there is no hope for any refuge on the planet. Others think that there will soon be a new solar maximum and then Sol will gradually return to its pre-Mindslip output. We have no way of knowing which scenario will be correct. There is no scientific evidence either way.'

Caroline went to ask a question, but Gren put a hand on her arm to advise her to hold.

'The project we've been working upon is to create some places of refuge which would allow humankind to continue to have hope into the future. Three of those refuges are based on the first principle, that the Earth and the sun will return to their historic behaviour eventually, although exactly when that might occur is one of the imponderable factors. The other principle assumes that Earth will never recover and that humankind must seek a home elsewhere.'

'Elsewhere?' asked Geoffrey. 'You mean Mars? Some people have said we should go to Mars.'

'No. Not Mars. Let me continue,' I said. 'What I'm telling you is confidential. The largest refuge will hold over ten thousand people and is nearing completion. It is in the centre of Antarctica. The official refuge is a British, US, Canadian, and French project. There are also several unofficial refuges on the continent. One Libyan, one being built by the European Union, but without France, one Argentinian, and we suspect others. Another is being established by the Russians, Chinese and Japanese on a huge island at the very north of Russia, inside the Arctic Circle. There's an enormous amount of construction taking place. The selected people for the official refuges have been notified.'

'We're too late to apply?' asked Geoffrey, looking reflective.

'No. It isn't a simple matter of applying. I should say that your father cannot be selected because all government ministers have taken an oath not to be chosen. I cannot be selected because I am on the management committee.'

'You'll have to die?' said Geoffrey thoughtfully.

'We have plans not to die, but let your mother finish first,' said Gren.

'What about the other refuges? Where are they?' asked Caroline.

'I hadn't quite finished. If Earth does not turn the corner and start to cool down, the refuges on Earth, no matter how far north or south they are, will eventually fail. The other three refuges then become humanity's only hope. Refuge two is on the moon. It is nearing completion and will house around eight thousand people. They, too, have already been selected.' I could see the stress building in their faces.

'Awesome!' said Geoffrey. 'The moon!'

'Refuge three is a huge space station which is now in orbit near the ISS. It will house up to four thousand humans. It is not yet complete but will be soon. Everyone selected has been notified. Both of those refuges will be unaffected by the climate on Earth. Even if everyone on Earth were to perish, those two refuges would still survive and if, in the distant future, Earth cools down again, the descendants of the moon and orbital refuges could return to recolonise our planet. There will even be animals in the moon refuge.'

'So, the only other one is leaving the Earth, but not going to Mars. Is that right?' asked Geoffrey.

'Yes. That's right,' I said, pulling the two certificate letters out of a folder I had beside my plate. 'These are your certificates. Both of you have been selected to become part of the crew.'

They looked stunned, but tentatively took the certificates and inspected them.

'Is it real?' asked Geoffrey, excitedly but holding it up to the light, examining the watermarks and integral metallic threads, as if it were fake currency.

'You mean it?' asked Caroline, more inquisitively.

'It's true. Your achievements in mathematics, botany and biology were crucial and Geoff's keenness to study physics too, was a factor. Your IQs were mandatory. No one with an IQ under 130 could be selected. You are exactly the type of people they want to crew the ship.'

'Where are we going?' asked Geoffrey.

'Probably Kepler-452,' I said, 'but it hasn't been finalised.'

'What's that?' asked Geoffrey. 'Sounds like a star. I've never heard of it.'

'It is,' I said. 'It is a star, very much like the sun, with a planet which is almost certainly Earth-like.'

'But that could take years to reach,' he protested. 'They say getting to the closest star could take more than a century.'

'That's true but they've been working on an ion drive which will help the ship approach the speed of light,' I said reassuringly.

'Years in a spaceship,' said Caroline, disappointment swamping her initial excitement.

Gren decided to whisper, 'It beats being dead, darling.'

Both looked from Gren to me to Gren again.

'This is serious?' asked Caroline. 'Not a wind up.'

'It is,' I said.

'How far is Kepler, whatever it is?' asked Geoffrey angrily.

'Kepler-452 B. One thousand six hundred light years,' I said and watched the shock materialise on his face.

'How long is the journey… for us, I mean? I take it there'll be time dilation.'

'There will. Honestly, you'll be unlikely to complete the journey, but, with any luck, your children might. Onboard time will be around a hundred years,' I said.

'What's this "onboard time" and "time dilation"? Speak English!' said Caroline, getting annoyed at her brother's knowledge of space and time exceeding hers.

'The starship will take almost two thousand years to reach Kepler-452, but because of relativity, the people onboard will experience only about a hundred years,' I said.

'I'll be spending the rest of my life in a tin can?' asked Caroline.

Gren broke in again, 'Beats being dead, Cas, and you'll be the first human interstellar travellers ever. Scientists are working flat out to give you that opportunity. They won't be going with you. They'll probably die on Earth but are making every effort to ensure you can survive. Don't demean their efforts.'

I noticed that Caroline had tears building in her eyes. 'You'll not be with us?' she asked, knowing the answer.

I lowered my voice. 'As I said, Caroline, neither of us is allowed to be selected. You will be travelling for us, carrying our hopes and dreams for the future. Conquering the universe. Or at least taking the first steps.'

I think the full impact of what I'd been telling them finally began to sink in.

'Nooooooooo! What will happen to you?' Caroline said, now in floods of tears.

Gren stood, walked around to our daughter and his arm encircled her shoulders. 'We'll be okay, darling. Your mum and I will be living in our little paradise here.'

I added, 'You've seen what we have. We've got the freezer lorry, the wind turbine, solar panels, air-conditioning, an entire river to keep our crops moist and we'll be dining on fresh lobster and crab while you'll be eating from tubes of NASA processed food!' I said, turning the last sentence into a joke.

'What if the sun never cools at all?' asked Caroline soberly.

'We have protective suits which will allow us to work outside in great heat. We'll survive,' said Gren

'What if the planet is no good?' asked Geoffrey.

'It's your children who will be worrying about that, not you,' I said, 'but it will be a great adventure. The Hubble and James Webb telescopes are concentrating on the planet almost full time, trying to learn more about it. It really does look promising.'

The questions and answers went on long into the night and it was well after midnight before we climbed into our beds, Caroline sobbing in my arms until sleep finally took her.

HEAT

43 Alaskan Space Center

Twelve square miles south of the Kuskokwim River at Crooked Creek, Alaska, had been acquired by NASA for the new space centre. The location had been decided upon owing to its latitude. The roasting temperatures would take longer to reach there than anywhere else in the United States. Building had begun as soon as the nature of the sun's increasing heat had been realised.

Today, there were six launch pads and a continual stream of Dragon and Starliner ships heading for the moon and the ISS. These were not the smaller launch vehicles which were used when the space station was in low-Earth orbit, but the massive rockets needed to fly to the moon or geosynchronous orbit. The moon project was well established, tunnels and caverns being opened up beneath the surface and a growing population of engineers were building the structure called Moon Refuge One. Progress was such that two thousand selectees were already living and working in the refuge.

Occasional launches were still being sent to the ISS in its new, safe orbit in the shade of Earth, but there were also an increasing number of flights of components and engineers being sent to construct the orbital refuge and the starship now named Kepler.

Thousands worked at the Alaskan Crooked Creek Space Center. It was a hive of activity, and everything was being undertaken at breakneck speed. It had been thought that there might be four or five decades to complete the project, but that had now been reduced to a single decade. New data predicted that much of Earth might not be habitable by 2050, just nine years from now.

I arrived on a flight from Anchorage with Caroline and Geoffrey. The reason for the visit was to give them some physical tests and I was to meet up with Harry. I'd called on an astronaut I knew to speak to the children about the ways of countering the physical problems during launch and freefall. We'd soon find out if it had helped as they were to be put through some gruelling underwater EVA trials, a trip on the so-called vomit comet, endurance experiments in the centrifuge and some manual dexterity tests.

They'd already experienced some of this at the Caithness Space Centre as part of a surreptitious NASA examination of likely selectees to ensure they would be suitable for final selection. They must have passed to have received the certificates. I was sure they would be fine on these final examinations, but there was always a chance that some defect in one or other of them might materialise and cause their elimination. I didn't know how they'd cope if either were rejected, and nor did I know how I would deal with the fallout for them and us.

I left them at the reception point and went to my hotel. It would be two days before I saw them again. The one good factor was that if there were to be a rejection, it would happen there and then. There would be no waiting period.

My duties on the refuge selection committee were now complete, so when I got back home, Gren and I would be able to relax back into a domestic life.

Perhaps it would be time to move permanently to Fetlar.

That evening, I met up with the head of NASA, Harry Kinsman, for an enjoyable dinner discussing a wide range of topics.

'How is the Kepler ship progressing?' I asked as we began to eat dessert.

'It's not easy. Internal parts for both the ship and the orbital refuge are almost identical and both are being constructed at worrying speed. I'm scared to death that we're going to get something critically wrong. We're still targeting early 2046.'

'What? For departure on the journey or just that the ship is ready to begin boarding?'

'Boarding late 2045 if things go well and the journey beginning soon into the new year. Your two children were selected, I understand,' he said, finishing his sticky toffee pudding.

'Indeed. We're so relieved. They're going through the final tests now. That's the other reason why I'm here. I'm dreading that one or other will be rejected.'

'If they've got this far, they should be okay unless there's some sort of physical problem, heart defects, disease, et cetera.'

I finished my scoop of chocolate chip ice cream and ordered a brandy. I had never recovered my love of malt whisky after Mindslip. My new tastebuds hated the stuff. Brandy was okay, but nowadays I tended to be a social gin or vodka drinker.

'How many working on the ship?' I asked.

Harry swirled his brandy in its glass, cupping the bowl to raise the temperature of the amber liquid. 'A couple of hundred in total. The health and safety is a nightmare and sadly, we're losing engineers regularly.'

'What? They're leaving?'

'God, no! They're dying.'

'Seriously?'

'It's more dangerous than any of us realised. On Monday we lost two. They were fitting exterior panels to the orbital refuge when one came loose. Almost in slow motion, it began to spin. One of the astronauts stupidly tried to stop it, forgetting that the lack of gravity does not mean a lack of mass. It pushed him into another part of the structure and smashed his helmet. His partner attempted to help, and her arm was sliced off by a sharp edge on the same panel. At least it was instantaneous,' he sipped his drink.

'I thought the suits were compartmentalised.'

'They are, but the panel hit at the shoulder joint. Instant decompression.'

'How often is this happening?'

'Too often. We've lost sixteen in the last twelve months. It's dreadful. Under normal circumstances we'd stop and reassess the procedures, but we don't have the time. You've seen the new climate projections?'

'I have. Not good – 2050 could be it for most of the world.'

'Indeed. What are your personal plans?'

'We have a hideaway with wind and solar generators, lots of spares and it'll be well stocked when we need to make the move permanent. Isolated too.'

'In the Arctic Circle?'

'No, Shetland, the islands north of Scotland. My pre-Mindslip son and his family are living in Norway, the Arctic Circle. A place called Vågnes. I suppose we're banking on Sol's misbehaviour coming to an end,' I said.

'Any sign of that?'

'No. Nothing. What's so frustrating is that we still have no idea why the sun is heating up. There's no rhyme nor reason to it. The week before last there were only two flares but as yet we can't tell if that was just a freak lull. Have you and Ellen made plans?'

'New Zealand South Island. We've a place there but it's not as well equipped as yours. I'll get onto that as soon as I can.'

'Gren has all the details of the turbine, solar panels, and storage system. Give him a call if you like. We also have a refrigerated truck which is connected to the power room. Huge deep freeze and chilled area within it.'

'Impressive. You growing anything?'

'We have a good water supply for continual spray irrigation, plus an air-conditioned chicken house. The spray irrigation is sensitive to rain, so only runs when it isn't raining. With the growing heat, we have to ensure the crop is irrigated continually. There's a nearby cove which supplies crab and lobster, although we don't know how long that will last with the warming seas.'

'No. See what you mean. What a horrible situation we find ourselves in,' he said, finishing his brandy.

'Yes, and we're the lucky ones who are able to do something. Most will be helpless until heatstroke or fire kills them. Can't imagine what it will be like. My pre-Mindslip daughter and her family are still in the south of England. They can't come with us and seem too complacent where they are.' I felt tears building. 'We've told them what they need to do in order to have some chance of saving themselves. Sandra's husband is quite resourceful, but we're worried about their lack of any plan of action. My son has moved to the Arctic Circle with his family, but Sandra and Malcolm don't seem to appreciate the threat. Gren and I have talked extensively about how we could accommodate them with us, but it just isn't possible. We don't have the resources. It would mean another whole house and the duplication of our power generation system. Also, Sandra isn't Gren's daughter. I don't know how to spur them into taking action.'

'They know what you're doing?'

'Yes. Shetland is not big, but our location is pretty secure. Hopefully, they'll devise something similar, but our hideaway is too small for anyone but the two of us. We knew we'd need to add a couple of rooms if our children didn't get selected, but we can't afford to extend to help a complete additional family, which might include other relations of Malcolm's. You know how these things can spread.'

HEAT

On that depressing note, we went to our rooms to sleep and, hopefully, not to dream, for dreams these days often morphed into nightmares.

∞∞∞∞∞∞∞∞∞∞

Two days later, Caroline and Geoffrey came bounding across the reception area and threw themselves into my arms. Everything was okay. Their certificates now bore a red stamp which announced:

FINAL APPROVAL

I was so relieved.

Our flight wasn't until the next morning, so that night we had takeaways delivered to my room and we sat around munching on a Big Mac with fries for Geoffrey, margherita pizza for Caroline, and a king prawn with cashew nuts for me.

'The vomit comet was really dope!' said Geoffrey. 'Some people were sick!'

'How were you?' I asked.

'No problem. Don't understand why they were ill.'

'Everyone's different,' said Caroline. 'I felt queasy but was fine in the end but I can understand why some didn't enjoy it.'

'Well,' I said, 'it's good to know you'll be alright in space.'

'I thought the underwater EVAs were brilliant,' said Caroline excitedly. 'Our instructor said I have a talent for it and would probably be part of the exterior engineering team when we set off for Kepler-452 B.'

'You think you'll enjoy that? Spacewalking can be dangerous, you know,' I cautioned.

'Yes, we know that but the whole adventure's dangerous, isn't it?' added Geoffrey.

'What else did you learn?' I didn't want to think about the danger they'd be in for the rest of their lives.

'Oh, loads,' said Caroline. 'We had two full lessons filling us in on the climate crisis. We're not allowed to talk about much of it.'

'It's okay with Mum,' said Geoffrey conspiratorially. 'She's in the know.'

'Mum,' said Caroline more seriously, 'Do you really think Fetlar will be okay when it gets *really* hot?'

'We hope so, darling. It's the best we can do. Your dad has even bought a couple of those silver radiation-proof suits. We'll be able to get to the trailer and power room however hot it gets,' I said reassuringly, knowing that the limits would eventually be exceeded. We'd worry about that if and when the time came.

We picked up the rubbish, the kids went to their rooms, and I tried to sleep because the flight to Chicago and home would leave the space centre airport at ten the next day.

44 Riot and Murder

Back in Britain, Gren and I were making more and longer trips to Fetlar. We now had the retreat set up how we liked it. In addition to our already massive library of DVDs, we also had many real books collected over the years, and downloaded an enormous selection of eBooks and films which we kept in a digital memory vault.

These were not stored in the cloud. Gren had purchased solid state servers which held our stash. There was no point in having everything in the cloud if our connection to the Internet was lost. We had no idea how long it would take civilisation to totally break down, but once it did communication infrastructure would likely go with it.

I suppose, when the history of the climate disaster were finally written down for posterity, if there were one, we might have a better understanding of the tipping points.

It was interesting to see how the general public were reacting to events. The country was abuzz with talk about the recent hurricane which tore through Cornwall and Devon, causing huge destruction in Plymouth, Penzance, and other towns along the southern coast. Then it was followed by the most enormous flood which left much of Bristol underwater when the Avon burst its banks during high tide on the Severn. At the same time, a tornado ripped its way through Kent, destroying medieval Canterbury Castle and ripping off part of the roof of the famous Cathedral.

Buchanan's protests were becoming more violent, but it was 2040 when demonstration morphed into revolt. Up until then, Buchanan had claimed that his eco-warrior group were peaceful, but had been infiltrated by undesirable elements. This time it was him and his key supporters who had the deliberate intention to resort to violence.

It started with a demonstration outside the steel gates of Downing Street. The crowd was becoming rowdy, and it was clear that the police were having trouble keeping order.

An emergency contingent of riot police arrived; hundreds of officers in hi-viz jackets with riot shields. Some with round shields for charging the crowd and others with almost full height shields to protect their bodies. They were expecting trouble, but not at the scale which followed.

The sun was setting when the first bricks and stones were thrown at the police. Protestors were screaming abuse at the government's failure to control the rising temperatures. At this point, most people still thought it was part of the ongoing climate crisis. The fact that it was increasingly looking like the beginning of the end of the world was still hidden. The PM and government advisers thought the truth was just too horrific to impart. What would be the consequences? What would people do if there was an announcement that everyone was going to die? There were rumours about refuges in Antarctica and the Arctic Circle, but no one had confirmed it officially, and there had been no announcement that the selection list had already been closed. How would people react to that?

HEAT

The police were being pushed back. Molotov cocktails were being thrown. This was clearly much better planned than the police had realised. Two policemen were showered with flaming petrol. Screams rang out. Officers rushed to extinguish the flames and pull their colleagues to safety while, all the time, the crowd was pushing forward, attacking the riot shields with cricket and baseball bats. This had been well orchestrated.

Some of the police were now being crushed against the Downing Street railings. There was nothing they could do. Many fell to the floor and were climbed over by the rabid mob. Then, a ten-ton truck ran towards the gates, it's horn blaring. Some of the crowd knew it was coming and jumped to one side or the other. The police were not expecting it. It ran into and over them causing screams and cries of pain and then it impacted the gates. Despite their strength and reinforcements, they gave way under the impact. The truck was in Downing Street.

The sequence of events after that is not particularly clear as closed circuit cameras became targets for paintball shots. What we do know is that the mob pulled the truck back and then invaded the hallowed tarmac of the world-famous street.

What happened next was reported live on social media. There was an explosion at the front of Number Ten and the mob dashed inside. Armed police in the hallway opened fire and several protestors fell to the ground. While some looked to run, others continued the charge, holding stolen police riot shields before them. In a minute or so, the lobby was clear, and the corpses of the police bodyguard contingent were being hauled out of the demolished doorway.

Later, two windows on the first floor were destroyed by small explosive charges, leaving a gaping hole in the grey façade.

Suddenly, three bodies were thrown out. None of them hit the ground. They were all hanging from nooses around their necks. One, the home secretary, Jack Easton, was still twitching. Thankfully, the prime minister Jenny McRoberts and cabinet secretary, Sir Joseph McKinley died instantly. These three figures, the elected representatives of the British people were hanging there, motionless, dead, murdered by a mob.

A banner was unfurled across the gaping hole in the building. It's message, STOP CLIMATE CHANGE and beneath that NO MORE HEAT!

The army arrived shortly afterwards and took control. More police arrested rioters and the leader of the riot, James Buchanan was cuffed and led away.

Before the night was out, government had been restored, but a video was being widely distributed on social media, showing the hanging bodies while Buchanan gave his message: 'We have been let down. Our leaders have continually told us that climate change is under control, yet, for the last ten years, we have seen average UK temperatures increase by nearly twenty degrees. They have lied to us. Heat elsewhere in the world is killing thousands of people every day. Don't let it happen to you. Join the CLIMATE REVOLT now. It is the only way!'

The video of the murders and the message continued to be repeated throughout the Internet, while Sir David Brenner and others tried to get the social media companies to take it down.

HEAT

2041

45 No Respite

As the spring of 2041 arrived, attitudes were beginning to change. Suspicion of governments reached a whole new level, and the rumours and conspiracy theories took on a life of their own. Almost no one believed that the climate was under control. Temperatures were rising at two or three degrees per year. Any belief in the story that emissions were falling, but the improvement in the climate was just lagging behind was gradually being shredded. Something was badly wrong. Fortunately, the extraordinary variety of conspiracy theories meant that no one could be certain which was true. The fact that our own sun was planning to incinerate us was lost within so many rumours.

Riots were happening worldwide. Equatorial countries were seeing their populations migrate north or south and their neighbouring nations were trying to prevent it. The military were guarding land borders and shooting anyone without a visa there and then. Thousands were dying. They couldn't return to their homes – they'd been burned down, been flooded by the rising oceans, or held no prospect of anything but starvation or death from heatstroke.

There were numerous instances of unarmed or poorly armed hordes rushing the military posts at borders, and many were mowed down by machine-gun fire. However, some got through and their stories were told elsewhere. Others were inspired to use the same tactics. The carnage was nothing less than hell on Earth. Soldiers had been told that they must protect their borders at all costs and the migrants knew it was break through or die. The consequences were obvious.

What began as just an equatorial disaster had spread into the tropics and would soon be as bad in temperate regions of the planet.

Southern European countries were no longer hiding the fact that they were repelling migrants. Boats were being sunk and those crossing land borders were taken back to the crossing points and released. What was happening at borders in Africa, Central America and the Far East would soon be enacted in the UK too. Where the odd concerted invasion occurred, the military were already acting swiftly, and the borders were secured.

While North America, countries south of Brazil in South America, European countries, those in the old Soviet Block, China, and Japan, still had food, as did Australasia, the news was full of reports of starving people trying to get to cooler regions. Such reports were suppressed to a degree, though even a few were enough to pull at the heartstrings, but nothing could be done.

The weather worsened. Violent storms, hurricanes, typhoons, torrential rain, and incredible heat all added to worldwide misery. Wales and Eire suffered a devastating hurricane, and the tidal surges were inundating coastal towns and villages. East Anglia was almost uninhabited after the last high tide.

How could any of this be reconciled with the reduction in emissions which governments were still claiming would soon start to show results.

It wasn't just Buchanan who was making accusations of lies and deceit, it was now occurring throughout the world.

Something had to give! Revolution began everywhere.

HEAT

2042

46 Training

It would be four years before the starship Kepler left the solar system with two thousand sons and daughters of residents of Earth, all chosen for their scientific ability. Training began at Easter and would continue until departure.

The whole process was thoughtfully planned. The residential blocks in Alaska had horses, lambs, dogs, and cats for the selected few to love, walk, ride and feed. I'd heard that psychologists wanted trainees to have knowledge and relationships with animals as there would be none travelling with them. Geoffrey was full of his growing environmental knowledge, understanding habitats, evolution, and animal husbandry. Excursions were made to farms and out to sea where they learned the ins and outs of fishing, both as a sport and as an industry.

The first generation on the starship would need to be able to pass on much of their knowledge to the second generation, some of whom would never set foot on any planet if the onboard journey time was a hundred years.

The starship would begin its journey with two thousand male and female crew; there was no hiding the plan that no female should have a third child unless there were deaths and that both children must have different fathers. This was to ensure that none of the genetic problems associated with inbreeding would be encountered. I remember Caroline's horror on learning that she would be compelled to have children with different partners. It was her eighteenth birthday and we'd flown over to see them at the Crooked Creek Flight Center.

'They want us to have children with different men,' she whispered to me when we were alone. Gren and Geoffrey were playing pool nearby.

'Not as bad as it sounds, darling,' I reassured. 'You won't be having sex; it'll be done by artificial insemination.'

'I know, but what if I fall in love? How will *he* feel about me carrying another man's child?' she dabbed her eyes. 'What if the one I love dumps me because of it. I couldn't ever share a boyfriend either. What if both fathers want a relationship with my children. I might hate them. I won't have chosen them to be my children's fathers, will I? It isn't fair.'

'None of it is fair, Cas.' I took her hand in mine. 'I do think you're likely to find *the* one, though.'

'Why should I?'

'It might have escaped your notice, but you are exceedingly beautiful, darling and you have the loveliest personality,' I told her. 'You'll find someone who will love you too.'

'It isn't just that, Mum. We've been told that we will only be allowed children at fixed intervals. It's all so awful. We're being treated like cattle. One at twenty-five and one at thirty-two and they'll all be half-brothers or sisters with different fathers and the fathers must be allowed to have a relationship with them, yet the fathers won't know who their children are until after they've been born.'

HEAT

'You'll enjoy being a mum, Cas. I was scared about childbirth, but when you came along it was actually quite easy and modern drugs make it pretty painless too,' I said. I decided not to mention that I had a hard time with Geoffrey. God, he took an age to emerge into the world. 'It's only fair that the fathers can have a relationship with their children. Just keep it formal if you don't want to share the experience.'

That evening, Gren told me that he'd had a similar conversation with Geoffrey, but he was perfectly happy with the situation. Gren had to spend some time hammering into him that he mustn't take advantage of girls. That sex is not always true love and that he should try to find one girl he could make a permanent connection with.

There was a tearful goodbye, and we flew home. Flights these days were erratic, and cancellations and delays made the experience less than enjoyable. It was a symptom of staff shortages. People were only working enough to keep a decent standard of living. Careers were no longer important. The spectre of death was looming over the horizon and the most intelligent and most innovative were trying to find ways to head northwards to delay the end.

When we arrived at Heathrow, we were both surprised to find Sandra and Malcolm waiting for us in arrivals. We'd been planning a train back to Guildford, but they knew which flight we were on and wanted to drive us home.

Once we were in the car, with the air-conditioning running and Malcolm driving, Sandra turned around to face us from the front seat.

'We wanted to give you some news,' she said. 'We're moving to Vågnes. Wils has found us a house beside them and I'm going to run an exclusive restaurant in the village.'

'How lovely. When do you go?' I asked. A huge weight had been lifted from my mind.

'The house contract went through yesterday so we're moving on the twenty-fourth,' she said.

'How did you get permission? In government, we'd heard that Norway was issuing no more visas,' Gren said.

'Wils managed to swing it for us. One of the Tromsø Idrettslag board of directors, you know, his football club, has a brother in the immigration office. One phone call and we were in,' said Sandra.

'Wonderful,' I said.

'Have you got the resources to equip the house for the rising heat?' asked Gren. 'Just being in the Arctic Circle will not be sufficient.'

'Yes, yes, we know,' said Sandra. 'Wils has told us he knows how to prepare with a turbine and solar panels. The two properties back onto each other and I'm sure we can come up with a way of producing some crops between us too.'

Malcolm spoke from the driver's seat, 'Working together, when the children grow up, it will be seven of us. We should be able to make a fist of it.'

'I do hope so,' I said, putting my hand onto Sandra's.

During the rest of the journey, Gren reminded them what we were doing at Fetlar, and by the time we got home, we all felt really good about their upcoming arrangement. We offered them a room for the night, but they needed to get home to pick the children up from friends in Beaulieu. It was only about ninety minutes this time of night.

HEAT

47 The Truth Will Out

Rioting continued unabated. The violence was against any form of authority and the government no longer met in London, but in a military base in some unknown location which looked a little like the Berkshire countryside.

After the murder of the three senior members of the cabinet in Downing Street two years previously, it was finally agreed that a truthful announcement should be made about the crisis. Sir Charles Browning, who had taken over as PM, was to appear on all networks of national television. He had, of course, also been the prime minister during Mindslip, so was the natural choice in a crisis. The USA, Canada, and most European countries were following suit. It was hoped that it might defuse the worst of the violence. I had my doubts.

The PM sat, in a lounge suit, behind a modern desk with a large window behind him. Outside, in the distance, oak and elm trees could be seen, sadly looking in poor shape from heat damage. Despite the increased rainfall, both in volume and frequency, most trees were finding it difficult to cope with the conditions.

He shuffled some papers and looked sombrely at the camera.

'Good evening fellow Britons.

'I am speaking to you tonight in order to give you some understanding of why the climate is so hot.

'Your government has done a good job of countering the effects of carbon dioxide emissions by reducing all use of fossil fuels whenever possible.

Wind, wave, tidal, and nuclear power took up the slack and, by now, temperatures should have been beginning to fall towards pre-1950 levels.

'Sadly, however, when Betelgeuse exploded in 2019, it did not just cause the frightening and disastrous swapping of minds, known today as Mindslip, but it also did something to our sun. The very best scientists in the world have been trying to understand the mechanism but, so far, without success.

'The sun reached its periodic solar maximum in 2025 and should then have returned to normal, something that had happened for as long as records have been kept. Unfortunately, it did not happen on this occasion, and we are now in the seventeenth year of continually increasing output. Our own sun is burning up the world and there is nothing we can do about it.

'Two years ago, a terrorist organisation murdered my predecessor plus the home secretary and cabinet secretary. I need you to understand that the heat is not their fault and never was. They had been working tirelessly to reverse it, again, without success. We were wrong to hide the truth from you but that should never have resulted in the death of people dedicated to trying to do the best for their people.

'I am now leading a government of national unity to maintain control. Riots and violence will be swiftly stopped, and the army will be assisting the police.

'You might be wondering what is going to happen about the rising temperatures. Work has been going on behind the scenes. Scientists tell us that the sun should return to normal at some point, but we do not know when that will be. It could be tomorrow, or it could be more than a decade ahead. Rioting and violence will not help anyone. It will most certainly not reduce the heat. In fact, the disruption caused will make life *more* difficult for everyone. That is in no one's best interests.

'It is your government's duty to plan ahead as best we can in a crisis for all of our people. You may already be aware that migrant boats are being turned away. We do this humanely, forcing them back to France, Belgium, Holland, and Spain. The main influx from the Mediterranean is not affecting us, but the northern Mediterranean countries have been repelling migrants for several years. They are, of course, trying to do the best for their own populations, but it is sad for me to report that boats crossing the Mediterranean are being sunk if they do not willingly return to North Africa. There have been many skirmishes, and much loss of life. The poor people are trying to escape death from heat far worse than we are so far experiencing here.

'Your government has been working with other nations to create four refuges. One is in Antarctica, one on the moon, one in orbit near the International Space Station and one is a starship heading for another Earth-like world called Kepler-452 B.

'I don't want to give false hope, so I will tell you right now that all the people going to the refuges have already been chosen. No government or civil service individuals were selected. The choice was made on academic ability, physical fitness, and intelligence alone. It was done anonymously, and no one was able to influence who was chosen and who was not.

'The rest of us must take our chances and hope that the sun will reverse its relentless output of heat. That includes me and all the ministers of the government of national unity. We will live or die with you. There is no special treatment for us.

'It is important for everyone that the economy does not completely break down otherwise we will all suffer even more, so, please, everyone, continue in your work for as long as you are able. If you cannot complete a full day's work, then do what you can. Anything you can do will help us all.

'I have made this honest broadcast to fully inform you of the situation. I'm sorry that it is such bad news. I promise to continue to update you in the coming weeks and months. Over the next few days there will be documentaries explaining about the refuges. They are the hope for the future of humankind.'

Sir Charles sat back in his chair, stared pointedly at the camera, and finished with, 'God save us all.'

2046

48 Departure

We had to change flights four times when we headed to Alaska for the final visit in 2046. It needed three stopovers, and we were actually stuck in Chicago for three days. We thought we might miss the final opportunity to see our children, but at the last minute, we got a connection into Anchorage and on to the space centre.

No hugs or cuddles this time. We were separated from Caroline and Geoffrey by a double-glazed glass wall. They'd been in isolation for the last three months to prevent any infections or diseases being taken into the community. Genetic banks of many diseases would be taken with them, of course, so that scientists would have something to work with if they encountered diseases on Kepler-452 B, but they were trying to avoid outbreaks during the journey. In such an enclosed environment some viruses and diseases could easily become rampant.

We had the memory of a final holiday at Fetlar before they entered quarantine. Those were the last hugs we would ever have from our children. There were, of course, floods of tears on both sides of the glass partition. We were in a room-sized cubicle so at least it was private. Caroline pressed her hand against the window, and I mirrored it with mine. Oh, how I wished we could touch each other. Is it possible to express love through a protective screen? We did our best.

The permitted hour seemed to pass in minutes, then one of the older crew came to take our offspring away to begin the rest of their lives in a starship. Geoffrey just twenty, and Caroline twenty-two. They'd never go for another drive in the country, stand on the rugged cliffs of Shetland, or feel the wind in their hair. They'd never see animals again, never cuddle a cat or pat a dog. So sad. Yes, it was also a great adventure, but I worried about that isolation from the real world I had enjoyed. Of course, the new real world was increasingly being burned to a cinder, and they were far better out of it.

Gren shouted, 'Love you always,' as they stood in the cubicle doorway and turned to look at us for that final time. Caroline mouthed her love to us and Geoffrey just waved casually and hurried away. I saw tears in his eyes. He was trying to be brave. So was I, and utterly failing.

We were ushered out of the meeting area and guided to a large theatre where we sat for the next six hours until one of the SpaceX Starships took off with our children and almost a hundred others on their journey into space. I couldn't hold back my tears and, to be honest, neither could Gren.

We felt a little better when the announcement was made that the ship had achieved orbit and was on course to the Kepler starship. The flights were all being made at the end of a flare cycle, so, with good fortune, they would not be harmed during the two-day journey.

It would take four flare cycles before the entire crew would be in orbit and on to the Kepler, the ship which would be first to see humankind break free of the solar system, but in the most horrible circumstances.

It took almost four days for us to get back to Lerwick and our lovely hideaway at Hermaness. Airports were becoming chaotic, and the heat was affecting the operation of even the most sophisticated planes. There had been many crashes in the last few years put down to extreme heat.

The next day at Fetlar was a really bad day. Outside the temperature reached fifty-five and we decided only to venture out briefly to visit the deep freeze and check that all the batteries were charging efficiently. Gren had bought eight additional batteries which were to be used as backups in case of breakdowns. He'd also installed a couple in the house for emergencies. I was now fifty-one and Gren pushing sixty, but we were both pretty healthy. We could do no more to secure our future and were relieved that all of our children were now as safe as they could possibly be, perhaps safer. I kept up to date with scientific news about the sun and was still hopeful that it would peak before all life on Earth were extinguished.

Hopefully, our careful planning would give us a decade or two as long as the sun continued to shine not too brightly, the rain continued to fall, and the wind continued to blow. Given the prevailing wind was in from the Atlantic, those latter factors could almost be guaranteed. Gren had laid in two radiation-proof, hazardous-materials resistant suits rated to 1,000°C. They had built-in respirators and could be sealed with hazmat tape. They would get us to and from the power room, fridge and freezer, in almost any conditions, although I didn't fancy the idea of trying to walk down to the cove in one. They were very cumbersome and quite heavy. Gren built a special wardrobe for them in the hallway so that we would not be seeing them every day as a permanent reminder of the horror which might be in store for us during the years to come.

    The wee burn which ran past the house to the sea was still fast flowing. The heat we were experiencing was matched by regular rainstorms, sometimes so torrential that the burn overflowed and flooded the garden area which faced the cove. The vegetable area and chicken compound, behind the house, were well drained and high enough to avoid flooding, as was the house itself, the steading and power room. The hens and cockerels seemed perfectly happy scratching around outside in the rain or sun, but we noticed that they regularly entered the air-conditioned coop through the hen flap. They might be stupid, but weren't daft.

    We were okay indoors during these deluges. The air-con coped with the heat and Gren had four spare aircon units stored with the batteries as emergency replacements. The cost had been phenomenal, but money was losing its value as the days passed anyway. We couldn't even sell the house in Guildford. It now sat empty and abandoned. The knowledge that my darling wife, the original Caroline, was buried under the cherry tree in the garden made me tearful.

HEAT

Two days later, the heat was back to a manageable forty-six and, in steady rain, we ventured down to the cove. We rowed out fifty metres to the lobster buoys. We'd be eating fresh lobster tonight and we had two more and a crab to add to the freezer supply. Lobster was our favourite meal and Gren had turned it into a new speciality, baking the lobster with herbs and vegetable spread, together with spiced potato rösti, and a soya based hollandaise sauce. We'd long been without dairy products although we had twenty-four pints of milk and six pints of cream in the freezer for when we felt the need to splurge. Gren's stroganoff was off the menu these days. The only meat readily to hand was chicken, although I had managed to shoot a rabbit now and again, but neither of us enjoyed preparing them for the oven. Gren kept threatening to shoot a deer, but no luck so far. There were some steaks in the freezer, but we considered them untouchable. Perhaps on a very special occasion. We knew that certain items in the freezer would possibly need to last us for the rest of our lives.

My biggest fear was that one or other of us would fall ill. We'd tried to mitigate that by having thorough checkups each year, including both CT and MRI body scans. Nothing showed up, but the worry would always be there in the future.

It was now too dangerous to go into Lerwick unnecessarily as there were increasing numbers of climate-migrants and food supplies were not keeping up with needs. People were starving or attacking each other over perceived injustices. We felt it was better to keep clear. Our electric all-wheel-drive vehicle could also be a target during periods of anarchy, and we wouldn't want anyone following us back to our hideaway either. A drawer in the hallway held two loaded revolvers and several boxes of ammunition. We had a taser and crossbow with bolts hidden at the back of the top shelf of our wardrobe plus the rifle and shotgun. Gren had removed the Fetlar and PRIVATE signs at the end of the track.

Our home was now suitably anonymous.

HEAT

49 Was Anywhere Safe?

The Kirkenes Snowhotel, which had been built from fresh snow every winter for decades was finally absent. For the first time ever, there had not been sufficient snow for its construction. In fact, there had been barely a centimetre of snow during the winter of 2045 and now the spring temperature was starting to climb.

The small town, only a kilometre from the Russian border, had a population of just over three thousand five hundred. The "just over" included a fair number of illegal migrants to whom the Norwegian government turned a blind eye. Many camped out in the woodland on the Bøkfjorden, an arm of a larger fjord which ran out into the Barents Sea in the Arctic. Among them were Destri, Bright, Mariam, and Edu. They'd been joined by Dirk, a South African who had married Mariam. She was now heavy with their first child but agonised over whether it was right to bring children into this apparently dying world.

Destri had found that he had a knack for sea-angling and Edu discovered that he was a dead shot and had developed a talent for hunting. With Dirk, the three men managed to keep the family self-sufficient with fish, deer, and rabbits. Dirk took rabbits into other encampments and traded them for vegetables, milk, and cheese.

Mariam and Bright looked after the two tents and kept the clothes clean and dry. Life was bearable. They'd been told that the temperature would still get to fifty Celsius in the summer, but it was so much better than it had been in the south of Sweden and

Denmark. There was no longer any news from Toase and Destri reckoned there'd be few people still alive there, so close to the equator.

What had happened to the world? This seemed worse than anything fossil fuels could have caused. He remembered his conversation with the doctor when his father had died from the heat over fourteen before. They'd wondered if this might be the end of the world. Looked as if it might be.

But they were safe for now. They had food, two tents for shelter, the heat was bearable, the fishing good, and Edu's skill with bow and arrow kept them in meat. Dirk was a great negotiator and anything they wanted, he could find for them, as long as the supply of rabbits held out – and, so far, that seemed endless.

50 Communication

I was reading a news site on the computer one afternoon, about three months after the children had blasted off for the Kepler. There was an incoming communication. I thought it might be Sandra or Wilson, but no, it was a video from the Kepler starship. I pressed play and there were Geoffrey's and Caroline's smiling faces. They were sitting on a couch looking towards the camera. In unison, they said, 'Hello, Mum, Dad. Are you sitting comfortably?'

I hit pause and called Gren through from the kitchen to see. We both pulled up chairs and watched the screen intently. We'd already had several iViz calls, but the last one saw the time delay becoming tiresome. Almost a minute and it would only get worse. Real conversations were impossible. Since then, communication had been by email. This recorded video was a new development.

I pressed play.

'Hello, Mum, Dad. Are you sitting comfortably?' they both said.

Caroline continued, 'We thought you'd like an update. I've been keeping a journal since our last live call. So, here we go. Geoff will chip in when he has something to add.'

They looked at each other and back at the camera. They both looked really well. Young adults now. They were wearing Bermuda style shorts and loose T-shirts with Kepler logos.

'We're still accelerating at just over one tenth of a gravity. The ship can't achieve more than that because of some Coriolis thingamy.'

'It's not a thingamy,' broke in Geoffrey. 'Mum will know what it is. Because we're accelerating forward and also rotating to provide some gravity, weird things can happen if you suddenly change direction inside the ship. So, at a tenth of a gravity it has hardly any effect unless you're near the hub. Dad, ask Mum. She can explain it to you.'

'Okay,' continued Caroline, 'This Coriolis thingy stops us accelerating faster. The captain tells us we're now out of danger from any flares and the water jacket in the hull of the ship is protecting us from deep radiation.'

'Deep *space* radiation,' said Geoffrey.

Caroline looked daggers at her brother.

'We're both keeping well and now have apartments side by side. I've made lots of friends in the botany section and I spend much of my time with them in the hydroponics gardens. Everything is going very well in there and it's compartmentalised so that any diseases can't spread. We must walk through disinfectant troughs if we're moving between sections.'

'Tell them about Joe,' insisted Geoffrey.

Now, Caroline looked really annoyed and scowled at Geoffrey.

'Shut up, Geoff. It's nothing.' She looked embarrassed. She continued in a softer, more gentle tone, 'I've been dating a guy called Joe. We're little more than friends, but we enjoy each other's company.'

'I caught them snogging!' said Geoffrey triumphantly.

'Shut up! Just 'cos you can't get a girlfriend,' she said and poked him in the arm, causing him to sit still. 'Anyway, there's a lot to do on board. We play basketball in one of the larger areas and that's when we do notice the Coriolis thingy. You throw the ball, and you can never be certain it's going where you're looking. Makes the game more difficult. It doesn't swerve by much, but it is noticeable if the distance is greater.'

'I play five-a-side football, and we see it happen sometimes too. There's also American football and it's worse for that with long passes,' said Geoffrey.

'Food is good,' said Caroline. 'We were both worried that it might be tasteless, but there are synthetic meats we produce on board, and they make a mean beefburger. We grow our own onions and tomatoes so we can make ketchup as well.'

'Hey,' said Geoffrey, 'I've found I'm pretty good at chess. There's a tournament next week. I'll let you know how I get on.'

'I'm luckier than Geoff with work, because we're carrying out real duties in the hydroponics…'

Geoffrey said, 'Yes. Most of the time I'm studying, but it's really interesting stuff. I've been helping a couple of physicists who are looking at ways to improve the ship's dust shield. That could be really important in the future when we're travelling at a decent fraction of the speed of light.'

'That's it for now. We have a file size limit on these videos. Bye, Mum, Dad,' said Caroline. 'Love you both.'

'Love you,' said Geoffrey.

There was a five second credit and ship's logo then the video ended.

'That was good,' I said. I turned and found Gren in tears. It really got to him.

2048

51 Belts and Braces

The heat was now regularly over fifty-five and trips outside were fewer and farther between. Sol was not giving us a break. I was one of the so-called experts who thought the sun would return to its normal output eventually, but I was changing my mind. It might well do so, but not before it destroyed all life on Earth.

The refuge in Antarctica had long since been sealed, apart from their monitored exterior compounds which could be visited for short periods when the heat was not too excessive. Eventually it would be 'no one in and no one out'. The residents were as safe as technology could make them, but it was a life which would have to be lived underground. Some of the selected residents had formed a military force which was responsible for repelling any aggressive attempts to breach the refuge's security. There had been several mob attacks, but they were now more seldom. The military had a policy to shoot on sight and that seemed to ensure their security – so far.

How long could we hold out in our Shetland retreat? As long as our power supply held good, the river continued to flow, and we could make short sorties to gather our crop and reach the refrigerated lorry, we'd survive. Gren had a second wind turbine on order, but it hadn't arrived so far, and we were concerned it might have been hijacked en route. We also continued to make dashes down to the cove to see if there were any crabs or lobsters, but the warm sea was having an effect on marine life and sometimes the firth was full of jellyfish. We'd tried collecting some and searched online for how to cook them but cleaning them was messy and difficult. They also deteriorated very quickly in the heat. Not bad eating, though, if you like unusual crispy Asian cuisine. There were fewer crabs in our baskets, but lobsters seemed to still be in good supply.

Our life settled down into a simple routine. Reading, watching our vast collection of DVDs, cooking, playing both computer and card games. When our satellite Internet was operating, we tried to keep abreast of worldwide events and downloaded documentaries and dramas. The signal was down increasingly frequently, and the news was full of dreadful violence as people tried to move north. Northern nations had taken to militarising their defences and starvation was now a big problem worldwide, particularly for countries in lower latitudes. It was dreadful to see all the starving people, including babies, but nothing could be done for them. Even the northern countries were struggling to feed their populations. Almost no news was emerging from Central African and Central American countries. India had declared war on Sri Lanka, and in the north of the most populous democratic nation, the people were trying to take over the Himalayas to get some respite from the rising temperatures. What a mess. The epitome of hell on earth.

At night, awaiting the arrival of sleep, we held hands or cuddled and speculated about how our children might be getting on aboard the Kepler. We hoped they were as happy as we were. Despite the horrible situation, we'd achieved everything we really wanted to do. Living in our little paradise on Shetland was enough for us.

HEAT

52 Speed and Distance

We continued to communicate with the children, sending videos every couple of weeks, and receiving theirs equally often. A new one had just arrived. Gren was in the power room so I called him on our walkie-talkie to come in as soon as he could. I was so impatient to hear what the space adventurers were doing now.

We used the short-range radio rather than mobile phones as the latter could be traced and we most certainly no longer wanted to be found. The authorities might still be able to track us, but it was migrants or criminals which worried us, and they'd be unlikely to have the technology to pick up short-range radio. Even Haroldswick was too dangerous to approach with gangs looking out for anything which they could steal.

'Fifty-two outside,' he said, pulling off a soaking wet T-shirt, towelling himself dry, and slipping on a clean one. He also pulled on a dry pair of shorts. He'd kicked his shoes off in the hall and leaned over the air conditioner for some instant respite from the temperature outside.

'Come on. Hurry up,' I said as I heard him fetch something from the kitchen. A pack of homemade crisps. I looked at the clock. I supposed it was almost lunchtime.

'Call from Kepler,' I said and hit play on the screen. Instead of appearing on the computer, I'd rigged it to appear on the main TV.

'Hi, Mum, Dad,' said a smiling Caroline. She had a small handset and pressed one of the buttons.

The video zoomed out and suddenly there were two people there. 'This is Graham,' she said.

I wondered what had happened to Joe, Pete, Antoine, David, and Percy. She was leaving boyfriends in her wake. There had been none mentioned recently.

'Hello, Mr Pointer and Dr Arnold. I'm Graham Hodder,' the young man said in an Irish accent. 'Cas and I have been an item for a couple of months.'

It was difficult to tell while he was sitting, but he seemed to be a fairly well-built lad. Blond hair, clean shaven, blue eyes.

'It's serious, Mum, Dad. We entered a civil partnership yesterday,' she said, proudly leaning forward and showing a gold band on the third finger of her left hand. She turned to Graham and kissed his cheek then encircled him with her arm and pulled him closer.

Then a real surprise for us. A ginger cat wandered across the foreground. Caroline laughed, 'That's Jasper, one of the ship's cats. He visits us sometimes. We discovered that some cats and guinea pigs had secretly been brought aboard for us.'

'Jasper loves Cas,' said Graham.

'He does spend a lot of time with us. Anyway, Graham and I knew it was the real thing. I do so love him, and I think he loves me too.'

'I do,' he interjected.

'And... guess what... we've been told we can start a baby as I'm over twenty-five. What do you think about that? I do hope you like him. He's lovely.'

I could see the boy blushing.

'I'm a year older than Cas,' he said. 'She wants me to tell you a bit about myself. I'm training to be an astronautical engineer and have an engineering degree. I work with a team of people keeping our air regeneration system in good nick.'

'He moved into my apartment yesterday. I've got more space than him. Do let me know you love him too,' she said. 'I'm sharing this file size with Geoff. You'll see him in a second or two. Bye to you two.' She waved, blew a kiss and Graham waved too.

Suddenly, Geoffrey was on the screen, sitting on his own on a couch and holding something golden.

'Hi, Mum, Dad.' He pushed the object towards the camera, and it was clearly a golden bishop, as in a chess set. 'I won the regional championship on Saturday. That's the second time. I'm in the Port Side finals in two weeks. Eight of us. If I can win that I'll go for the Kepler championship. I'm good, but not sure I'm *that* good. There's a girl called Joanna Baker and she's brilliant. I've played her six times, and she's wiped me out every time.'

He reached over to the side table and put the bishop into the precise centre of it, moved it a millimetre or two each way, then adjusted it so that the mitre faced the camera. He'd always had a touch of OCD.

'You know about Cas and Gray. He's quite nice and he does seem to get on well with her. They've been given permission to have a baby soon, so I'll be an uncle. I know I'm uncle to Emma, Pat, and Linda, but it'll be different when Cas has a baby. Closer somehow.'

He slouched back into the couch and continued. 'I've got a new girlfriend, Jessica.' He leaned forward and thrust a picture of a very attractive blonde towards the camera. It went out of focus, but she looked very pretty.

'She's learning to chef. I told her about my half-sister, Sandra being a Michelin-starred chef, and she was soooooo impressed. Might ask Sandra if she could send a few words of encouragement to her. She didn't reply to my last call. Will you mention it to her. Jess would be so appreciative.'

He picked up a small tablet and touched the screen. 'Thought you'd like to know, Mum. We just passed one hundred billion miles from Earth. Billion, not million, and the gauge in the leisure dome says we're doing over fifteen million miles per hour. We just covered more than forty thousand miles while I was saying that last sentence. That's over four thousand miles per second. Can you believe that?' He laid the tablet down and looked a little sad.

'Hope you're both well. I often think about your hideaway and going down to the fjord to get lobsters. Take care. Running out of file size. I'll see if Jess will talk to you next time. Byeeee!' The screen showed the usual Kepler logo and went blank.

'Well,' I said. 'I'm glad Cas has found someone nice. She seems excited about the baby.'

'Yes,' agreed Gren. 'She was concerned about having to have a child with a donor. Much nicer that it's a love child.'

'I didn't know there were ship's cats. That's nice,' I said.

'It is. Nice touch. She mentioned guinea pigs too.'

'I suppose their small enough not to eat too much and it's lovely for the passengers to have a few pets,' I said.

Gren squeezed my thigh. 'Must get back out to the power room,' he said, jumping up. 'I was halfway through swapping two of the batteries.'

'Is that really necessary?'

'Sure is. Use each one sparingly and they'll last longer. Want anything from the lorry when I come back in?'

'Yes. A tub of vegetable spread, half a dozen eggs, and some bread mix. Thanks, Gren.'

HEAT

53 The Storm

We believed we'd thought of everything, but, as always when you're feeling as if you've covered every eventuality, something totally unexpected spoils the party.

In November 2048, the days in Shetland were approaching their shortest, fewer than six daylight hours, and the heat continued to be relentless, rarely dropping below fifty degrees. Venturing outside at such temperatures had to be restricted to as few minutes as possible. The air-conditioned henhouse still provided us with a good supply of eggs and continual spraying of the garden allowed some vegetables to survive, although, sadly, potatoes were one of the casualties.

A continual flow of winter low-pressure systems pushed in from the Atlantic and it rained almost continually. We wouldn't suffer from any lack of water, that was for sure.

On Sunday, the twenty-second of November all our plans turned to stone. It was still dark, nine in the morning, when a brilliant flash coupled with an enormous explosion somewhere outside shook the entire house. The air-con stopped immediately. The lights flickered twice then died, yet the kitchen, where I was standing was lit up with a flickering orange glow. What could it be? I quickly realised that the power room was on fire.

Fear filled my heart. 'Gren! Fire!' I screamed.

He ran through in his dressing gown, and we looked in horror at the blaze. 'God, the turbine's gone,' he said.

'Stopped?'

'No, look! It's gone! Completely gone.'

I squinted past the burning power room and could see that the turbine tower was truncated. At about five metres it was broken in two leaving jagged fragments of fibreglass pointing accusingly towards the heavens. It really had gone.

The sky lit up brilliant white as lightning struck part of the solar panel array. We almost jumped out of our skins. The crash of thunder rolled on for almost a minute and torrential rain fell. Thankfully, it seemed to be having a beneficial effect on the power room fire. The flames were subsiding, doused by the persistent warm deluge.

'I daren't go out in this,' said Gren.

'No,' I agreed as another bolt of lightning struck the remains of the turbine tower. The noise was deafening.

'I'll get dressed,' said Gren, dashing out of the kitchen. He returned a minute later in denim shorts and a T-shirt which looked bizarre with his wellington boots and shoulder length hair and beard.

'Wait for the storm to pass,' I said. 'You don't want to get struck by lightning.'

'No,' he agreed, 'but get your wellies on ready. I'll need help when I venture out.'

'Air-con's off,' I said.

'The cable from the power room must have shorted. Might be a trip switch. I'll check it all out when we can leave the house.'

Trip switch my arse, I thought. He's trying to soften the blow.

HEAT

The fire was dying, and the pale glow of Shetland's winter sun was spreading over the horizon. It didn't ease our concerns. The roof of the power room seemed to have been ripped off. The turbine had fallen onto the lorry's roof, partially demolishing that too, and then it had rolled over onto the bank of solar panels destroying them. This was not a good situation. Could it be repaired?

I heard a noise from the hallway and found Gren using a torch to check the two spare batteries in the store cupboard.

'These are okay,' he said. 'I knew it was wise to have two on charge in the house.'

'Are they charged?'

'Oh, yes. Both full,' he said as he checked out the isolating switches. 'The charge input switch tripped but nothing worse.'

He pulled on an isolating lever which snapped shut and the lights flickered and came on. A minute later, the barely audible whoosh of the air-conditioning returned, and it slowly began to battle the heat indoors which had begun to rise worryingly swiftly.

'How long will those last?' I asked.

'Forty-eight hours unless I can get a connection to the remaining solar panels,' said Gren. He went into the lounge, cut the air-con unit and lights, came out, closed the door, then did the same with the bedroom. 'Leave the bathroom and kitchen doors open. I'll cut the units in the hall and bathroom to save power. The kitchen air-con unit should be able to cope with that much volume.'

HEAT

'Do you think it's fixable?' I asked, looking into Gren's eyes. His expression held little hope.

'We can't do anything until the storm finishes. We need to inspect the battery room.'

'I'll make some breakfast,' I said and began to prepare poached eggs on toast and coffee.

We sat in silence at the kitchen table as daylight finally took control of the sky. It was amazing how much heat and how little light it provided this far north in winter. The thunderstorm eased itself slowly eastwards, God's flashlight occasionally lighting up the firth and the distant hills towards SaxaVord.

We could do nothing but wait. Eventually, the thunder faded into the distance. Had the storm finally passed us by?

'No lightning for a while,' said Gren shortly. 'Think we'd better take a look outside.'

We both tugged our wellies on again, pulled light plastic macs over our shoulders, opened the front door, and stood in the porch to get used to the heat before venturing to the power room.

'The Henhouse is burned out,' I said.

Gren followed my gaze. The henhouse backed on to the power room and had obviously caught fire at the same time. I cried. All our lovely, faithful laying hens would have been incinerated. Gren put his arm around my shoulders and pulled me to him. 'And the Range Rover, look!'

The car was burning, not as wildly as the chicken house had done, but it would never be driven again. The lightning must have struck it through the charging cable.

HEAT

We stood in our embrace. Each with our own thoughts for a minute, but with the oppressive heat, we knew we needed to get to work. It so sapped your strength. We bowed our heads and ran to the power room door. Gren unlocked it and when he pulled, it fell off its hinges almost knocking us over. It caught Gren's arm, and I saw blood.

'You're hurt,' I shouted.

'It's nothing. One of the batteries must have been thrown across the room and was leaning against the door. There must have been a veritable explosion inside when the lightning struck.

The roof was gone, and rain was cascading over the equipment and bouncing off the floor. The eight batteries were burned black, and the switching gear had been incinerated. Strands of heavy electric cabling were blackened and bared. Despite the rain, it was still smouldering. I didn't need Gren to tell me that the power room would never work again.

We walked around the outside and climbed the steps to the door of the refrigerated lorry. Gren pulled it open, and a flood of water rushed outwards almost sweeping us off the steps.

'Both of the skins of the roof must have gone,' he said. 'The turbine must still have been spinning when it fell. We'll need to salvage some food.' He picked some boxes off the floor and shook his head. 'What a mess!'

'What about the solar panels?' I asked above the sound of the rain pounding the remains of the lorry's metal roof.

HEAT

We clambered down the steps and ran over to the main array. 'Half a dozen might be okay, but the cables are burned out.'

'There's still those on the house roof,' I said.

Gren's expression did not encourage me. 'It's winter. They won't even power what we're running now. Let's get inside and assess our situation.'

Gren quickly inspected each of the remaining solar panels, then we ran back to the house and ducked into the kitchen where we shook off our plastic macs and drank some iced elderflower cordial to bring our body temperatures back to normal.

'What do we need to do?' I asked but when I looked up for his response, I could see that he was in floods of tears. I knew it must be hopeless. Gren was an amazingly resourceful individual. For him to be in such a state, our circumstances must be dire.

I pulled my chair around the table, butted it up against his and encircled his shoulders. We both cried. Other than the sobbing, the silence continued, only disturbed by the faint whooshing sound of the air-con running in the background.

Eventually – was it minutes or close to an hour – I asked, 'How long have we got?'

He sat upright and held my hands on the tabletop. He said, 'The panels on the roof will give us about a third of our power needs. The batteries in the cupboard will last about two days. We'll be out of power by Tuesday morning, so we have today, and Monday.'

We sat quietly. I asked, 'Anything we can do to mitigate that?'

'I don't have enough cable to connect the undamaged panels to the house system. Even if I did, it wouldn't add more than half a day,' he replied. 'The turbine was essential for the winter.'

'I guess the one on order is lost in transit.'

'Yes. Probably stolen. We've no way to get to town. Certainly not quickly enough and very few businesses are still operating. The generator would need to be imported. Angie has gone to live with his children in the Faroes. He's the only one I could call upon for a lift into Haroldswick. We've hidden ourselves away too effectively. There might be some heavy duty cabling available at Mackays, but that's not going to save us. Why on Earth didn't I chase that spare turbine harder?'

'Don't blame yourself. There was nothing wrong with our planning. It might have been struck too if we did have it.'

'Bad mistake not having a second turbine,' said Gren, holding his head in his hands.

'I wonder if Wils or Sands could take us in?' I mused.

'I was talking to Wils. I've been right through his plans with him. There are three of them and now Sands is there, that makes seven. They've barely enough space and resources for themselves. Taking us in could make the difference between failure and success.'

'No. We mustn't burden them.'

'Anyway, I don't fancy a thirty-mile hike in this heat to try to find another vehicle. We'd need to get to Lerwick, really, and that's out of the question. And what do we do then? Cross the North Sea somehow? We'd just be more illegal immigrants!'

I shrugged.

'Coming back here, loading up with anything useful and then trying to get to Norway through hordes of panicking migrants... no, it isn't on. Someone would rob or kill us.'

'You're right,' I agreed. 'Better make the best of it here.'

'We've had it, haven't we?'

'Think so,' I replied, and we sat quietly, holding hands.

Our silent pondering continued for another hour.

I jumped up. 'Come on,' I said. 'I need things from the lorry. Come with me.'

He looked a broken man when he gazed up at my sudden enthusiasm but pulled himself to his feet. 'What do you need?'

'Never you mind. Just come and help,' I said, pulling on my wellington boots and kicking his over to him.

Gren followed me as if in a daze. I carried a couple of supermarket shopping bags and headed for the broken refrigerator lorry. Again, water flooded out of the door. It was quite dark inside and I'd brought the large torch.

I picked my way through the debris from the roof to the freezer section at the rear of the trailer. I tried to open it, but it seemed to be jammed.

'Can you help?' I asked.

He grunted and squeezed past me to yank on the door. Eventually it gave way to his attack and as it opened, even more water flooded along the floor. The freezer section, too, had a hole in the roof.

I gave him the torch and said, 'Point it where I'm looking.'

I filled the first bag with three frozen quarts of milk, a couple of frozen pints of cream, two blocks of butter, then turned to the opposite section and took some fillet steaks and the two lobsters we'd kept from our last foray to the cove. I passed the full bag to him and continued to select delicacies from the shelves.

As we passed back through the fridge area, I took canned new potatoes, frozen asparagus, tins of rice pudding, mushrooms, and more vegetables, a dozen eggs, olive oil and some dried herbs.

'That's it,' I said. 'Let's get back.'

I hurried back to the house with Gren still following me, lethargic and disinterested. In the kitchen, I sorted through the goods then went through to the lounge and bedroom and turned on the air-con again.

'What are you doing?' he asked, trying to hold me back. 'You're just going to drain the batteries.'

I gripped his arm, spun him around, pinned him to the wall by his shoulders, and said, 'Darling, we've a couple of days left to live. I'm not going to spend them trying to eke out the power or eating poorly. Tonight, its fillet steak, mushrooms and roasted new potatoes and tomorrow the lobsters cooked in cream with herbs and spices.' He looked at me as if I was mad.

'Go and get a bottle of that Margaux and let it breathe. Life is for living, let's live! Put a bottle of Gewurztraminer in the fridge for tomorrow.'

'But…'

'No buts, go get the wine, it's already getting dark, and I want to watch one of our favourite films before we eat.'

He looked at me, wide eyed. I smiled and kissed him. 'Do you love me?' I asked.

'God, yes.'

'Then *show* it! We knew this day would come, it's a shame it was sooner than we'd hoped. I've no regrets. Have you?'

He stood in silence, looking lost and bemused, then I saw a strange transformation come over his face, and he smiled, chuckled, and began to sing, 'Regrets, I've had a few, but then again, too few to mention…'

I laughed, punched him playfully in the ribs, and said, 'Oh, God! Stop singing. It's worse than the heat!' He laughed too. We hugged and he said, 'What do you want to watch?'

'*As Good as it Gets*. It's crazy enough for both of us.'

'I'll go find it!'

'I'll do the prep for dinner. Real steaks! Can't wait,' I called after him.

Gren busied himself searching our DVD and digital collection.

∞∞∞∞∞∞∞∞∞∞

'That was wonderful,' he said after our lobster meal the next evening.

'Yes, you can't beat lobster and so good to cook with real cream, such a treat. Didn't realise how much I'd missed it.'

'You got the herbs just right – perfect! And the wine was superb. I forgot I had that bottle of Hugel Gewurztraminer Vendange Tardive.'

'Yes. Perfect,' I said. He stacked our plates and took them to the sink.

I heard him fussing around in the kitchen and went through to find out what was holding him up. He was washing up.

'Bit of a waste of time,' I said.

'No. Wouldn't want anyone to find the place untidy, Beth. One day survivors may come looking. Could even be one of your two trying to find us.'

He was right, of course. I dried the last of the cutlery and we went through to the lounge. The rain had paused, and a full moon's silvery luminescence was intermittently reflecting off the firth through the breaks in the cloud cover. It looked so beautiful. With the air-conditioning running, we were isolated from the outside and its brutal, almost alien, environment.

'How lovely,' I said, standing in the window. I felt his arm encircle my waist, sliding under my loose top.

'Beautiful. I wonder how the children are doing,' he said.

'As long as they're happy. We could do no more for them. They're now travelling at millions of miles per hour. They're about twenty times the distance of Pluto now.'

The moon disappeared behind a bank of clouds and suddenly there were colours in the sky. The misbehaving sun was treating us to the most amazing aurora, pink and green bands wheeled around above the northern side of the firth.

'Wow, astonishing,' said Gren.

We watched for twenty minutes until the clouds moved north and again revealed the moon and its sparkling reflections on the waves in the cove.

'Stunning,' I said.

It clouded over and I sat at the computer.

'Thank goodness the Internet is back,' I said.

I hammered out a goodbye reply to Kepler's last message while he stood and watched, telling me to add this or that into the message. It probably wouldn't reach them for weeks. I repeated it for Wilson and Sandra. I hoped they'd have more luck than us. At least they were inside the Arctic Circle.

'That's done,' I said. I turned the computer off and disconnected the router.

'What did you say to your two?'

'Told them all it was the *big goodbye*, and they mustn't come looking,' I replied.

'Guessed so. Best thing really.'

We walked over to the window, stood hand in hand, and stared out as the clouds broke and allowed another glimpse of the moonlit cove, the shadowy cliffs, and the sparkling waves tumbling lazily up the firth.

'We have our little paradise,' he whispered.

'Make love to me.'

HEAT

'My thoughts entirely,' he responded, pulling on my hand as he led me through to the bedroom.

Our final lovemaking was not quite as frantic as our first, but possibly even more beautiful. We lay together, holding hands, legs intertwined, and talking in whispers.

He got up. I admired his nakedness as he opened the chest of drawers and took a couple of small white boxes from where he'd secreted them at the back of the drawer. He showed me them. 'Time for these?' he asked.

I knew what they were. Government ministers had been given them when the decision was made that officials could not be selected for the refuges.

'I guess so,' I said and kissed him for a final time.

There was one each. We talked for a while, remembering happier and more amusing times. We reached a natural break in our remembering. There really was nothing left to say. Our love for each other said it all.

We swallowed the tablets with a drink of water. They promised to be effective in six minutes. Painless, just like falling asleep.

Time was passing. So little of it left.

'Life was good, wasn't it?' he asked.

'Wouldn't have missed it for the world,' I replied.

We looked into each other's eyes. I saw his eyelids flicker and droop. His head fell limply onto the pillow. The end must be close for me too. I squeezed his hand as tightly as I was able.

HEAT

54 Kepler-452 B

The Kepler spent half of its journey in reverse, slowing down at the same rate at which it had accelerated during the early part of the trip. At the midway point, the entire ship swivelled through one hundred and eighty degrees. Then the bridge faced backwards, and the ion drive was burning its way through the scarce molecules of empty space before it, destroying anything which entered the ejected material now being allowed to fan out to cover the whole diameter of the main disc of the ship. If the scientists had got it right, this would protect the vessel from dust impacts. At close to the speed of light, a collision with a grain of sand could cause huge destruction.

Automatic systems guided the enormous spinning starship through interstellar space, carrying its precious cargo of human beings searching for a new start in an unforgiving universe. As the Kepler-452 system started to separate into individual planets and moons, the computers began their analysis, still more than a year before arrival. A region of asteroids and heavy dust was encountered, a landmark for the vessel, it was now in the system which was intended to offer the new home and new hope.

Next, two gas giants, one a turquoise hue and another with a ghostly rosy ring, its gaseous atmosphere almost glowing with a welcoming honey tint in the light of the central star.

The four inner planets were not all small and rocky. Planet C was another gas giant, not as large as those in the farther reaches of the system, but almost the size of Neptune. It bore dozens of gas bands in all the colours of the rainbow, a beautiful, but deadly world with enormous gravity and noxious atmosphere. The other three were rocky worlds.

D was a cold and desert grey world in an eccentric orbit which indicated that it might have suffered a collision some aeons previously. Planet A was burned to a crisp. Too close to Kepler-452 to ever have had an atmosphere, and locked in its orbit, one side permanently facing the star and hot enough for lakes of molten metal, while the other at -241°C, was close to absolute zero.

The invading spaceship was approaching planet B, its designated target, having twice circled the inner gas giant in order to shed the last of its great velocity. Now, it travelled at a more sensible speed, and began a four-month journey between C and B. It was on final approach.

It entered orbit, almost two hundred miles above the surface of the planet. If anyone had been standing on the bridge, the view would have been mesmerising, but the bridge was deserted, the only signs of life were intermittent clicks, buzzes and many glowing LED lights indicating that the systems were operational.

Below, a world a smidgen larger than the planet Earth, was covered with pristine white clouds in formations which all residents of Earth would have recognised immediately. Jet streams moved weather systems across the surface, one of which had the distinct signature of a hurricane. Electronic sensors measured wind speeds and atmospheric temperatures. A small ice cap showed similarities to the Arctic but was in the south. The northern pole, with a similar mass of ice, was currently hidden but would come into view as the two-hour orbit progressed.

Beneath the clouds there was land. Some appeared brown or ochre suggesting low precipitation, but other areas were visible through the weather systems showing many shades of green. This world had life, even if only plant life. If there were plants, it was likely that there would be animals if evolution had progressed as it had on the human home world.

All was well with the planet. Temperatures were within tolerances, wind similarly. The atmosphere was primarily nitrogen but with sufficient oxygen to support humanity. There were seas and oceans. Rivers indicated rain and freshwater. This could be a perfect replacement world for the exiled population escaping a fiery death on Sol-1 C – Earth.

For two weeks, the starship had been orbiting. Why was the bridge empty? No one was on duty, no one looking at the stunningly beautiful world beneath, no sounds of civilisation, no voices, mechanical or real. There were just the clicks and buzzes of relays opening and closing, circuits cutting in or out and the odd crinkling metallic sound of equipment casings expanding or contracting as they warmed up or cooled down.

Where were the residents? The plan was for there to be between two and four thousand living souls on board. Where had they gone?

Find out in *KEPLER-452 B*

THE END – or perhaps not?

Tony's Books

Thank you for reading HEAT. Reviews are very important for authors, and I wonder if I could ask you to say a few words on the review page where you bought this book. Every review, even if it is only a few words with a star rating, helps the book move up the rankings.

Other books. They include a trilogy, a series, some stand-alone novels, and some non-fiction works.

MARK NOBLE SPACE ADVENTURE SERIES

THE FEDERATION TRILOGY

STAND ALONE NOVELS

TONY'S NON-FICTION BOOKS

COMPILATIONS (Not all available in paperback)

Reader Club

Building a relationship with my readers is the very best thing about being a novelist. In these days of the Internet and email, the opportunities to interact with you are unprecedented. I send occasional newsletters which include special offers and information on how the various series are developing. You can keep in touch by signing up for my no-spam mailing list.

Sign up at my webpage: **Harmsworth.net** or on my **TonyHarmsworthAuthor** Facebook page and you will know when my books are released and will get free material from time to time and other information.

If you have questions, don't hesitate to write to me at Tony@Harmsworth.net.

Printed in Great Britain
by Amazon